AN EDUCATED DEATH

AN EDUCATED DEATH

V. & D. POVALL

An Educated Death

Published by Dragonfly Media. Oceanside, CA

Library of Congress Control Number: 2023949107

ISBN (paperback): 9781662945755
eISBN: 9781662945762

CONTENTS

━━ ∙ ◆ ∙ ━━

CHAPTER ONE

I woke in the hospital, cracked ribs bound, face lacerations stitched, bullets from my thigh and shoulder removed.

But Cecilia was dead. For that I could never forgive myself.

A DOJ errand boy handed me an official memo placing Special Agent Justin Pierce on indefinite leave until fully recovered from "bla-bla-bla," followed by something about "a full psychological evaluation before reinstatement."

"Fuck reinstatement," I barked, and threw the forms in the man's face. My injuries screamed.

On that note, I plunged headfirst into a swamp of misery.

I certainly didn't deserve round-the-clock care in a state-of-the-art hospital while she decayed in a box, buried in some remote place the Bureau refused to disclose for fear I'd do something inexcusable.

I lingered under medical care for three more weeks, but as soon as my legs felt strong enough to prop me up to something resembling a standing position, I checked myself out. Then, with a load of rage, guilt, and anguish strapped neatly across my shoulders, I fled.

I escaped to Seaview, my safe harbor for many years, with the specific purpose of hiding. Unreasonable, I know, but despair and reason never see eye to eye.

Nothing ever happens in Seaview, California—and *nothing* was exactly what I wanted.

For a month, I'd languished at my beach house. The weather had mimicked my state of mind—gray and depressing, plus abnormally cold on top of the typical June gloom of the southwest coast. So, as on countless previous afternoons, I parked my aching carcass on the deck and stared across the ocean toward the invisible horizon. I'd grown used to the leaden, dismal, flat look. Ignoring everything around me had become my newest specialty. From the seagulls and sandpipers poking around for food in the sand to the strands of seaweed that denoted the high-tide boundary, nothing mattered. Today, that included a dead walrus that now floated on the rising tide below the cliffs of the Pacific Sunset Hotel south of my place.

Truth be told, I didn't give a damn about any of it.

A woman screamed.

Another yelped, "Stay away!" The anguish in her voice, along with the stranger's scream, yanked me out of my stupor.

I recognized Mrs. Sandusky, the hotel manager, who trotted down the steps toward the overlook above the beach as fast as her seventy-year-old legs could carry her.

Less than thirty yards from my seaside hideaway, and just below the hotel bungalows, the walrus rolled and bobbed as the waves pushed it along.

Only then did I realize it was the body of a man…*my bad, no walruses in California.*

As the afternoon had waned, a mere handful of diehards roamed the beach, but within moments, people sprouted from everywhere. Irrepressibly curious onlookers gushed toward the body.

"Get away from there!" Mrs. Sandusky's strident command compelled everyone to make an involuntary pause. From her perch above the beach, she glowered toward the gathering crowd then down at the few grains of sand that encroached upon her sandals. "I called the police. They'll be here any minute."

The imperious quality of her voice had an uncomfortable tone of meanness difficult to ignore. But a dead body is an irresistible magnet, and the group's quest for an up-close view resumed before the last sentence left her lips.

Instinct forced me to my feet. A sharp reminder of my condition stabbed me in the left ribcage and caused me to grunt as the wind erupted from my lungs. I forced some briny air back into them and moaned my way to the railing. I ignored the pain in my thigh and limped to within a few feet from the gathering crowd.

The body had dropped anchor about fifteen yards from the south end of my deck, and within seconds a dozen or so gawkers gathered round it, and more were on their way.

One guy decided to document the event with his cell phone. "Jee-sus! Would you look at that, honey? Get over on the other side."

No doubt the footage of the man's wife posing next to the bloated dead body would flash across screens on the late-night news and social media in a matter of hours.

One of the onlookers upchucked her dinner. The crowd gave her a wide berth that offered me a glimpse of the body. A middle-aged man, well over six feet, bloated by the time spent in the water, in a dark blue suit with narrow pinstripes, a deep gash over the right ear, left shoe missing, and fly open.

Mrs. Sandusky tiptoed toward the scene and grimaced at the offensive sight—encroaching sand and a corpse with open fly all in one afternoon—what's the world coming to? She proceeded to bark orders to the remaining employees, but no one listened. The corpse allowed no distractions.

Mr. Newsreel and his cell phone grew more intrusive by the second, filming from every imaginable angle. A fierce resentment began to surge inside me and, in my state, it might cause me to become unpleasant. Refuge in a stiff drink presented a far more desirable alternative.

I dragged myself back into the house and heard the wail of sirens along I-5.

At least this death won't go on my tab.

I splashed some Crown Royal into a glass over some ice and got the fireplace going. I scarfed down the whiskey, but it changed nothing, so I poured another.

Mere feet from my house, a man lay dead on the beach, surrounded by strangers to whom he signified nothing more than coffee-klatch conversation, proof of divine intervention, or fodder for a horror story. In the next few hours, however, some unsuspecting relative would receive a call from the Seaview Police Department to inform them that their next of kin had been found in a state of irreparable damage, officially referred to as *deceased*. That's when we're hit with the cold facts of mortality.

My increasingly morbid mood screamed for another drink.

By now, the only light that remained outside came courtesy of a sliver of orange-red reflected under the clouds across the rim of the Pacific. Since the fireplace matched it just right, I left the house lights off. I slid to the floor and leaned against the sofa, emptied half my glass on the first try, then let my head drop back, and stared at the ceiling. As I approached dream state, the ice in my glass popped a couple of times and snapped me back. It took me a few seconds to get my bearings. My whiskey had at last done the trick.

I'd promised myself not to slip, yet again, into the artificial comfort of a drunken stupor. But after the appropriate self-recrimination, I decided that, when mired in grief, one is obligated to dull one's pain, so I started greasing the slide. After all, hadn't the events on the beach reopened my wounds and made them bleed?

Not my fault—blame death.

After pouring another refill, I stretched out on the leather armchair and took another sip.

Something flashed outside the window and, with a moan and a grimace, I rose to take a look.

The police prowled the area in force. Several of them milled about the body on the beach. Others set up perimeter lights. The area had been cleared for police activity, but the crowd resisted all attempts to disperse them. A dozen or so cops combed the beach with flashlights.

A balding man in his early fifties by my estimation approached the stairs that lead from the beach to my deck. He projected that Hollywood central casting look of the overworked, underpaid cop, thirty pounds heavier than his health could tolerate, and a slouch that forecasted defeat before the game had even begun.

I flicked on an outside light then stepped out onto the deck to meet him halfway. "Hi."

He took a deep breath as he looked up at me. "Good evening." He tugged at the breast of his coat to emphasize the police badge dangling from the pocket. "Sergeant William Haskell, Seaview Police Department."

"Justin Pierce." I nodded toward the table and chairs at the end of the deck. "Care to sit down?"

"Won't be but a minute, Mr. Pierce. Just a couple of routine questions."

A cloud of rancid sweat engulfed the man and his clothes looked like they hadn't been pressed since he bought them. He had a chronic case of ring around the collar and an air of rehearsed indifference. He glanced through the window as he crossed the deck.

"This your residence, Mr. Pierce?"

I nodded.

"Nice place," he said with what seemed sincere admiration. "Bigger than most others in this area."

"It's on a double lot, and it's also closer to the ocean than the others."

"How's that?"

I forced a smile. I knew such arrangements were now illegal and, of course, so did he. "It was the first place built on Playa Vista in the early forties. The ban on double lots was passed in '57. So, until dry rot, high tide, or termites knock it down, it's legally illegal."

He chuckled. "Legally illegal. I like that. I like that." He stuck his hands into his coat pockets and looked down as if searching for something on the deck. He took two slow steps toward the railing, then squinted toward the sight where the body lay behind a makeshift screen.

"Nasty business, a body washing up like that. Good for the hotel, though. The Sunset'll be packed to the roof for the next three weeks is my guess." He produced a pack of cigarettes and a book of matches from his left pocket and showed them to me. "Mind if I smoke?"

It wasn't really a question. He stuck one in his mouth before I had a chance to shake my head, cupped his hands against the wind, and lit it on the second attempt. He glanced toward the ocean.

"I understand you were out here when they first found Mr. Devon's body. Don't happen to know him, do you?"

"No, Sergeant. Sorry."

He nodded as if it were the answer he'd expected. "Crowds always gather 'round. One fella was even shooting video. Funny how people like to do that. Damned cell phones do just about anything except make calls." He took a deep drag on his cigarette and turned to face me. "I hear you left in kind of a hurry. Care to tell me why?"

His tone was as indifferent as before, but the content seemed to have acquired a sharp edge that I didn't like. I wondered if I should call my lawyer. Only I don't have a lawyer.

"That idiot you mentioned," I said, "the one with the cell phone. Turning a man's death into a travelog to show his friends back home over beer and chips was more than I could stomach." I came across more aggressive than I should have and a little voice in the back of my mind screamed for me to back off.

He sucked on the cigarette. "What's your line of work, Mr. Pierce?"

"Industrial insulation. Latin America mostly. I come here anytime I get a break."

"Sounds exciting. Lots of traveling."

"Yeah. Starting to get old, though."

"Really? I had you pegged for about thirty-six or so."

"I meant the traveling is getting old." I didn't want to tell him how old I really felt. None of his damn business anyway.

"You're joking. A man with your good looks can really score south of the border, if you catch my drift." He winked.

"My looks?"

"Hey, blue eyes, brown hair, wide shoulders, the works. And what are you, six-foot-five?"

"Six-four."

My good looks, as Haskell put it, inherited from my father. At times helpful, often a burden. A label I didn't enjoy but that had affixed itself. My physique, on the other hand, is a result of my stint in the Marine Corps and years of training with Special Forces. Despite my current state, I must've looked somewhat daunting to Haskell.

"What's with all the bruising and cuts?" He pointed towards his right temple.

"Disagreement with a buddy."

He scowled.

"Over a girl," I added. Maybe "my looks" could come in handy.

He sneered. "Must've been a hell of girl and a hell of a fight."

"Yes, on both counts."

He pushed off the railing and glared at me from under bushy eyebrows. "Anyway, you're absolutely certain you didn't know Mr. Devon?"

The look and the implication made my blood boil, and I was too tired and too drunk to control it completely, but I did the best I could. "That's what I said, isn't it?"

He raised his eyebrows at me, then shrugged and flicked his cigarette out onto the sand below the deck. I watched the wind blow it back a few feet into a pile of seaweed. When I turned to him, he was already on his way back to the beach.

I flicked the outdoor lights off and ambled back inside to the security and comfort of my drink. I filled the glass to the rim this time. Number three by my count, maybe four, or five. I dropped to the floor and leaned my head against the sofa.

I'd overreacted to Haskell's attitude, an approach I'd used often enough myself when questioning suspects. But my defenses were down, and that made me irritable. I needed a friendly face, and I thanked God for Demetrio.

Over the years I've been through my share of downs. Comes with the territory. I often fail to recognize the downward spirals. Demetrio gets me and recognizes them right away. Our close friendship spans our entire lives. Earlier that morning, in a two-hour phone conversation punctuated by periods of silence and convulsive sobbing, I'd spilled my guts to him. I begged him not to come, but he ignored my plea.

"Listen, *gringo pendejo*, the university owes me more vacation time than it can afford to pay. So, make sure you're sober enough to pick me up tomorrow."

"Don't come, please. I think I need to be alone for a few days."

"*Carajo*, you think too much, that's your problem. I'll catch the late afternoon flight. *Hasta mañana*."

It now gave me great comfort to know I'd see his cherubic, malicious smile the following evening.

The flames in the fireplace leaped and fluttered across the logs, and exhaustion hammered its presence into every cell of my body. It wasn't the mere physical injuries. The emotional exhaustion had clawed its way deeper each day. Agony invaded everything, my body, the air, sounds, and smells…Cecilia had the scent of the sea on her skin the last time I'd held her alive. Far different than when I cradled her lifeless, delicate body. Remote as childhood, vivid as yesterday.

My nightmares had mutated into a flickering kaleidoscope of life and death. Her body melded with mine in a whirlpool of laughter and love, only to shrivel away into anguish and lifelessness. Staying awake didn't help. I saw her in everything. Smelled her everywhere.

Damn guilt. The bastard gnawed at my soul, reminding me that I should've shielded her from danger and didn't. I'd convinced myself I needed her as part of the operation. But the truth is I wanted her with me, so I persuaded myself she'd be safe. She was, after all, a professional like me. She understood the risks. We both did. And we made the fatal mistake of believing that, for a while, we could live like regular people.

I downed the last of my drink as the shadows flickered across the bricks and beams like defective neon lights. For some reason I thought of *Fantasia*, and it became my nightmare as I drifted into sleep.

"Justin!" Cecilia yelled.

I lurched out of my dream and into an instant pain that jarred me. My head throbbed and my neck was so stiff it refused to turn to the right. A cold perspiration soaked my shirt and my entire body shook. My heart struggled against the confines of my chest, blood pounded in my ears, and thumped at my temples. Something crawling along the crossbeams of my mind urged me to cry. I dismissed it. Anger felt more suitable, manlier. I slammed my fist against the floor and a remote part of me gave thanks for the heavy carpet.

I forced down a few deep breaths, pulled my miserable body to its feet, and made my way to the guest bathroom. Flicked on the light, filled the sink with cold water, and submerged my face. Cupping my right hand, I scooped the water over my head and the back of my neck. Stood there, hunched over the sink, watching the streams dwindle from threads to droplets. I raised my head and faced myself in the mirror.

An abhorrent creature stared back. The monster that killed the only person I ever truly loved.

A real man would kill it.

The realization horrified me and tears burst into my eyes. I shuddered. In seconds I was convulsing. I shriveled to the floor shaking uncontrollably. I hit the floor and walls with my fists, the pain encouraging the flow of tears, and satisfying in some minute way the need for punishment.

As my rage dissipated, I became depleted. Empty. A threadbare rag hurled into a corner, expendable and superfluous.

"Augh!" I bellowed. "Cut the crap, asshole!"

I forced my self-pity up onto my back then dragged what was left of me up the stairs and into my room. I sank face down onto the bed and, for the first time in weeks, slept a dreamless sleep.

CHAPTER TWO

A cell phone rang.

My body refused to budge, and I possessed neither the strength nor the inclination to force it.

The sun was up, and the glare from the hallway shot into the bedroom with painful sharpness thanks to a floor-to-ceiling window with its panoramic view of the beach and sea. It always seemed a waste to me, that window. Other than passing glances as one walked from room to room or up and down the stairs, no one except Demetrio spent any time appreciating it. But to shroud it with an unsightly curtain felt sacrilegious.

The phone rang, and I ignored it as payback for waking me. Wondered about the time, but didn't really care, so I didn't move. The phone went silent at last. I'd check the voicemail later.

I felt dampness on the bedspread under my mouth and chin. *Great, I'm drooling.* A habit that annoyed me so much as a child that I'd learned to sleep with my mouth shut to avoid it. Last night, however, the "shut-yer-mouth-ya-drooling-toad" command short-circuited.

Hadn't moved a muscle the entire night, so I wiggled my toes, relieved to find them still there. I folded my legs and one at a time took inventory of each limb…hands…check…arms… check…head…attached but nonfunctional.

I willed myself onto my back then rolled my aching mass to a sitting position. Every inch of me felt alien, like it belonged to someone else. I heaved a deep sigh and recoiled at the revolting odor I produced.

"No wonder I feel like garbage," I mumbled. "I'm rotting."

The phone rang. Didn't answer it this time either.

I rocked my head from side to side and my vertebrae cracked as they did whatever it is that makes them settle and adjust. My brain sloshed about as I rolled my head around in a painful attempt to stretch the neck muscles. Still resisted the turn to the right. Arched my back and stretched my arms then sighed. My knuckles, swollen and bloody, pulsed with a dull throb. Bloodstains marred the bedclothes.

The phone started again. Coffee took precedence. I slithered my gelatinous mass down the stairs to the kitchen.

The breakfast nook displayed windows on three sides, and the morning sun burst through with a vengeance, a feature I'd missed over the past month. It made the kitchen oddly cheery, which I enjoyed once my eyes got used to the blinding glare. I soaked my bloody hands in cold water, then fashioned a pot of industrial strength coffee and stepped out onto the deck while it dripped itself ready.

No vestige of the angry clouds from the previous day. With luck the sun would remain, clouds would stay away, and I'd be blessed at last with a glorious day in paradise.

The phone rang.

The fresh morning air felt invigorating, but the realities of the previous evening couldn't be denied. I'd forgotten about the unfortunate victim that had floated up the beach to my house. The uninvited recollection blasted the wind out of my sails.

A large area along the beach remained marked off by yellow strips. A handful of weary investigators milled about aimlessly, some below my deck. A couple eyed me with suspicion. My access to the beach had been taped off as well.

A handful of local TV news crews buzzed about ambushing any unfortunate passersby that strayed into their web. I wondered if the persistent phone meant reporters were trying to get my side of the story. *DEAD BODY FOUND NEXT TO LEGALLY ILLEGAL BEACH HOUSE. Police question suspicious resident.*

A couple dozen onlookers lined the boardwalk and several hotel balconies featured more guests who pointed and discussed. Fearing they might notice me, I turned away and absconded to the safety of my kitchen.

Enough coffee for one cup. I sugar-and-creamed it and attacked it immediately. The caffeine activated cogs and wheels and seconds later joints and muscles made their appreciation known. My aching hands with their swollen and scraped knuckles refused to chime in.

I glanced at the clock on my way to the front door—11:40. I'd slept twelve or thirteen hours and, save for a nasty hangover and painful body parts, felt almost normal.

I peeked through the peephole. No reporters were poised to ambush me. I snatched up the paper. Closed the door and perused the headlines. Our quiet little beach dominated the front page. A circle of people, clad mostly in beach attire, surrounded a large black object that, upon closer scrutiny, resembled a body.

A corner of my house filled the background. *Fuck.* I tossed the paper aside in disgust.

Feeling more alive than I had in weeks, I determined not to allow bad news to wrestle me back down. Experience assured me that endless repetition of the same story would flood the TV channels, so I opted for the fifties radio station instead. My brain recoiled at the cacophony. I clicked it off and settled for scrambled eggs and ham smothered with Tabasco to ward off the hangover, then poured another cup of my nuclear-strength brew.

The phone screamed for attention, and I ignored it just to teach it a lesson.

After a shave, a very long, very hot shower, and clean clothes, I came close to the cliché of feeling human again.

For the first time in weeks, I found myself deliberating what to do next. Staying in the house threatened to suck me back into the feelings I'd faced the previous night. Lounging on the deck put me at the mercy of bloodthirsty reporters. Plus, the cops might decide to question me to break up the monotony of their routine.

An escape to the golf course presented the best alternative. With Demetrio due to arrive in the early evening, that left enough time to practice a little and attempt to gain a bit of flexibility over nine holes. Perfect.

The phone rang and, in good conscience, I couldn't let it go unanswered any longer. After all, I was cognizant again.

"Hello."

"So, you're in town. Where the hell have you been? I've been calling all morning!"

My sister. But instead of her usual cold-fish tone, she sounded intense…desperate.

"Good morning to you, too, Carrie. What's up?"

"Thank God you're in town! Justin, Justin!" She sounded distressed.

"Carrie, calm down." I could tell she was crying. My sister never cried. "What's going on?"

"It's Paul. He's in the hospital. Somebody smashed his head in. Please come over."

The sincere anxiety in her voice left me little choice. "Sure. Where are you?"

"Scripps Memorial. Do you know where it is?"

"Yeah. I'll be right there."

"I'm in the ICU waiting room. Please hurry." She hung up.

The image of the body on the beach flashed in my head. I stood there with the phone in my hand, stunned.

She'd divorced Paul a good twelve years ago, but they never quite moved apart. He'd adopted the role of protecting her like a doting brother—something I never did. Never. With infinite gratitude for good old Paul, I'd allowed myself not to worry about her. I never understood why he tolerated her. She belittled him constantly, ordered him to do petty chores, run errands, or deal with people she didn't want to face. He never complained and did whatever she wanted with a smile. The panic in her voice told me how important he really was to her. I wondered if he'd been hurt defending her.

I revved up the Explorer and sped out heading for La Jolla. Memorial Hospital sits west of Genesee Avenue, off of Highway 5, not far from La Jolla. I arrived at the hospital in a little over twenty-five minutes, parked in the visitor area, and locked the car.

I scanned for the route to the ICU. Three arrows pointing left read: *Neurology. ICU. Waiting Room.*

Aside from my recent stint in Cozumel, I've only visited two ICU waiting rooms in my life. Each time, I lost a parent. They make me very uncomfortable, and I never know how to react. There's a leaden silence about such places as if speaking will awaken the tube-riddled patients to their reality and somehow hasten their departure.

I trudged my way to the waiting room where Carrie nursed an empty cup of dispenser machine coffee and stared at the floor. She hadn't changed one iota since I'd last seen her. Her brown hair cascaded loosely about her shoulders, her blue eyes remained as icy as ever—despite the swelling and puffiness—and her long legs were exquisite to look at. Even with the constant *"go fuck yourself"* vibe that emanated from her every pore, she was a stunning woman.

After a deep breath to summon courage, I headed in her direction. She spotted me first and bolted to her feet.

"What the hell took you so long?"

"Fine, thanks, and you?"

"Huh? What are you talking about?"

I needed to cut her some slack. "Want a refill? You look like you could use another cup."

I started toward the machine but didn't get very far.

"I don't give a damn about coffee. For Christ's sake, I have some serious stress going on here. Can't you see that?" As per usual, her tone seemed to imply that I'd turned out a little slow—maybe way slow.

I regaled her with my most amenable smile. "Okay, tell me about it. What's up with Paul?"

"I need a cigarette," she said and reached for her purse. "Under the circumstances, you won't mind if I smoke."

"You can't smoke in a hospital."

"God. You're a pain in the ass."

She produced a cigarette and put it in her mouth but didn't light it. She glowered at me and sighed. A moment later she yanked it out of her mouth and tossed it into her purse. She lunged at me, threw one arm around my neck, and sobbed with unconstrained convulsions. Her abrupt reaction shocked me. Not even when our mother died did I ever see her give into tears. It brought home in an instant how little I knew about her true feelings and how deft she'd become at concealing them.

"Hey, hey. It's okay." I endeavored to sound convincing as I placed my hands on her arms to indicate that she could release me, but she remained locked on. "Want to tell me about it?"

Her sobbing ebbed and she let go, then reached into her purse for a handkerchief. I patted her shoulder to reassure her, more for my benefit than hers.

She glanced around the room then nodded toward the hallway. "Let's go outside."

I followed her, unsure whether to put my arm around her shoulders or just stay close by. It was clear that Paul's predicament had shattered her. She stayed next to the wall as we plodded along.

"How is he?" I asked.

"He's in a coma," she whispered as she fought back a new onslaught of tears.

Her reply knocked the wind out of me. "A coma? What the hell happened?"

She shook her head as she struggled to regain composure. "I asked him to repair a light fixture in my bathroom. It had a short in it. He said he'd come over about 10:30, fix it, then take me to lunch if I could sneak away from work. When I got home about eleven, I found him lying in the dining room in the middle of—" She stopped as the tears overwhelmed her. She cleared her throat and continued in a very quiet voice, "Tons and tons of blood. There was a gash in his head. I thought he was dead."

"Did he fall?"

"No, of course not. For God's sake, Justin, get real. Isn't this the sort of stuff you're supposed to know about?"

I chose not to notice the jab and moved on. "What do the doctors say?"

"Too soon to tell. They need to, you know, run tests and all that crap. First, they have to stop the hemorrhage inside his skull. The next two days are critical, they say."

"And you?"

"Okay, I guess. Shocked, mostly. Must've been thieves. Every drawer in the house was on the floor. The closets emptied, the clothes all over the place. It's a mess. Someone must've broken in and attacked him. Or maybe he surprised them when he entered the penthouse."

I was starting to get the picture. "What did they take?"

She shook her head. "I don't know. I didn't look. All I could think of was to call 9-1-1."

"What do the police say?"

"Nothing. Maybe they're still there looking for clues or something." She sighed and glanced over at the nurse's station, then back at me. Her eyes widened and a stunned look appeared on her face. "My God, Justin! What the hell happened to you? You look like shit!"

"It's nothing. I'm fine."

She shook her head. "Really, Justin. This is too much. Wait here."

She approached the nurses' station and leaned over the counter. One of them, a large woman in her forties, pointed to the left and made a gyrating movement with her hand. Carrie nodded and returned to me.

"She says there's a place across the street. I could use a drink. You look like you could, too."

It turned out to be one of those eateries that pass for a Mexican restaurant. In all fairness, the food at some of them has improved substantially over the years, but not at this one. They did serve margaritas however, and that's all Carrie really wanted. I ordered some enchiladas to give me something to do and a Dos Equis beer to wash them down.

Carrie stared at the table in silence until our drinks arrived. Her eyes were glazed and she sipped her drink automatically. Seeing her this vulnerable was new and unsettling for me. Keeping her engaged with Paul appeared to be the best approach—at least for the moment.

"Does Paul have any family around here? Anyone we should notify?"

She shook her head. "A brother in Boston. I already called him."

"Is he coming out?"

She seemed to think it over. "Uh, no. He just asked me to keep him informed," she said and sipped her margarita. "I guess they're like us." She managed a painful smile. "I mean, look at us. You're beaten to a pulp, and can't even manage a "hello-I'm-okay-sis" phone call or email. Lovey-dovey siblings, aren't we?"

I always feared having that "about us" conversation with Carrie. Maybe the dread that some unknown hostilities would erupt to the surface and make us end up further apart. I didn't imagine that such a conversation could occur at this particular moment and the prospect made me nervous. I watched her stir her margarita with the plastic straw.

"Nothing to tell, Carrie. The job sometimes gets a bit rough. That's all. I look like shit, feel like it, too, but I'm okay. Tell me about Paul."

She looked up at me as if reeled back from some distant thought. "What do you want to know?"

"I'm curious about you guys, your relationship. Why have you stayed so close?"

Her eyes wandered to the margarita. She pinched some salt from the rim of the glass between her thumb and forefinger and licked it off. Her demeanor suddenly turned calm and detached in an eerie way as if she were observing us from some far-off place. Finally, she looked up.

"It's simple, really. Paul loves me. He's nicer to me than anyone ever has been. I feel safe when he's around, like someone cares." She looked down and sipped her drink. "I wish I loved him the same way he loves me. But I can't." She escaped into another sip then sighed and looked at me with a painful smile. "Well, there you have it. I love him like a brother or something like that." She placed the straw on the cocktail napkin and sipped from the glass.

"Is that why you split up?"

Another shrug. "That… and some personal stuff. Nothing you'd understand."

This time the jab hit home. I disguised my annoyance. "Why don't you try me?"

She produced a sarcastic smile. "You're just like Dad. You're too fucking—" she shook her head and tried to utter the words a couple of times with no success. "And I'm just like Mom," she said at last. "I hate it."

I would have said the exact opposite. But this was neither the time nor the place for that exchange.

Our waiter passed on his way to a table behind me, and Carrie indicated she wanted another margarita. I declined his offer to bring another beer. When he left, I rested my elbows on the table and leaned toward Carrie.

"Tell me about Mom."

"What about her?"

"Did she talk about Dad? About me?"

She stared at me for a moment then emptied her glass and placed it back on the napkin, making sure they were symmetrically arranged, then crossed her arms on the table and leaned toward me. "She was perpetually drunk, as you remember. Depressed, as I'm sure you guessed. God only knows what all she took over the years to cope." She sighed and shook her head. "Half the time I didn't know what she was saying, so I didn't pay attention. Certainly not when it was about Dad. I hated him. Still do." Her mind wandered back to some distant memory. She straightened up abruptly. "I don't want to talk about them."

Dead end. "Okay." I took a swig from my beer and slumped into the corner of the booth. I studied her. I thought I could read guilt on her face. About our father or about refusing to talk?

Probably about Paul, I decided. She took the stem of her glass between two fingers and rotated it by precise quarter turns and stared at it. She'd locked herself shut.

There we sat, miles apart across a narrow table in silence until the waiter brought my food and her drink. I dug into the enchiladas with a vengeance. Lost in her own thoughts, Carrie picked at the chips and salsa with deliberate slowness, selected the occasional morsel from my plate, and chewed with a sluggish cadence, her eyes glued to her glass.

I realized I had seen this very image countless times in restaurants all over the world. Couples, usually, married, I assumed, who sat across from each other, with never a word uttered between them. I wondered if this was how they'd reached that point, one reluctant to speak, the other reluctant to press, until, over time, silence became the way of things. As I watched her, I realized how easily this moment might become perpetual for us. Solidifying into ice, pushing us further and further apart, perpetually spinning our drinks while an ever-growing chasm spread between us, a canyon too wide and too dangerous to cross. In time we'd cease to even say "hello" and reduce our relationship to the occasional nod. One day, not even that.

I had to force myself to care enough to keep that from happening. I felt tightness in my throat. Maybe losing Cecilia had ignited a cinder of concern, a minute flame of caring, a tiny spark of need. It was clear that I must make the effort for both our sakes. Long years of purposeful indifference had built a barrier impossible to smash. But she was, after all, my sister. My only sister. Scared and in pain. I'd never seen her in this kind of emotional distress.

I needed a tool, a lever to pry the door open before it slammed shut forever. But nothing came to mind. She appeared unassailable, too well fortified, and much too fragile. Armed as I was against her sarcasm and coldness, I now found no leverage to pry open the tiniest of cracks in our mutual silence.

She came to my rescue in a most unexpected way.

"First Jerry, now Paul."

"Who's Jerry?" I asked in a tone of complete confusion.

"Haven't you read the papers? My God, it happened right down the beach from you. What kind of agent are you? Or whatever the hell you're supposed to be. Jerry Devon, for Christ's sake. Don't tell me you don't know." Her tone carried more than a little disdain.

The realization made my jaw drop and my breathing catch for an instant. "You knew that guy?"

"Sure. We worked together."

"Were you going out with him?" I asked incredulously.

"Oh, for God's sake, Justin, get real. The man was over 300 pounds. Jerry was a nice guy but we were just friends. Colleagues. Our respective offices collaborated. End of story." She failed to maintain eye contact with me and looked back at her drink. "We were at a college party together on a private yacht sailing around the harbor. You know how that is."

I shook my head. "No, I don't."

"Anyway, that was the last time I saw him."

"How long ago was that?"

"Friday before last."

Her comments aroused the investigator inside me. "A little less than two weeks ago. Did anyone else see him after that?"

"Not that I know of. His office was all a-buzz about the fact that he seemed to just disappear. I figured he'd left on vacation. After all, summer had arrived. Others speculated that something was going on at home. Several people tried calling him, but he'd vanished."

"Did you tell the police?"

"Certainly not. I wouldn't anyway. He's not one of my employees. His supervisor should've. But why would anyone do that anyway? We figured if anything had happened to him, we'd have heard about it." She began to fidget with the straw in her drink.

"So, now you have," I said with more than a hint of contempt. It created a prolonged silence.

"Did you see him?" she asked at last, without looking at me.

"Briefly."

The straw fidgeting increased.

"What have they found?" She tried to sound uninterested.

I had to smile if only to myself. "No idea. You probably know more than I do. Have the police questioned you yet?"

That aroused her indignation. "Of course not. Why on earth would they question me? You're very dense today."

"You were one of the last people to see him alive, Carrie, and the cops usually want to talk to such people. Especially if you were alone."

"Well, we weren't. Good Lord, give me a break. It was a party on a yacht the president threw to close a three-day seminar for administrators. The entire leadership team was there."

She stopped as if there were nothing left to add so I prompted her to continue. "Go on. What kind of party?"

"A typical, bureaucratic type party. You know, everybody trying to get laid or drunk or both. Most people got smashed with all the free booze flowing. By midnight half of them could hardly walk." A look of astonishment came over her, and she brought her free hand up to her mouth. "Oh, my God! He must have fallen overboard. That's it." She almost seemed relieved.

I shrugged. "I doubt it, he had a nasty bump on the head."

"That shoreline is covered in rocks. Or haven't you noticed, dearie? You can clearly see it from your place. That's it, that's it! He must have hit one of the rocks as he tried to swim ashore." She added lip biting to straw fidgeting.

"Carrie," I insisted, "why are you so nervous?"

She shook her head. "It's the shock." She glanced at her watch and pretended to be in a hurry. "Thanks for coming, Justin. I should get back to Paul." She looked around for our waiter but he was nowhere to be seen. She glanced again at her watch. "How long will you be with us this time, darling?"

Her demeanor had changed completely. Her bitchy, condescending persona had returned, and she'd reverted to the cold fish I'd been accustomed to.

I shrugged. "I don't know. A while."

"I'll go back to the hospital. You don't have to join me. I'll be fine on my own." She finally located the waiter and signaled for the check. "You'll take care of it, won't you?"

"Carrie," I whispered.

She glanced back at me with artificial smile number four on her face, the one she uses when she wants to appear patient while letting you know that you're a pain in the ass. "Yes, dear?"

"Would you like to stay at my place for a while?"

She flashed me smile number seventeen, the one that means, "aren't you sweet, you poor, useless creature."

"Thanks, but no thanks. I already reserved a room at the Marriott down the street. The police should be done with the penthouse soon. I'll be fine. Really."

As she scurried away, I realized that one of my most useful skills had kicked into gear. Suspicion reared its menacing head. My sister in distress, Devon the dead man on the beach, and now Paul attacked in her flat, connected a perfect trilogy of events. The hairs on my arms bristled. Devon, murdered? Or, as Carrie so desperately wished, the victim of an unfortunate accident? Whatever had happened to the man linked Carrie and the place she worked for, that much was clear. But what could possibly happen at a university that warranted killing? And how did Paul fit in?

It was quite clear that Carrie didn't want to tell me the entire story. She'd recoiled when I suggested a connection between her and Devon, and I could smell her fear a mile away. But why not tell me what she knew? I could attribute it to her character, her personality. It was possible she didn't want my help. Carrie had never asked for anything in her life. Certainly not from me. She simply commanded—her most irritating characteristic. Anyone who dared contradict her she dismissed as either stupid or liberal, never to be addressed socially again. If there's a streak of unselfishness in her at all, it's reserved exclusively for small animals, usually cats.

Three trips down the aisle had done nothing to mellow her out. She possessed an extraordinary talent for emasculating her husbands, leaving them miserable and substantially poorer than when she'd married them. She'd kept souvenirs from each—her last name from the first, friendship from the second, and a penthouse condo in La Jolla from the third. Paul, her second legal victim, was the only one who remained in the San Diego area. In fact, he lived in La Jolla, one street away from Carrie, and continued to be her whipping boy to this day.

I'd attributed her attachment to Paul to a dread of getting old. At thirty-nine, three years older than I, and on the threshold of the big four-O, Carrie requires incessant affirmation of her beauty and astuteness. Paul fulfills that need effortlessly. I never did. I can't abide that superficial crap. So, our relationship— barring the period when we were children and she could still beat the crap out of me—devolved into meaningless and sporadic contact. We've never been close. Except, on occasion, geographically.

Given our history, the fact that she'd refused to tell me the entire story about Devon didn't surprise me. But my suspicions had been aroused, and the genie wouldn't return quietly to its flagon.

Golf was now out. Pity. The trade-off didn't excite me, but as I sat contemplating our familial world, I remembered that I'd grudgingly promised my mother before she died that whenever Carrie needed me, I would be there. Unless this whole Devon-Paul-Carrie connection turned out to be one miraculous coincidence, she needed me now, even if she preferred not to.

As for the shape such help might take, I had no idea. It needed to be without her knowledge. For now, at least. I remained huddled in the restaurant booth nursing my beer, to give my brain an opportunity to figure out how to handle this new information.

As to the promise made to my mother, I've honored it, if only in part. For years my work has kept me away from Seaview and environs for extended periods of time. Work that in a twisted way I inherited from my father—the man my sister hates—causes the same contempt she has for him to be directed at me. Because of that she'd reject any help I offered out of hand.

I understand her resentment. God knows I've harbored the same resentment toward my father most of my life. The irony is that in the end my choice to follow in his footsteps widened the barrier between us.

Following in a father's footsteps generally means a career in medicine, the law, or something socially acceptable like that. But my father, although socially acceptable, was different, very different. He'd been posted to the U.S. Embassy in Mexico City since the early eighties. His official title was Cultural Attaché. At least that's how the official line read at the time of his death. The truth, however, proved to be vastly different.

Carrie and I were born in Mexico City and registered instantly at the U.S. embassy to guarantee our American citizenship when we reached adulthood. We attended an expensive and exclusive bilingual school. Unfortunately, when Carrie hit puberty, she became involved with a Mexican movie star reputed to be a heavy user of drugs and an incorrigible womanizer. That relationship placed my dad in an untenable position that compelled him to exile her to the U.S. with my mother. They were banished to San Diego, close enough for him to exercise some control, but far enough from Carrie's entanglements. My mother never recovered from their unfair expulsion, and my sister still hasn't forgiven him. It remains the principal cause of her resentment towards him. But one never argued with my father.

From that point on, I only saw Carrie and Mom at Christmas or some sporadic holiday. My father rarely joined us. At times, Mom would fly to Mexico for a few days to celebrate my birthday or to disappear with my father for a couple of weeks to some unknown destination. In the end there were always copious tears, violent quarrels, and vast amounts of alcohol involved. It wasn't until I reached my early twenties that I finally understood why.

No doubt my parents loved each other, but something secret drove an insurmountable wedge between them. I now see a clearer picture of the culprit, but as a teenager the lack of details filled me with confused imaginings and deep resentment.

Our house in Mexico City had *secret* places. Rooms that only my father could access, sound proofed, guarded by electronic security, where *important people*, as he called them, gathered. Often for hours. And each time they met, a heavy gloom descended over my mother. She'd drink herself into a stupor, order the maids to put us to bed, and stumble off to bed herself. Then she would cry. Good God, how she cried.

As I grew older, I realized that our house seemed to always be watched—heavily armed men, some American, some Mexican, in large impenetrable-looking vehicles stationed at the corners of our street, across from our house, or outside our gates. From time to time, there would even be military or police vehicles along the entire street. The house itself stood surrounded by a wall, easily fifteen feet high, studded with shards of glass across the top and barbed wire above that.

I lived in this fortress from the day I was born, and during childhood, it never struck me as unusual. In adolescence, however, I began to realize, with significant prodding from my best friends, that very few people in the city lived in similar circumstances. Those who did were either top military or political types, pariahs not well liked by the public, or individuals with powerful enemies. Often, all of the above.

One day, not long after Carrie and my mother's expulsion to San Diego, I had the temerity to ask my father about this unusual living arrangement. I'd spent the afternoon with Demetrio, Alex, and Javier, my three best friends. We'd been disappointed by my father's refusal to let us hold a dance at the house for my sixteenth birthday. For the first time, both Alex and Javier had voiced a long-repressed curiosity about the characteristics of secrecy that surrounded our house. Their speculations ranged from the atrocious to the fantastical and none of them were positive. The worst part was that they'd given voice to my own misgivings and assumptions. It made me angry. Frustrated really. My friends and their families were always generous to a fault. I visited Alex's ranch several times a year. Javier's family invited me constantly to their country estate in the mountains. And I hung around Demetrio's place all the time sharing anything and everything from girls to money to weed. But I never obtained permission to invite my friends to our home for any occasion.

The day my youthful world imploded began when I emerged from the television room as Dad started up the stairs. I watched him, my heart bursting from my chest, hands soaked with cold sweat while I summoned enough determination to challenge him. I sauntered up behind him and cleared my throat. He turned to face me. Then I spoke.

The images branded into my mind as a result of this encounter colored my relationship with him for years until long after his death. In some ways they still do. Try as I might, I don't remember exactly what I said. Something to the effect that he had no right to stop me from having a party because this was my house, too. I do remember how he came slowly back down the stairs, planted himself before me, and glared. He smacked me so hard, I went sprawling across the marble floor. He lifted me by my shirt and squeezed my face with such force that I had finger marks for days after.

"In this house you do as you're told," he said in a monotone.

My entire body shook. But my indignation required more than a mere command.

"Why do we live this way? Are you a criminal? My friends say you're a criminal!"

He stood there glaring into my eyes. I remember thinking he looked almost sad. His free hand smacked me with even more vigor than before. Only his grip on my shirt prevented me from collapsing to the floor. My eyes watered from the pain.

He seemed eerily calm as he released me. "A criminal would kill you," he said. "Son or not. Remember that." He turned away and trudged up the stairs as if the weight of the world had abruptly descended upon his shoulders.

I never asked him anything again. And when he died unexpectedly two years later, I felt relieved enough to celebrate, and sad enough to cry.

Carrie reminds me of him. She displays the same air of detachment. Even when she smiles, one has the feeling that it's an exercise in lip movement. I resented him, but Carrie hated him. She still does.

My one sincere regret is that his death deprived me of any chance to talk, to have it out, as it were. As I've reexamined what I remember of him, analyzed his professional actions, and acquired a deeper understanding of his activities through my own experiences, I've come to see a far different man than I did on that unfortunate day. I now see a lonely man. A tired man who hugged and kissed his sad wife with longing and affection when he thought his children weren't looking. A man who sobbed at night when he thought everyone was asleep. A man who missed the entire lives of his children and maybe even his own. A man who believed he was doing something so vital, so important, that only someone of unflinching courage and patriotism could carry it out.

Years later, I learned that my father was, in effect, a CIA operative, a Station Head, responsible for one covert operation after another throughout Latin America. The irony is that it was precisely my resentment toward those activities which, once I graduated from college, led me into a similar line of work on behalf of both the Mexican and American governments. To be in the service of two countries had to be a nobler endeavor than my father's. Bigger and more admirable. Or so I told myself.

Like father, like son. Amen.

Or could it be like father, like daughter? Carrie's reaction at the hospital bewildered me. Why on earth had she cuddled up to me with such affection? Or was it despair?

By three o'clock, I realized that my brain had reminisced but failed to come up with any useful way of helping her.

━━ ◆ ━━

CHAPTER THREE

With Demetrio scheduled to arrive in a few hours, it seemed a good idea to stock up on some provisions. We dine out sometimes, but when we're together we eat, drink, and talk in prodigious quantities and prefer to prepare our own meals. Demetrio can make a mean steak tartare if he has some quality meat, and my mole enchiladas can make a grown man cry. Besides, shopping offered a good way to kill an hour and help me clear my mind.

I drove back into town and noticed that, despite my year-long absence, everything looked the same as I'd left it.

An hour later, I opened my front door and retrieved the shopping bags from the back of the Explorer. It required three trips to get them all and line them up along the counter. I'd just emptied a rather hefty bag filled with cans of juice when I heard the surf pounding outside, which meant the deck door had to be open.

I found no one out on the deck, but the door stood ajar. I vividly remembered closing and locking it. Since nothing seemed amiss, I shut it tight and locked it just to prove to myself that I knew how. Normally I only engage the house alarm when I intend to be gone for an extended period of time. No way of knowing if anyone had paid me a visit or I'd simply been negligent.

Out on the street some idiot revved up his car and screeched off into the distance.

All afternoon I'd nursed an uncomfortable feeling about Carrie's reaction to my enquiry as to why she seemed so nervous. It rattled me more than I cared to admit. I returned to my storage duties in the kitchen, my mind still in search of what to do about Carrie. Something had crossed her mind, and she'd become prickly about it on the spot. On the other hand, she sometimes uses exaggeration as a ploy to garner attention. The more I thought about it, the more I vacillated between disregarding her reaction entirely or trying to dig deeper, which I didn't particularly relish. Carrie, skilled at rejecting any attempt to get close to her, had erected a wall of superiority that most people, myself included, found repulsive. Under this persona, everything she says and does has the stench of artificiality about it. As a result, I'm never quite sure if she's acting to avoid contact or if she's simply lost in her own lifelong performance.

There's a hitch in this two-bit analysis of mine, and his name is Paul. He's not a stupid man, yet he's never strayed far from her and tolerates her abuse in a way that no self-respecting person ever would. Paul's one of those rare individuals capable of an intelligent in-depth conversation with anyone from a toddler to a scholar to a wino. Carrie, I tell myself at times like these, must have something that I'm simply too dense to see or else Paul is not as bright as I give him credit for.

My phone rang.

"Hello?"

"¿Qué pasa, *gabacho?*" It was Demetrio. I almost jumped through the receiver.

"Where are you? The airport already?" I asked with amazement.

"*No, qué va,*" he chuckled. "I'm calling from the big pay phone in the sky. I feel like I'm the voice of Quetzalcoatl calling to the bearded conquistador. *¿Cómo estás, hijo mío?*"

"*Jodido,*" I said. "When do you land?"

"The paleface at the controls, Capitán Santos, whose name, by the way, is not in the least reassuring, informed us that we will arrive fifteen minutes early. This means that we will be cruising through your downtown San Diego office buildings in about twenty-five minutes."

My enthusiasm jumped another 200 percent. "*¡Perfecto!* I'll pick you up outside the terminal. What airline?"

"Well, I hate to brag, but it's my airline."

I gave him a sarcastic chuckle to queue his punch line. "Oh?"

"It just so happens that my father's brother, Alejandro—you remember him, the unwavering bachelor that owned those hotels in Cancun? Anyway, he purchased Aeroméxico stock back in 2020 after Delta stepped in to save it. I am proud to say I've always been his favorite nephew."

"Probably because you took him on the original digs to uncover those Mayan ruins in Belize."

"*Es posible.* With sadness I tell you he died last year. The good news is that he left all his stocks to me. Thanks to him, I now own an insignificant percentage of the airline."

He said something I didn't quite get, and a muffled female voice responded.

"María Luisa says hello."

"Tell her that if she's smart, she'll stay away from you."

More muffled exchanges at the other end.

"She says to tell you it's too late, and that you can pick me up at terminal 2."

"Okay, Don Juan, I'm on my way. *Nos vemos.*"

I hung up and ran around the kitchen storing the remaining groceries. I felt giddy with anticipation.

Demetrio is an oasis of sanity in a world of inhumanity and possesses the gift of life. No other person I know is able to squeeze so much enjoyment into every second with so little effort. Decadent, intellectual, caring, and impossibly erudite, he retains boundless information and, unlike any professor I ever learned from, he understands the actual significance of his knowledge. He keeps me bolted to reality. He always shows up when I need him, and I needed him now more than ever.

Anticipating that the evening might be a tad cool for what I was wearing, I dashed upstairs to get a sweater. As I opened the drawer, a cold shock darted through me. My clothes lay askew. I've never been a neat freak, but over the years I've found that rumpled clothes annoy me. Therefore, anything that goes into a drawer gets placed with at least a measure of care. Someone had riffled through this drawer.

I pulled out the others with the same results. With a jolt, I realized that the intruder might still be somewhere in the house.

The deck door. A sense of utter vulnerability shot through me. *Shit! That'll teach you to set the damn alarm!*

I rushed to my bedside table and released the gun compartment concealed under the drawer. The Browning Baby fell quietly into my hand. I checked the chamber and made my way to the closet. Nothing.

I continued room by room until I'd checked every inch of the house. To my relief, I found no one. Once done, I examined the deck door. No sign of forced entry. Whoever it was either entered by some other means or was a skilled professional.

I found the lock to my gun chest intact. I opened it and found nothing missing. I removed the Sig Sauer P226 and shoved it into my waistband, then returned the Baby to its hiding place and made another quick inspection.

This time I engaged the alarm before I left the house.

My heart sped much too fast for comfort, my lungs worked overtime, and my hand shook as I placed the gun inside the armrest. I pressed the ignition button and pulled out of the driveway.

Rush hour traffic clogged the freeway, but luck was on my side, and it took me a mere forty minutes to get to the airport from North County. Demetrio stood at the curb, tapping his feet with mock impatience as I pulled up. He tossed his two bags into the back seat and clambered into the front.

"Our marriage is doomed if you are always going to be late, sweetheart."

"An unexpected visitor. Sorry."

Demetrio could tell the exhilaration of our phone conversation had been replaced by cold professionalism.

"Anyone I know?" he prodded.

I shook my head.

After a moment, Demetrio added, "I am ready. *Soy todo oídos*. Tell me what has happened."

In spite of myself, I smiled. His slight Spanish intonation, coupled with his literal use of the English language, produces a melodic effect irresistible for women and always comforting for me.

By the time we reached the house, I'd brought him up to speed on the events of the last twenty-four hours—Devon's body, Sergeant Haskell, Carrie, Paul, and my unexpected visitor. We lugged his bags upstairs and tossed them on the bed.

"I can unpack those later," he said. "Time to enjoy a drink. We both need one, I think."

"Amen."

Demetrio and I grew up drinking tequila, often more than we should, and it remains our poison of choice. The drawback is that I prefer it with a chaser known as "little blood of the widow," or *sangrita de la viuda,* as it's called south of the border.

Impossible to find a good one anywhere north of Tijuana. Lucky for me, Demetrio knows a killer recipe, and I made sure the ingredients were available for him. He started mixing it while I poured us a couple of shots of Patrón Silver tequila. We started sipping it before he'd finished the chaser. My entire being relished the comforting liquid. I smacked my lips and sighed.

"What puzzles me is the way this all seems interconnected. Carrie must be the key."

"We are ruling out coincidence?" he asked as he squeezed three entire limes into his concoction.

"You tell me. What are the odds?"

"Well, let us think about that." He furrowed his brow. "Let us start with the body on the beach."

"Devon's been dead a couple of weeks, so—"

"Why wait until now to go after Carrie, or Paul, you may ask?"

"I have no answer for that."

He gestured as if to say, *there you have it,* before going on. "Thanks to the tide, Devon washes up at your doorstep. Coincidence. You did not know him from Adam. Right?"

I nodded.

"Paul gets assaulted at Carrie's house. Another coincidence. Because, if the same people were after her, they would have attacked sooner. Yes?"

"It's possible."

"Someone breaks into your house, but you return before they have a chance to steal anything. The only damage is a few messy drawers. What is the word you Americans use for that? Eh, something…dipitty."

"Serendipity?"

"*Exacto.*"

I shook my head at that one. "No. Whoever it was, didn't come here to steal. They were looking for something in particular."

Demetrio mulled that theory over for a moment.

I pushed on. "It's possible the same people that went to Carrie's were after whatever it is they want, and Paul happened to show up." I grabbed half of one lime and sprinkled it with a little salt.

He rocked his head from side to side. "Then the question is, what were they looking for? Agreed?"

I nodded and took a sip of tequila then sucked on the lime.

Demetrio tested his mixture and moaned with approval. He took two glasses and filled them with the *sangrita*. "Maybe it was a thief," he said as he handed me one. "*Salud.*"

"*Salud.*" We each sipped the tequila then the *sangrita*. It tasted better than ever. "Mm, you nailed it."

He picked up the pitcher of *sangrita* and motioned toward the living room. "In my opinion, we have too many questions and too little information for any resolution to be reached."

I grabbed the bottle of tequila and a bowl of pork rinds and followed. "Yeah. Annoying as hell."

Demetrio settled into one of the large leather chairs that stand at each end of the sofa. I placed the bowl and tequila on the table where we could both reach them and plopped onto the sofa.

This has forever been our ritual, and it's one that I find particularly comforting at moments like this. We've found ourselves in similar positions quite often over the years. During these sometimes endless chats, we've discussed everything from the beauty of women to the meaning of life. I know almost everything there is to know about Demetrio, and he knows everything about me. We never hold back. There's no vanity or competition between us. We're free to criticize because we've learned that's what the other expects. If either of us ever pulled a punch, it would spell the end of our friendship.

"Okay," Demetrio said, "let us put Carrie aside for the moment since we do not have the necessary answers. Agreed?"

"But—"

"No, no. *No hay pero que valga,* Justino. I made this trip specifically to hear about your pain, your loss of Cecilia, and this anger and depression that are eating at you. Time to unload with Tata Demetrio."

Demetrio is quite simply Mexico's most outstanding archeologist and specialist in pre-Colombian history and languages. With the same patience he displays when he painstakingly excavates his way through newly discovered ruins, he questioned, prodded, dug, and sifted, forcing me back and forth into the tortuous memories I desperately sought to forget.

A small man, no more than 5'5" in his custom-made shoes, with a cherubic face that beams with an almost constant smile, a full head of thick black unruly hair, and a nasal voice that can break through the din of even the loudest gathering. His infectious personality is impossible to resist. Although no one would deny that the man loves to hear himself talk, especially when there are females to impress, he's also the best of listeners when it matters most.

"Tell me," Demetrio went on, "what causes the most pain, the most fury. Start from the moment Cecilia and you first made contact at that out of the way restaurant you told me about, La Sandunga, then go all the way to the end."

The rage, the sadness, and the pain of reliving it all churned like a cauldron inside me. I shook my head.

"Close your eyes." When I hesitated, he insisted. "Please, *gabacho*, close your eyes and take a deep breath. Start with the plan of action."

I did as he said and forced myself to relive the experience.

He listened for over five hours, interrupting only for clarification or when I rambled. I related every detail I could remember of that awful afternoon.

I confessed how my plan to ensnare the Calavera cartel had backfired, and Cecilia had fallen into their hands.

"Wait. Your plan? Didn't you tell me Cecilia offered to infiltrate the gang?"

"Yes. Nonetheless, my plan."

"Your superiors did not approve?"

"They did but—"

"Okay, I get it. Go on."

I described Cecilia's desperate cries intended to lure me in so they could kill us both. "I decided, why not oblige them? My only course of action was to try and save her."

"It meant suicide, of course."

"Yeah, but least I'd be with her on the other side. With luck I'd take some of them with me."

"An unlikely scenario, no doubt," Demetrio whispered.

"Right. All my options played to their advantage. Worst of all, the cracked ribs, the loss of blood from bullet wounds and lacerations to my face, not to mention the sweltering heat of Cozumel, made it all the more difficult to pinpoint her location and formulate a strategy. Time was running out."

"Your backup team?"

"No sign of them."

"So how did you get out of that mess?"

"I've told you about the 'fight or flight' reaction."

"You said the mind shifts into a kind of alternate reality."

"Yeah. Suddenly I became acutely aware of my options. Not in a way that I could translate into words, but in a way that my subconscious and my training understood. In simple terms, I became a weapon wielded by a power far greater than myself."

"Instinct took over."

I nodded. "The drawback with that state of mind is that it causes lapses of memory and later, when you need to remember, the full picture of what happened isn't there."

"So, you have no recollection of what you did?"

"All I remember is that when the last Calavera bastard dropped, I had one bullet left in my weapon, one lodged in my thigh, and one more parked in my left shoulder."

"And?"

"By the time I dragged myself to her side, Cecilia was dead. Torture had left her unrecognizable. I heard the backup team rushing toward us. Too little and much too late. Then my world faded to black."

"Until you woke up in the hospital."

I nodded and slumped back, tears streaming down my face. Reliving it all had caused the rage and despair to surge inside me, and I cried out.

Demetrio remained silent until my tears ceased to flow.

"I understand better now," he said at last. "But hearing what actually happened that afternoon is not enough. That is not the only thing that distresses you, is it? History is important as well. Take me back to the beginning. What did you two speak about at La Sandunga?"

I wanted to blow him off when her image crept into my mind, and an involuntary grin shaped my lips.

"Why do you smile?" he asked with a tilt of his head.

I stared at the floor, momentarily lost in the memory. "She looked more beautiful than ever that night. Her eyes sparkled."

"Particularly after she told you she had asked for the assignment when she found out you were leading the team. Am I right?"

Another smile along with a nod.

"It would have made me feel excellent as well." Demetrio winked as he toasted to her memory. "A woman like her wanting me? I can only dream such a thing will happen sometime in my future."

Of my three friends, only Demetrio is privy to my true activities on behalf of the Mexican and American governments. Not the details of the missions, of course, but my affiliation with both governments. And though I never shared the original details of any operation, he knew the outcome of many of them. Not from me. His family, the entire Rubio Dávalos clan in fact, was and continues to be steeped in political tradition. They're one of the pillars of the ruling Mexican class and can boast of having produced more secretaries of state, ministers, politicians, and diplomats than any other family in the history of the country. Two of the most outstanding Mexican physicians are Demetrio's uncles. His oldest brother is the Minister of Agriculture and his younger brother was an author on his way to greatness before his untimely death in a questionable automobile accident. The family owns silver mines in Guanajuato, hotels in Acapulco and Cancún, and a ranch in Michoacán. In short, if anyone has access to confidential information it would be the Rubio Dávalos family.

"Tell me again how the two of you first met," he asked as he leaned back in the leather chair.

"You know that already," I protested. I gulped down my Tequila unwilling to go there again.

"Humor me, Justino. It is good to find the place of origin of such things and look for their meaning. Do not refuse the archeologist in me, trust this old man."

I sighed by way of surrender. "Okay, have it your way, *viejo*." I emphasized the last word as a feeble jab to encourage him to desist, but all he did was arch his right eyebrow.

"Our paths originally crossed during a contraband bust in Tijuana a couple of years ago." I smiled. "We hit it off instantly. Realized that we worked well together. There you have it. The whole enchilada."

He ignored my attempt at humor. "How did you 'hit it off'?"

I shrugged and searched for the answer. "I don't know. Our styles were similar somehow. We complemented each other. She's something fierce, that woman." I paused when I realized what I had just said. "Was, she was," I corrected myself.

"Go on," Demetrio insisted. "How long did you work together on that scene?"

"What does it matter?" I grumbled.

"Humor me, *gabacho*. Please."

I wiped aside a couple of tears and nodded. "Okay, okay." I sighed. "I came in at the tail end of the operation, about four or five months."

"This part you have never told me. When did you fall in love?"

I shook my head as a memory took shape. "Then and there, I'd say. But we didn't acknowledge it. Instead, we jumped into bed. A celebration of the strenuous and dangerous work that led to the successful bust and a perfect excuse for what we felt. No need to talk of love. We went at it with full knowledge that it couldn't last. That sooner or later she would have to go her way and I mine. The nature of the job."

"Then when you met again in Cozumel, you picked right up from where you left it. No?" he said with a smile.

I nodded. "Yeah. This time we did talk about it."

"She knew you loved her that night at La Sandunga?"

"Oh, yes. And I knew how she felt." I shook my head. "We should've asked to be replaced. Requested that other agents take on the operation." I shrugged. "But that meant going our separate ways, and we needed to be together, wanted to be together. So, caution—" Tears welled in my eyes, and words proved difficult to come by. "My fault that she's dead."

"She knew the risks," Demetrio whispered.

"So what? I'm the senior officer. My call. My operation. I should've—"

"Did you try? Did you talk about it?"

I stifled a sob and nodded.

"And?"

I shook my head. "She wouldn't have it."

"That fierceness in her. No?"

"That, and the desperate need we felt for each other." I slumped forward, my face buried in my hands.

"Okay. Let me see if I understand." He paused to make sure I caught his drift. "Given what you've told me, her death wasn't an operational mistake on your part. She chose to go forward and—"

"Yes, but—"

"She chose to go forward against your better judgment."

"I know what you're trying to do, Demetrio," I snapped back. "It won't work."

"If you truly understand what I'm trying to do, *cabrón*, you wouldn't go on and on and on," he yelled. "Now, answer me this. Did you and your superiors agree to her suggestion to infiltrate the ranks of the—"

"¡Carajo, sí! Yes, yes, yes! But we were wrong. I was wrong!"

"And why is that?"

"Because she died."

"*Escúchame*, Justino. She died in the line of duty doing what you or any other agent would have done. Am I right?"

"No! She died to save me!"

"That is not what I heard. I must have missed the part where she did that."

I sprung to my feet. "Demetrio!" I yelled. "It won't work. You can't excuse my actions. She died to save me!"

He rose and pushed me back onto the sofa and glared down at me. "*Cállate, pendejo.* Listen to me, and listen well. She died to give you the chance to exterminate the vermin you were after. She did *not* die to save you. Had it been you in their hands or any other agent, you would have done the same thing. ¡Por Dios, hombre! Honor her courage, her commitment. Do not reduce her to a mere victim by denying her sacrifice. She died to bring that cartel to an end. She died a hero in the line of duty. You owe her that much, and nothing less."

With that, he allowed me to whimper on my own. He refilled our glasses with the last of the tequila and *sangrita*, and placed them on the table, then snuggled back into his chair.

"Justino, listen. Countless times in the past you have described many 'adventures,' as you call them, similar to this. From that I have learned that you are a methodical man. You are never rash. Always in control. True that you change your approach and tactics in creative ways from time to time. But you reduce your risks to a minimum and always do exactly as you and Cecilia did in Cozumel."

"And what is that?"

"Whatever is necessary to complete the mission. This fact has been the same, except"—he sipped his drink—"except that in this particular case, you were in love with the person who did what she was supposed to do and gave you the opportunity to finish off Calavera and his thugs. She kept them busy long enough for you to find her. She made it possible for you to eliminate her killers and destroy the cartel because that was her mission. Her duty. If either of you had acted differently, both of you would be dead, and the mission would have been a failure instead of the success it turned out to be. Countless lives have been saved as a result of her actions."

After another sip of tequila followed by the *sangrita*, he placed the glasses on the table and continued. "You are now having trouble accepting the reality that you must live with this." He leaned forward and placed his hand on my forearm. "And you know why?"

I shook my head.

"Then I will tell you. You have rediscovered yourself, my friend. That is the real gift she left you. If you deny it, if you throw that gift away, then it is *you* who has made her death a waste. And I guarantee that if you do, it is the one thing you truly could not live with."

I thought it over but the concept refused to sink in. "I don't—"

"Stop. I will spell it out for you since you have chosen to not recognize it." He leaned back into the chair. "Do you remember the last time you gave a damn what happened to you? Before Cecilia, when did you care about anyone, including yourself? Answer me honestly."

All I could muster was a blank stare.

"Come on, Justino. When did you last want something for yourself?"

I shrugged. "Truth is, I don't really need much."

"Bullshit, as you gringos like to say. You need love. And I do not mean Cecilia's love. That is gone. I mean your love, the love of life, the love of purpose that you used to have."

"What the hell is this 'love of purpose' bullshit?" My patience with my pseudo psychologist was thinning. It happens when he gets too close.

"Some years back, you lost your interest in life. Everything outside the 'job' no longer had meaning for you. Agreed?"

What he said made sense, and in spite of myself, I nodded.

"Any idea why?"

His question stumped me. A heavy silence settled between us. Demetrio didn't speak, didn't move, and maybe didn't even breathe. He waited for me to search for the answer.

"Too much death," I whispered at last.

He sighed. "*Exacto*! You needed to connect with life again, and Cecilia gave you that."

"But now she and it are gone."

"Only if you let it. The least you can do for her is to make sure you never again give into that place of darkness."

"And how the fuck can I do that, Demetrio?" I roared. "Tell me how the hell can I do that?" It sounded more like a threat than a question.

He leaned toward me. "You must honor Cecilia's love enough to care."

"Care?"

"Care."

"She's dead, I can't—"

"Yes, you can. How do I know this? Because you have already started. Look at your concern for Carrie. That is a form of love. Caring for you sister whom you have neglected for years and who is alive. That is a way of loving and living. You had lost your way, and Cecilia offered you the road back. She was the first woman to get close to you since your mother died."

He peered deep into my eyes before he continued.

"Listen to me, Justino. For years now, I have watched you slide away from life. I saw you take greater and greater risks, challenging your own mortality. You have been killing much more than just your enemies these past few years, my friend. But more worse, I could see the death wish in your eye. It filled me with great pain because I had no idea how to make *you* see it. Somehow, Cecilia got close enough to show you a glimpse of who you once were and could still be. Use that now to care for your sister. It may be your best chance to find your way back to yourself."

I felt tears flood into my eyes as I stared into his.

"Justin, please give yourself as much love as Cecilia did. Do not run from it. Be alive. Let yourself feel the pain, yes, but use it to heal the wounds so you can give some love back to those of us who love you."

Like the night before, I felt fury and pain too great for my chest to contain. "I can't do it, Demetrio. I swear to God, I can't do it." I banged my fist against my chest. "There's nothing in here. Just death. Death upon death. I'm steeped in it. I look over my shoulder, and it's all I see. My life now means nothing but death."

I swayed aimlessly, and I tasted my tears as I spoke. My senses so acute that I could see shades and lights on objects as if they were photographs. Every breath triggered pain as I gasped for air. I wanted to lash out. Smash everything in sight. I settled for smashing my hands into my legs.

Demetrio dropped to his knees and clamped his hands around my wrists. I collapsed forward, my head between my knees, my sobs exploding through my throat.

Little by little, all emotion drained from my body. As with the previous night and so many nights before, I ended up depleted. No emotion, no strength, only a leaden emptiness that dragged me further and further down.

Demetrio stuffed a handkerchief into my left hand. Such a tender gesture. He placed his hand on the nape of my neck and leaned his head against mine. He said nothing. After a few moments, he released me and rose to his feet.

When my breathing finally subsided to something close to normal, I slumped back and let the cushions embrace me. It was comforting to feel the softness. My throat was on fire. Everything felt congested. Eyes, mouth, and face swollen. My body had plunged into the depths of exhaustion.

Demetrio went to the kitchen and drew some water. He returned and held out a glass. I sipped it, letting my throat savor every cool drop. He downed half of his own glass of water in one gulp, then placed the remainder on the table, and sat on the arm of the leather chair.

I glanced up at him and a smile came to my lips. I shook my head and turned away. It was an awkward moment.

The room seethed with a despair that needed to claw its way out. Anything said would be trapped there forever. We both knew it, and in agonizing silence, we both let it go.

——◆•◆•◆——

CHAPTER FOUR

I awoke before dawn and stared at the ceiling. Demetrio's words replayed over and over in my mind. He was right, I'd plunged into a quagmire of self-pity. Cecilia's death had contributed to that. But now, for the first time, the realization that I'd inhabited that deep abyss for years became undeniable. The more I thought about it, the more I recognized the pattern.

Misery had been the force that steered my every action.

The anger I felt when I first discovered my father's activities had driven me into the same business, in a futile attempt to atone for what I'd concluded were his and the agency's atrocities. With dogged determination, I'd contrived to place my father at the center of every political upheaval I could remember, from the removal of president Allende of Chile and the endorsement of Pinochet's brutal rule, to the perpetuation of Noriega's murderous regime in Panamá. With each distorted recollection, I detached myself further from him.

Such stigma demanded retribution. I'd show him and his kind that there were better ways to achieve peace and protect us from the evils of the world. I threw myself, body and soul, into defending the honor of America, and later Mexico, against what I imagined to be a one-sided, self-serving intervention— my father's kind of abuse as I'd chosen to interpret it. I'd prove to him that I could work for the betterment of both countries without upsetting the natural balance. After all, I'd been raised bilingual and bicultural—a significant feather in my hat that my father never donned. And a clear advantage.

My education into the harsh reality began almost immediately. On my first assignment into the jungles of Guerrero, those who recognized the name Pierce were quick to point out how the father I loathed for his indifference and cruelty had, in fact, saved this village or that family or that freedom fighter. I later discovered that his actions stood in direct contradiction to his express orders. Despite my self-proclaimed convictions of his corruption, I came across the same pattern of admiration almost everywhere I went. By the end of my second year in the field, I'd been forced to reassess my opinions of the man I so wished to despise.

At the same time, an increasingly clear picture of my own employers emerged. Their corruption was at times so encompassing that it defied belief. Not everyone, not everywhere, not every time, but pervasive nonetheless. Vast sums of public money gushed into the private coffers of officials—on both sides—to carry out their personal agendas. In Mexico, presidents, high-level military, government officials, and ministers were on the take. At the end of their tenure in office many had amassed fortunes large enough to place them on the lists of Latin America's wealthiest men, while their countrymen remained mired in poverty, ignorance, and disease.

American officials and diplomats, along with corrupt investigative and intelligence agents, also took full advantage of the under-the-table money game.

Hard lessons for a son seeking to erase the stigma of his father's actions. Confronting the realities of *the game* gradually pulled me down, but the definitive blow came from the guilt over my delusions about him. *Justin's self-pity served to him on a silver platter.* I'd talked myself into this line of work—my choice, mind you—to defy my dead father and atone for his faults, only to uncover that he wasn't the monster I'd made him out to be. Squeaky clean? Not even close. But neither was he the demonic spreader of destabilization I'd envisioned.

I must've drifted back to sleep, because when my eyes crept open, the sun blasted through the curtains, and the invigorating aroma of fresh brewed Mexican coffee penetrated my senses. I rolled out of bed and found Demetrio in the kitchen, scanning the newspaper. He has his own way of making the strong brew, which includes cinnamon and cloves, sweetened with a little brown sugar. I headed straight for it.

"*Buenos días,*" I said in a voice that reverberated with morning gravel. "*¿Cómo estás?*"

"*Bien.* I think this will be a good day. The beach already shows signs of becoming interesting."

I glanced through the window, and sure enough, the multicolored bikinis already speckled the sand, all evidence of the unfortunate events of two evenings earlier now completely gone.

I glanced at the clock on the wall over the sink. The short hand was north of eleven and the long hand pointed south of three. "I caught up on my beauty sleep."

I climbed onto a stool down the counter from my friend and closed my eyes as I sipped the strong black coffee. It provided exactly the jolt of electricity my system needed. In an instant, all the cogs and levers inside shifted into gear. I felt alive. Two more quick sips confirmed it. Even my brain whirred into action.

"Anything in the news?" I asked.

"Mm."

From experience I knew that meant, "Shut up, I'm reading." I slipped away and let my eyes wander to the beach.

In spite of myself, I found enjoyment in the radiant day in Seaview. The morning haze had given up and allowed the blue sky to make an appearance, dappled with a few high clouds here and there. No wonder the sun worshipers raced to stake out their claims—sunburn weather's triumphant return demanded to be celebrated.

"The police have established that your Mr. Devon never stepped off the yacht," Demetrio said. "He got on, but never got off."

"No trouble narrowing down the suspects, then."

He continued his abridgment. "The passengers and the crew will be questioned… 'extensively,' I think it said. They expect it will take several days, but the chief is optimistic that his men will have this sorted out in no time." He held the paper out to me. "Would you like to read it?"

I savored my coffee and shook my head. Demetrio folded the paper and placed it on the counter behind him. He stretched and groaned then rolled his head from side to side. He finished with a loud grunt then looked at me and smiled. "How are you feeling?"

I shrugged. "Amazingly well. Thanks for the therapy session."

Demetrio slid off his stool to get a refill. "Are you hungry?"

"Mm hmm. You gonna cook?"

He poured some coffee and scooped an additional heaping teaspoon of brown sugar into it, stirred the mixture, and returned to the stool. He peered at me through squinted eyes, his mouth puckered in a mock effort of serious consideration. Finally, "No, *compadre*," he said. "I have decided I want to grow up and be like you. I will start with one of those decadent American breakfasts they offer over at the hotel that is made with everything that is bad for you. After that you need some exercise to strengthen yourself. You are looking too weak. You will drive us to the nearest golf course, where we will spend four or five wonderfully meaningless hours chasing a little white ball through trees, miniature beaches, and artificial lakes. Doctor's orders."

"Okay, doctor," I said. "Let's do it. Don't know if I can manage eighteen holes, but I'll give it a go."

After cleaning up well enough to appear in public, we sauntered up the hill to the Mirador coffee shop at the Pacific Sunset Hotel. The hostess, a charming young woman named Judy, nodded to us the instant we entered. She always takes care of us even when there's a crowd. Today, there was a crowd.

"You're just in time, Mr. Pierce. Another two minutes, and I would have had to cancel your reservation. Hope you're feeling better and that the doctor here is caring well for you." She smiled at Demetrio. "Please follow me, gentlemen. Right this way."

She flashed us an impish smile, plucked a couple of menus from the case, and escorted us through the line of waiting patrons to a small table that overlooked the gardens. The ideal setting.

"Thank you, darling girl," said Demetrio as he took her hand and kissed it.

"Gosh, doctor. You shouldn't do that, you'll have me thinking I'm a grand lady." She glanced disapprovingly at me. "What happened to you, Mr. Pierce? You look awful."

"Fortunately, you look beautiful enough for both of us."

"Sorry. I didn't mean—"

"I know, I know. Just yanking your chain."

"He tried to stop a speeding truck when he went sleepwalking," Demetrio interjected. "I am here to make him all better."

"Thank goodness for that. Hope you heal quickly. Enjoy your meal."

Demetrio all but drooled as Judy glided off. "She is the real reason I come here for breakfast. With a woman like that, a man is content before he even orders." He watched her make her way among the tables. "Do you think Mrs. S. would have any objection to her granddaughter going out with a distinguished college professor-doctor type?"

"Only if it's you."

The Mirador will never make anyone's best food list, but it has a charm that more luxurious hotels lack—Mrs. Sandusky's touch. The service, the food, and the ambiance are professional enough to deflect complaints, but not so polished that you have to know which utensil is for what dish. She also makes it very clear to guests with children that if said children can't behave in a public place, room service would be a far more acceptable alternative. Over the years, this has resulted in a clientele among whom children are conspicuously absent, and the few who do appear are always quiet and courteous.

Demetrio's idea turned out to be perfect. The surroundings, the lush vegetation outside the window, the din of hotel guests and service personnel, even the decadent breakfast of eggs, sausage, pancakes, and potatoes, all conspired to insulate my emotions and pull me out of the doldrums. By the end of the meal, I was laughing at Demetrio's humorous anecdotes and looking forward to a splendid day on the golf course.

Demetrio adjourned to the men's room, and, as I loosened my belt to accommodate my expanding waistline, the somber figure of Sergeant Bill Haskell materialized next to the table. Without asking, he took an empty chair from an adjoining table and sat down.

"Mr. Pierce, nice to see you again. You don't mind if I sit down."

Obviously, not a question.

"Looks like you already have," I answered none too kindly. "What can I do for you?"

"I was wondering if you happened to know a Mrs. Carrie Harding."

"She's my sister, but you already know that."

"It seems she was one of the last people to see Mr. Devon alive. You know where?"

"I'm sure you have compelling reasons to ask me this instead of her." I didn't try to hide my dislike for him.

"Oh, nothing special. I seem to recall you saying you didn't know the man."

He ran his tongue along his teeth under his lips then made a sucking sound out of one side of his mouth.

My distaste for him grew by the second. "I didn't," I replied at last.

"Really? And she never mentioned him?"

"Why should she?"

"Let me get this straight. Your sister works day after day for, I don't know, several years anyway, with the same guy, and she never even mentions him to you?"

Haskell looked down his nose at me.

"Do you have a point to make? Because, if not, I have an important engagement that I can't put off."

Haskell glared at me and manufactured a sarcastic snigger. "Well, I'll speak to you again, Mr. Pierce. Hopefully when you're not so pressed for time."

"Good luck with that. I'm a very busy guy."

He shot me a curt smile then sprang to his feet and walked away, leaving the chair where it stood. He rammed into an elderly woman, almost knocking her to the floor. He was pissed. And pissed cops are dangerous.

Demetrio returned in time to see Haskell storm off. "He is even more charming than your description."

I took a deep breath. "I'd better avoid any dark alleys."

Demetrio laughed. "Amen."

It took me a couple of holes at Mar Vista Golf Club to shake off the encounter with Seaview's protector of society. My muscles had loosened up after the quick warm-up and now thanked me for the much-needed physical exertion. Some sporadic shots were good enough to delude myself into believing that I could actually play the game. Demetrio hates golf because he can't perfect it, and it showed each time he failed to execute the shot he had in mind. Despite that, we had a fun time, took it slow, and granted the effort "perfect therapy" status. We returned to the house by five.

My experience of the previous day had left me more than a little paranoid. I roamed the house and checked everything as soon as we opened a couple of beers. To my relief, nothing seemed amiss. There was, however, a message from Carrie. I'd been calling her on her cell off and on with no success. Her message conveyed a single purpose—stop calling, I'm okay, don't fuss over me.

Demetrio and I spent the balance of the evening talking about Cecilia, and for the first time since her death, I found myself able to smile at the mention of her name. Demetrio, the miracle worker.

Next morning, the Southern California sun glared across the Pacific with a vengeance as if it realized how desperately everyone needed it. The abnormal winter of torrential rains and wind almost fading from memory.

Demetrio and I ate breakfast out on the deck. By the time we finished, the beach swarmed with sun worshipers while surfers dotted the waves that swelled majestically before dying upon the shore.

The paper and TV news provided limited information on the Devon case. A spokesperson for the SPD stated that preliminary analysis of the body indicated that Devon had died between eight and twelve days before he washed up on the beach. The body had been submerged for much of that time. The coroner was carrying out an in-depth analysis, the results of which would be forthcoming. Until then, it could not be determined whether the victim had died as a result of foul play. The last time Mr. Devon had been seen alive was thirteen days earlier on board a party yacht during a staff celebration of Ocean Crest University. The police were still questioning all those present at the party and had no updates at this time.

"There are no coincidences," I said, as I sipped my coffee.

"What?"

"These things are all related. Devon, Carrie, Paul. They're linked. I need to find out how."

"I'm not sure I like where this is going," Demetrio replied with a slow, deliberate cadence. "You are on required leave and your superiors on this side of the border would not like it if you did not obey. You could get into a lot of trouble. Plus, your Picasso-style face with its scars is scary and—"

"I can't let it slide, Demetrio. If Carrie's a target, I need to do something. Even if she's flicked me off."

"Something like what? What about your bullet wounds?"

"They're pretty much healed," I lied. "No internal damage."

"You're still sore and—"

"I'm not going to a fight."

"Then where are you going?"

"I don't know yet. But she's hiding something, and that's not good. Especially if she knows why Devon was killed. I'll need you to keep an eye on her while I dig around. Can you do that?"

His face contorted in disapproval while he studied me. After a deep sigh, he nodded. "*Claro, compadre.* Whatever you need."

"She can be a real pain, you know."

"No, no. Your sister and I, we get along like two pea pods."

"*Gracias.*" Demetrio and his botched axioms never fail to amuse.

"Time for a dip in that blue ocean. Want to join me?"

"You dip. I need to patch my face. I'll get back to you when I locate Carrie."

He threw up his arms. "*Está bien*. If you insist. I think you are worried over nothing."

CHAPTER FIVE

Unable to reach Carrie on her cell, I headed toward the hospital, where I found her at Paul's bedside, meek as a faithful dog and completely out of character. His condition remained critical but stable, even though he lingered in a coma. The catheter in his brain continued to drain well and, at least for the moment, the prognosis was cautiously optimistic.

Carrie glanced up as I entered and quickly turned away. "What are you doing here?" Her bloodshot eyes offered undeniable evidence of a sleepless night of crying and concern.

"We need to talk, Carrie." She shook her head. "This is important. Please. I insist."

After much persuasion on my part, she reluctantly gave in. We left Paul in the care of the nurses and deemed a bland cup of hospital coffee at the commissary preferable to a cup from the machine or the would-be Mexican place. We made our way down in silence and secured a reasonably isolated table beside a window. The small, landscaped patio outside offered an oasis of greenery in an otherwise sterile environment. The bird feeders that attracted an endless stream of feathery creatures added a bucolic touch and a glimmer of cheerfulness. They hopped and flitted about in some kind of unrehearsed dance that made us smile in spite of ourselves.

I broke the silence. "Have the Seaview police questioned you about Devon yet?"

She made a face of disgust as if a bad odor had wafted in. "If you can call it that. They brought us into some makeshift conference room in groups of eight to ten and asked general things. Did we notice anything unusual about him or about the people around him, did we know of anyone who had a grudge against him, when was the last time we remembered seeing him. Stuff like that. A waste of time, if you ask me."

"What did you tell them?"

"The truth."

I leaned toward her to ensure no one around could hear me. "Carrie, when I asked you about Devon, you got upset. Why?"

She stared at me for a moment as if I had insulted her and spat out, "I did no such thing."

I reached for her hand. "Carrie, I realize this is uncomfortable, but I need you to listen to me for a second. There's more going on here than some overweight bureaucrat falling overboard because he couldn't hold his gin." She shot me a look of disdain. "Somebody broke into my house yesterday," I added.

She tensed and pulled her hand away.

I pushed on. "It's possible that the same people attacked Paul. Maybe not, but we need to be sure. You have to tell me whatever you know about Devon."

She nibbled at the corner of her mouth. Her eyes reflected the whirlwind of activity going on in her mind. She leaned closer to me and placed her hand on mine. "Are you sure?"

"Call it experience. Call it instinct if you want. There's too much going on for all this to be mere coincidence. If I'm wrong, no harm done, but if not, I need to find out. I need to make sure you're safe."

She mulled it over for a very long moment then nodded. "Okay. Devon was a straight-shooter kind of guy. The type that believes that laws and regulations are there for a reason and need to be enforced. He made some enemies a couple of years ago when he found that some faculty had been defrauding the college."

"Fraud? At a university?"

"Don't act so surprised. We handle lots of money in many ways and from a slew of sources." She flashed me frown number ten—*you jerk*.

"Okay, okay. I get it. Describe the fraud."

She shifted uneasily and glanced around as if deciding whether to confide in me or not. "They were cooking the enrollment rosters for some off-campus classes."

I shrugged. "I don't get it."

She nodded. "In simple terms, these so-called professors claimed they had students enrolled in their classes, when in reality the students didn't exist. They were getting paid for work they weren't performing."

"What did Devon do?"

"He stopped them immediately. But they banded together and initiated a vicious slander campaign against him. They thought they could intimidate him into backing down. When Jer informed their supervisor—"

"Not you, right?"

"No, of course not me." Smile number ten showed up briefly before she went on. "He reported his findings to the Vice President of Academic Affairs. She supervises all faculty. Anyway, he told her what he'd discovered and suggested that she should report it to the authorities. He was ordered not to make waves and leave them be. Uncovering their scheme and stopping them was enough, she told him. No need to sully the university's reputation with unnecessary investigations. As a result, all he could do was cancel their classes. It incensed him. These guys were stealing money, and nothing would be done. He wanted to hold them accountable."

"Devon's job, same as yours? Research?"

The left eyebrow went up, a telltale sign of smirk number eight—*are you kidding, you stupid creature*? "No. Dean of Enrollment Management. He didn't have the college degree to be at my level. Plus, what I do isn't 'just' research, it's strategic planning, accreditation, and—"

"Sorry." I apologized, not because I meant it, but to prevent her going off on a tangent. "What happened once he canceled their classes?"

"They filed grievances against him with a bunch of bogus claims. Eventually the grievances were all dismissed, but it tied his hands as far as taking any other action against them. It would look like retaliation, which was exactly their intention."

"I understand. Go on."

She looked down at her cup and began to rotate it by quarter turns. "Jeremy was not about to let it lie. He began an in-depth analysis going back almost ten years. Discovered all kinds of evidence of other schemes these guys were involved in and decided to save it in case he needed it."

"What kind of evidence?"

She shrugged and shook her head. "I don't know the details. He only hinted about it a few weeks ago. My guess is that they were collecting cash from students and running their own for-profit business."

I must've had a blank expression because she felt compelled to explain further.

"They could've asked students to pay cash for in-class fees and pocketed the money or required students to pay cash directly to them for special seminars or materials in order to pass the class. Things like that."

"I assume teachers can't do that because…?" My turn to raise an eyebrow.

"Fees and tuitions are regulated and must be collected by the bursar—the cashier for the college. Faculty shouldn't collect cash, let alone make up seminars on the fly and get paid directly."

"If he revealed this evidence, what would happen to those teachers?"

"Assuming the evidence was bulletproof? They'd be fired. As for being accused of fraud, I don't know, maybe criminal charges could be brought against them. The legal steps to fire a professor are almost insurmountable and take forever. The expense often prevents academic institutions from pursuing that kind of action. Then you have to face the very powerful union that protects its own, as it should."

"What else?" I asked.

"That's all I know, really."

"Do you know these teachers?"

"Sure, everyone knows them, and with all the grievances they filed, we all knew what was going on."

"What about the evidence?"

She looked away as if the answer was flying somewhere around the room. "I don't know. He let slip one night when we were working late that he'd been collecting it."

"Wait, why would he be working late with you?"

"I needed enrollment data to complete a report, that's all. I was having trouble making my computer understand me, and he helped me. He mentioned the evidence while he worked on the damned thing. He said he'd found the smoking gun. Didn't tell me what, just a passing hint. He was dying to share it with someone. But didn't tell me."

"Is there anyone else he might have given this information to? Someone who would know he'd collected this stuff, whatever it might be?"

She looked at me, then gave a reluctant shake of the head.

"I've got to know this, Carrie. Think about it. Devon's dead, Paul's in a coma, your condo's been trashed, and someone broke into my house. We're talking about fraud. Granted it's about a few corrupt professors stealing from innocent students and the college, but it's a crime, nevertheless. And it looks to me like they're very concerned about that evidence being made public. Now, talk to me."

She bit her lip and shook her head again. "I'm not sure."

"Carrie, listen to me. If you know about this, then somebody else knows, too. That person may face the same fate as Jeremy Devon, and trust me, that's a burden you don't want to live with."

She hesitated. After a couple of heart-felt sighs, she gave in. "Okay. There's one person that might know. She's a clerk. She was his…friend. I don't think he would tell anyone else. I'm not supposed to be aware of it, either. He made a passing comment while he was helping me. Really, that's all."

I didn't like the emphasis she kept placing on this accidental hint from Devon, but now wasn't the time to go into that. I needed more details, so I pressed. "Carrie, in my experience, the more secret the information is, the more people know about it. What's her name, where does she work?"

After some hesitation she answered. "Nancy Drier. She's in enrollment services."

"What about those teachers?"

"What about them?"

"I need their names."

She stared at me then sighed and pursed her lips. "Justin, is this really necessary?"

"You said it isn't a secret given they filed all kinds of claims through the union and launched a campaign against Devon. So why not give me their names?"

She looked down at her coffee then up at me. "It's a secret in that bad actions like that aren't shared outside the university. We protect the reputation of the institution."

"And I'm here to protect you and see to Paul's well-being, not to talk to the press or spread rumors."

She smiled, a shy, thankful smile—one I had no number for and didn't remember seeing before.

After a long pause she nodded. "Okay Justin, but you never heard these names from me." I nodded in agreement. "One is a health and fitness professor named DeLane Ruthskin. The other one is a dean—if you can call what he does management. He also teaches business part-time, a real mean bastard named Karl Hanley. Both have reputations for messing with their female students, but nothing ever sticks. In the end, the victims always change their stories or decline to testify."

"Did Devon give you any of his evidence?"

"Justin, I've already told you."

"Yeah, yeah, he just hinted. Can you think of another reason why they'd break into your condo?"

That hit home because her eyes opened wide. She thought it over for a moment, then gave in. "Okay," she said at last. "Colleges are cesspools of gossip. Folks have way too much time on their hands and like to keep entertained making up stories."

"You lost me. What does that have to do with you?"

"I'm pretty high up in the organization—upper management, a vice president—if that means anything to you." She stared at me, both eyebrows raised in an implied question.

I nodded. "Okay."

"The fact that we spent time together didn't go unnoticed. Work stuff, mind you, that's all. In some areas, my work and his merged. Although my subordinates dealt with him most of the time, there were occasions when I had to oversee things. Jer was very thorough, and I liked that. I'm a stickler for perfection. Folks knew I liked his work, and the fact that I stood up for him in our senior staff meetings when he was under attack got their attention, too. You know how it is. They see you standing up for someone and immediately slap you with an affair."

"But he's not your type. I'm sure they could see that." Carrie was feeling increasingly vulnerable and pinned in. I needed her to trust me.

She gave me a little smile, one I hadn't seen since she was eight or nine. A pang of caring stirred somewhere deep inside me.

"Did you tell the cops about this evidence of his?"

"It wasn't my place."

"Carrie—"

"Justin, I didn't. End of story. Now leave me alone."

With that, our sharing session came to an abrupt end, and I realized that I'd get nothing more from her. For the moment, at least. "Okay, let's get back to Paul," I suggested by way of escape.

She nodded, and we lumbered our way back to his room. Given that his condition remained the same, the nurses suggested she'd be better off calling in for updates rather than waiting there. Her reluctance was evident.

"Why don't you stay at my place?"

"No need. The police have finished with my condo and said I can go home."

"Did they find anything?"

"So far, they've got nothing, but said they'll be going over all the forensics they collected and keep me informed. San Diego has La Jolla police way understaffed, so it could take forever."

"You could stay with me until your place is straightened out. Besides, Demetrio's here and—"

"What's he doing here?"

"Little vacation."

She frowned. "Is he tending to your bruises?"

I nodded.

"He's good at that." And the little-girl smile crept up again.

Equipped with this new caring persona that had overtaken the old Justin, I persuaded Carrie to leave the hospital and take me back to her place so I could take a look.

By the time we reached her penthouse, she'd made it clear that she had no intention of coming to stay with me. No real surprise. Not once has she ever accepted my invitation. But seeing the mess Paul's attackers had left behind, particularly his blood splattered all over the floor, elicited a sense of vulnerability that I suspected she'd never experienced before. She filled two suitcases faster than I thought humanly possible, which left me little time to investigate the scene. I promised her that I'd take care of the cleanup as soon as she settled in.

We drove to my beach house in silence, her mind occupied with Paul and now, thanks to me, with Devon. Mine was occupied trying to figure out what bothered me about this whole convoluted picture. The crimes that Ruthskin and Hanley might have committed didn't add up to a motive for murder, as far as I could see. Double homicide if Paul died. From Carrie's description, the Seaview police didn't seem too thorough in their interrogations. And Haskell? He brought out the worst in me, which in and of itself made him worth looking into.

The minute I opened the door, Carrie flew into Demetrio's arms, tears and sobs as if on demand.

"*Mi niña, mi niña, pobrecita, pobrecita,*" he said as he caressed her hair. "*No te preocupes, Papá Demetrio está aquí, solo para ti. Ven, cuéntame todo.*" He guided her gently toward the living room.

In no time, Demetrio had Carrie eating out of his loving hands—the father she never had, the brother she never cared for, the friend she always trusted. How could I have missed this obvious bond between them?

I let them be and went about setting her up in the extra bedroom, the one always reserved for her, even though she'd never set foot in it. I never imagined she'd ever actually use it, but my mother would've approved. I dropped Carrie's suitcases on the bed and checked the adjoining restroom for towels and such. All was in place, waiting for Goldilocks to make her long-awaited appearance. I now appreciated how well my cleaning lady had kept it. The room was immaculate.

I returned downstairs to discover that Demetrio had lured Carrie into a walk on the beach. I watched from the window as they strolled hand in hand in the opposite direction from where Devon's body washed up.

Thankful for some time alone, I stepped out onto the deck, removed my shirt, and allowed the sun to rain down a few rays of hope. The rhythm of the ocean, the caress of the breeze, even the squawk of seagulls, all conspired to engulf the uptight Justin in a much-needed moment of peace.

As the sun began to set, my charges remained far down the beach engrossed in what appeared to be animated conversation. I wrote a note for them not to expect me for dinner and drove back to Carrie's place.

CHAPTER SIX

My sister's absence allowed me ample time to sift through the chaos left by the intruders and police. I picked everything up, placed all her clothes in the closets and the knickknacks on any available surface. At least she'd find some semblance of order when she returned home. At first glance, it didn't appear they'd found whatever they were looking for.

I did find something, however—a hitherto undiscovered side of my sister.

As I cleaned and inspected the penthouse, it became apparent that on the handful of previous visits, I'd failed to take any real notice of her apartment, due mostly to an overwhelming desire not to be there in the first place. Her *Town and Country* condo displayed impressive original art on the walls, counters, and shelves, most of which had been moved about, although nothing appeared to be damaged or stolen. All the pieces fit together with a thoughtfulness and sensitivity I never thought her capable of. Even the large sculptures weren't ostentatious and served to enhance the place with an uncanny simplicity despite the significant value of most pieces. An unpretentious Carrie?

Hard to believe, but I couldn't refute the evidence before me. Her choice of furniture dovetailed nicely with her taste in clothing, and the colors throughout the apartment blended effectively with her soft skin tones and streaked brown hair. A gentle grace permeated the bedroom, which she'd managed not to spoil by overdecorating, and allowed the wall-to-wall window with its enviable view of La Jolla and its beaches to dominate the space. I always knew she had good taste, but this evident subtlety came as an unexpected surprise to me. A warmhearted Carrie dwelled here.

Her wine cellar—a small temperature-controlled room—boasted a sophisticated international reserve. Carrie the connoisseur.

The library, a room dedicated exclusively to her expansive collection of books, welcomed visitors to relax in any of its antique cushy sofas, read by the vintage floor lamps, or simply enjoy the fireplace. She'd created a cozy room despite the posh furnishings, and by the look of it, this is where she spent considerable time. Carrie the intellectual I knew well, no surprise there.

The intruders had toppled and emptied her desk but hadn't damaged it. Its contents were strewn all over the library, so I gathered and painstakingly examined each and every item. Amongst the disarrayed files, I found her hidden collection of old family photos and news clippings. Carrie the sentimental.

The journey through Carrie's visual collage of our family revealed many joyful memories. It felt odd, however, to come to the realization that, despite the fact that there had been many good times and real familial love, both of us had chosen somehow to ignore those stretches of happiness. Instead, for some deep-seated Freudian reason, we'd elected to spit out venom about each other and our parents. I wondered why, when all our expressed memories reflected anger or disgust, she'd managed to collect and store all this confirmation to the contrary. Could this be Carrie the melancholic? I certainly could relate to that.

As the room regained order, I noticed that one important thing was missing. A computer. A researcher like Carrie would require a computer to complement and catalog all the papers, files, charts, and documents I'd painstakingly gathered and reorganized for her. I assumed she had a laptop, but it didn't seem to be anywhere in the condo. Had they taken it?

With little else to do, I headed home with more questions than answers.

The next morning, I decided not to tell Carrie that I'd visited her place. I didn't want her to leave. I needed her to be where I could keep an eye on her. As it turned out, there was no chance for conversation. She'd rushed off, explaining that she would barely get to work on time after stopping at the hospital. Paul's condition remained unchanged. His predicament weighed on her to the degree that she even seemed soft at times. If she didn't love him, whatever she felt for Paul came awfully close.

At breakfast, I filled Demetrio in on the rest of what I knew so far—precious little. I assigned him the task of keeping a close eye on Carrie. For all I knew, there could be another attempt, if whoever broke into her house thought she had something they wanted. He happily accepted his mission. He'd enjoy "toying with the academic types," he said. We rented him a convertible Mustang to ensure that the local *bellezas* wouldn't miss him, and off he went to college. One less thing for me to worry about.

Time to get down to serious business. A couple of years earlier, during the operation in Tijuana where Cecilia and I first connected, I had done several *favors* for Martin Sauers, my CIA liaison in San Diego. Since then, we'd exchanged *favors* on various occasions. The kind of favors that leave one indebted to the other for life. As a result, we'd developed a close friendship at a professional level that eventually leaked into a personal one. I gave Marty a call and asked him to get me everything available on a Sergeant Bill Haskell. His price, an evening of tequila and *sangrita* some weekend in the near future, met Pierce's strict guidelines for bribery, and that sealed the deal.

I swallowed some painkillers to avert budding aches and pains throughout my body, did my best to disguise the remaining bruises and visible scars, and headed for Ocean Crest University.

My adrenaline flowed pretty well now. Two nights ago, I'd sobbed myself to sleep. Now, my unease about Carrie had taken precedence over the events that had so impacted me in Cozumel. The effect, born of my concern for my sister, took me by surprise. For the first time in years, maybe ever, I'd finally focused on the real her, and not my resentful boyhood impressions. Could this be brotherly love? Not sure, since I'd never experienced it before. Perhaps I liked being the threatened wolf protecting what was mine.

All evidence pointed to Paul being in the wrong place at the right time, which meant he might have taken her place. Whether by accident or design remained unclear. Self-preservation, if that's the correct label, once ingrained, shifts into gear without conscious intent. In a way, that's good. Your guard is never completely down. It's also a problem because you can never look at things the way normal mortals do. But when those close to you are threatened, a far deeper instinct takes over. Defense mode becomes attack mode, and suddenly the predator emerges, fangs bared, claws at the ready. The unexpected realization that Carrie meant enough to me to kick that instinct into high gear, filled me with…I didn't know what to call it, but it moved me.

Perched on the rolling hills that overlook the lagoon and with a perfect view of the ocean, OCU, as Ocean Crest University is referred to, was built in the seventies, but also laid claim to some newly constructed buildings amongst its numerous structures. These newer structures were meant to be some kind of modern version of Spanish Colonial, but they looked more like glorified warehouses. The campus appeared clean and lacked the graffiti and other battle scars so typical in other colleges, no doubt due to the high-end neighborhood. I drove the perimeter of the entire campus to get a good take on it. The south and east bordered a large park with baseball diamonds and picnic tables that bled into a golf course, complete with lakes and a driving range. Beyond that were ravines outlined in the distance by housing developments, the kind where differing shades of paint are the only means of identification. The northern side of the campus was bordered by Carrillo Avenue, which in turn led to the freeway a few miles away. Howard Drive ran along the western side of the campus.

I left the car in the student parking area, and about a hundred feet away, I spotted the Matheus Hall sign that listed the services to be found within: Student Affairs, Counseling, Enrollment Services, Financial Aid.

I entered the U-shaped courtyard and located the two entrances. The one nearest me led to a long counter punctuated with windows behind some of which stood clerks tending to a few students.

I made my way along the counter checking signs and personalities.

Behind the window marked "Counseling," an efficient-looking Asian woman, who I estimated to be in her late twenties, smiled and nodded at a young man as she replied to his questions. He seemed annoyed by her answers. When he finished giving her a piece of his mind, he gathered his belongings and stomped off toward the exit, muttering. With no one left to approach the window, I took my chance. She glanced up as I approached. Her name pin said Kim.

"Can I help you?"

"I hope so. I'm trying to find someone 'cause this friend asked me to deliver a letter to her, and I don't know where to find her." I searched in my pockets hoping some long-forgotten piece of paper would emerge. It didn't. *Note to self, next time come prepared.* "Must've left it in my car. Anyway, her name is… let me see." I looked at the ceiling, then back at the young lady. "Uh, Drier. Nancy Drier. Do you know where I could find her?"

"She works in another department, I think." She glanced around the desks that filled the entire area behind the counter, where some twelve or so people carried out a variety of assignments from phone calls to computer operations. "Wait here, please."

She ambled over to a desk at the opposite end of the room, where an overweight woman with flaming red hair sat slumped over the desk with a phone receiver in her hand. When she noticed Kim, she put her hand over the mouthpiece and listened to her. She glanced in my direction, then said something to Kim. Moments later Kim returned to the window.

"Nancy's out sick. She hasn't been in this week at all. Sorry."

"You know if she has any close friends I might speak to? Don't think I'll make it out again before I leave for New York."

She thought it over for a moment. Little by little she started shaking her head. "Sorry. I don't know who I could send you to."

"Don't suppose you could give me her phone number."

She tilted her head and smiled. "Sorry, can't do that."

"Thanks, anyway." I didn't want to seem too pushy, and I exited into the courtyard. Maybe the personnel office could help me connect with her.

A group of students laughed boisterously as one of the girls chased a lanky blond boy around one of the many columns that lined the courtyard. The tallest young man leaned against the wall, sipping something from a red can.

"Hi. Could you tell me where the personnel office is?"

He gave me a bewildered look, as if I'd extracted him from some world-changing thought, then nodded and appealed to his comrades. "Hey, Carlos, where's the…what did you call it?"

"Personnel," I said to the group in general.

His friends each shrugged in turn or shook their heads. The tall one summarized. "I don't know man, maybe that building on the other side of the library. There's a bunch of offices in there."

I thanked them and set off in search of the biggest building nearby. I spotted it and confirmed its purpose by a sign in big brass letters that read Library. I rounded the building into a smaller version of the courtyard I'd just left. A concrete sign with chiseled letters in the middle of a flowerbed gave indications as to the direction to follow for different offices. The President's Office arrow pointed right to Prentice Hall, Public Relations in the same building, Administrative Business Services and Human Resources in Bower Hall, directly ahead.

I entered Bower Hall and looked around. I perused the building map and headed to Human Resources. A counter that should've been occupied by a receptionist stood unattended. Partitions behind it did a woeful job of concealing the desks that filled the room in all directions. All desks displayed computers. Set against the back wall I saw a large printer, a sizable copier, and off in the left-hand corner an even bigger area separated from the rest by more partitions. As I scanned in search of my target, I heard a voice at my side.

"You're looking for Nancy?" The overweight redhead that Kim had spoken to stood beside me. Almost as tall as I, she owned the deepest violet-colored eyes I'd ever seen.

"Uh, yeah. Do you know where I could find her?"

"Well, she's out of town for a few days. If you give me the letter, I'll see that she gets it." She seemed uncomfortable and glanced around a couple of times.

"I'd kinda like to deliver it to her myself."

She was really nervous now. "I can give it to her when she comes back to work. That's all I can do." Her mouth was like cotton. She stared at me for an anxious moment then decided to scurry off.

I'd gotten nowhere fast, so I figured it was worth the risk. "It's from Jeremy Devon."

She stopped cold. After more anxious glances she walked back to me. "When did he give it to you?"

"The day before he was killed."

The color drained from her face so fast, I expected her to faint. Suddenly, she spun and stormed out the door. She was almost running by the time I caught up to her and matched her pace.

"Give her a message for me," I whispered. She slowed down. I tried to smile in case anyone was watching this foot race. "I think she needs help." The woman came to a stop and looked at me. Her name pin said Alice, and she kept looking around with honest apprehension. "Alice, I take it you're her friend?" I asked.

She considered how to answer for a moment. "I know her."

"I work for someone very close to Devon," I said.

She held a clipboard with a notepad and a pen clipped to it. I gestured toward it. "May I?" She gave it to me. I wrote a name—Connors—and a cell number, then handed it back. "Tell her another man was attacked a couple of nights ago. I think it may be related to Devon. I need to talk to her."

She tucked the clipboard under her arm and glanced over each of my shoulders, intense fear reflected in those violet eyes. Without a word, she turned and rushed away.

I figured she might be headed to the office where I first saw her, so I rushed in the opposite direction and trotted around the library in time to see her enter Matheus Hall. No one followed her that I could see.

Pretending to be lost, I glanced in all directions with a gesture of confusion on my face then hooked my head and wandered toward the campus map a few feet from where I stood. I found Brontis Hall, where the Academic Affairs offices resided.

A receptionist materialized at the front counter when I approached. An athletic-looking woman with an obvious taste for colorful clothes. She flashed me a practiced smile and tilted her head with excessive politeness. "Can I help you?"

"I'm looking for a Mr. Hanley."

"Dean Hanley?"

I nodded.

"Dean Hanley isn't in yet. Would you like to leave a message?"

"How about Mr. Ruthskin?"

"He's in class, I think. Hold on." She turned toward one of the clusters of dividers and called out. "Sandra!"

"What?" The voice came from some buried corner.

"Is Ruthskin in class?"

"Yeah."

"Thank you." She spun back with an apologetic look on her face. "He's still in class. Sorry. You could catch him after lunch, probably. Can I have your name?"

"Connors. I'll try him again later. Thanks." I started out the door, but an idea prompted me to return. "Where can I get a schedule of classes?"

She leaned over the desk and pointed with her chin. "We're all out of extra ones here. They're gone after one week into the summer session. See that building straight ahead? That's the library and they usually have loads left over. They can give you one."

I nodded my thanks and headed toward the library. There were some class schedules in bins that hung on the wall. I took one and left. On my way out, I crossed over to Matheus Hall, walked toward the counseling offices, and glanced over at Alice's corner. She wasn't there. I hoped I'd guessed right. The fact that she appeared so nervous meant that she might be acting on someone's behalf. The question was whose.

The class schedule told me Ruthskin taught a health class in the Paul J. Firmin Fitness, Recreation, and Sports Center in room 2418. Following the map on the back of the class schedule booklet, I made my way to the building. The place stood two stories high, so I surmised that the 4 referred to an area on the second floor. I strolled into the lobby.

I found myself in the middle of a high atrium topped by a skylight that bathed the room in glorious sunshine with the metal frames casting their shadows artistically in geometric patterns across the floor. A wide central staircase led to the second floor. At each of the four corners of the atrium, hallways on both floors ostensibly lead to the classrooms. Varnished wooden benches lined the base of the staircase.

I headed down the hall to my right and read the number on the first door, 1322-A. I assumed that the ground floor rooms started with the odd numbers and the second floor with the even, so I headed up the staircase. The scraping of my shoes echoed with each step—the kind of place that tempts you to yell so you can hear your voice bounce off the walls. I resisted the temptation.

I headed to the right toward 2402-A, moved along the walkway overlooking the atrium to the hall that ran parallel to mine, above the one I had investigated below, and found 2422-A. Halfway down the hall I found 2418—no A. The door didn't have a window, so I had no way of knowing if Ruthskin was actually in there, and barging in seemed a bad idea. Better to wait. Footsteps echoed on the staircase and bounced along the halls. I traveled all the way around the rest of the hallway to make sure Ruthskin had no other exit. A few minutes later I found myself back at 2418. There were no exits other than the staircase and an elevator a few feet away.

I decided to stake my claim to one of the benches on the first floor, but as I emerged from the hall into the atrium, a man approached me from the left.

"Who are you?" he asked me, in a subdued voice.

I sized him up. The only threatening thing about him was his attitude. "Steve Connors. Who are you?"

"What do you want with Nancy?"

I decided to give him the pleasant approach, and I smiled. "Right. Well, the thing is, a friend of mine asked me to get in touch with her. Why?"

"What friend?"

"Maybe you should tell me why you want to know."

He tried to look as threatening as he could, but I stood at least six inches taller than him and probably outweighed him by 30 or 40 pounds. I leaned against the railing and smiled. His aggression dissipated only slightly.

"Are you a friend of Nancy's?" I asked.

"Yeah, you might say that."

"I might say just about anything. The point is, are you a friend of hers?"

"Yeah, I'm her friend." He was calming down and acquiring some confidence in the process. "You knew Devon?"

"Briefly. Did you?"

"Yeah, I knew him." His answer rang with contempt. "How come he gave you a message for Nancy?"

"No one else available. Can you get me in touch with her?"

"I'll give her the message for you. If I see her."

I looked away and shook my head. "I don't think so. See, thing is, I've only spoken to four people since I got here, and two of them have offered to take her my message. Why should I trust either of you?" I gave him an inquisitive look and waited for the reaction. It made him nervous again.

After a moment, he gathered all his courage and looked me straight in the eye. "If anybody tries to hurt Nancy, they'll have to answer to me. Is that clear, Mr. Connors, or whatever your name is?"

Behind him, I spotted the door to the men's room. I nodded toward it. "Let's talk in there."

He glanced over his shoulder. By the time he looked back, I was on my way in. I shoved the door open and made a quick check. Six stalls, all empty. I waited. Nothing. I went to the door and peered out. He stood there, trying to summon every ounce of courage he could muster. "C'mon," I commanded.

His reaction to obey was automatic.

I decided to give him some space and retreated to the far side of the restroom. He inched in and stayed as close to the door as he felt he could without betraying his fear. It didn't work.

"What's your name?" I asked.

"Mike Marinaro."

"Are you her boyfriend?"

His forehead furrowed, and I surmised I must've asked the wrong question.

"I am her friend. And she had nothing to do with what happened to Devon. So, leave her alone."

He was getting aggravated again. His determination to defend her seemed authentic enough, but I needed to be sure. "If you want to help her, take me to her. I can protect her."

He cackled sarcastically. "Ha. You cops can't protect anybody. Leave her alone."

"You do know where she is, don't you?"

"Listen," he said in a deep growl, "I don't care if you are a cop. If you don't get out of here, I'll…I'll…throw you out." He came at me with determination.

It convinced me. I grabbed him by the collar and brought him up a few inches off the floor and almost dropped him when my wounds screamed, *We're still here, stupid.* I set him down and straightened the wrinkles caused by my grip then fixed the knot of his tie. "I'm not a cop."

His eyes widened so much, I could read the small print of his reaction. I went on. "I'm not a friend of Devon's, either. But the people who got him killed may be after Nancy. I want to help her."

He stepped away, his breathing doing double-time. He needed reassurance that confirmed that I really was on Nancy's side. I decided to give him more to chew on. "A friend of mine knew Devon. Thing is, someone tried to get to this friend, too. I need to know who, and I need to know why. Something tells me Nancy can help."

Enough for him to mull it over. Whatever had motivated him to approach me in his quixotic endeavor to protect Nancy hadn't prepared him for the deep fear or the complications he now faced. Clearly, he had visions of walking up to this stranger named Connors, armed with the info Alice had shared, and scaring him off campus far from Nancy. A commendable but decidedly foolish action.

Now he found himself confronted with a dilemma that presented much more of a threat than anticipated. Instinct told him that he faced a man who could take him out in a second, if forced to. A terrifying prospect for any normal human being. His mind raced. I needed to slow him down before he lost it altogether.

"Can Alice be trusted?" I knew the answer, but it would make him focus along the line I needed him to follow and stop his wheels from spinning. It took him a couple of seconds to digest the question.

"Yeah. Yeah, she's Nancy's best friend."

My question had produced the desired effect. He slowed down. As his breathing subsided, I could tell he was reappraising me. His courage returning.

"Who are you?" he finally managed to say.

"Doesn't really matter, does it?"

"Why should I trust you? I don't even know you."

"You have to trust me because I may be the only chance Nancy has. Listen." I took a step in his direction, and he instinctively recoiled. "Somebody is doing nasty things to people you and I care about. Nancy may know why. She also may know who. Now, and this is very important, I can find her without your help, but it'll take longer, and she may not have a lot of time."

"What if she doesn't know?"

"She knows. That's why she's hiding."

"Who said she's hiding?"

Time to make the point hit home. I locked my eyes onto his and slid across the floor like a python stalking its prey. "I'm only going to say this once, so listen carefully. If you want to play hide and seek, Mr. Marinaro, stay out of my way. But if you really are her friend and want to keep Nancy safe"—I grabbed the pen from his shirt pocket and wrote my cell number on the palm of his hand—"call me at this number. You have six hours." I brushed by him and exited the men's room.

I left the campus and headed back to my place.

—•◆•—

CHAPTER SEVEN

The high-pitched ring of my cell phone woke me from yet another Cecilia nightmare. No idea how long I'd been asleep. Didn't even remember dozing off on my deck lounger. I lay there for a moment attempting to force the grim images to fade.

The ring of the cell phone persisted until it left me no choice but to react. After such deep-anchored sleep, my stiff muscles refused to respond for a second, and after two failed attempts at sitting up, I opted to roll across the lounger and scoop up the damned thing, if for no other reason than to stop it from yelping and quivering on the nearby table.

"Yeah?" My tongue felt like a loaf of bread, and my voice reverberated in my head like the echo in a dungeon.

"Pierce?"

It was Sauers.

"Hey, Marty. How's it hanging?"

"You been drinking?"

"No, no." I had to laugh. "Catching up on my beauty sleep, but it's not working. I think the next step is surgery."

He laughed.

I pulled my legs around to a sitting position and wiggled my toes on the floorboard. "Whatcha got?"

"I need to know something first. Are you running an official op here? If you are—"

"I told you, it's strictly personal."

"Okay. Then here it is. Strictly personal, you're not gonna like it. Officially, you could work with it, but personal is troublesome. Your Mr. Haskell's in the doghouse with your Seaview PD over his shitty personality and a little matter of some missing funds from a sting operation three years ago. Word is he's rotten through and through. His arresting methods produce a lot of injuries, too. He's got a little brother. Goes by the name of Al—Albert Haskell. Now, baby brother Al resigned from the force after the missing funds incident. My guy says no charges were brought 'cause Lewis, the then local chief of police, was seeking election as a councilman and didn't want any bad publicity. The Haskell brothers and Lewis cut some kind of deal, and Albert took the fall. The Haskell boys were known as Monster Mash. You fill in the blanks. Anyhow, Al ended up as a security officer. Billy Boy stayed on, but keeps getting into… let's call them clashes. So, he's been frozen out. But he's a leech, so they keep him at arm's length."

"What kind of leech?"

"Litigator type. When he whiffs that they're closing in on him, he slaps them with a lawsuit and stops them cold. I suspect he also knows where the bodies are buried, so to speak. Bottom line, they put up with him because they have to. Unfortunately, it's a bureaucratic disease endemic to the system. But that's another story. Net result, Bill Haskell collects a handsome salary because of his years on the force, but is only used in cases where he stands on the sidelines and can't cause any damage—window dressing. What's your interest in this piece of garbage?"

"He rubbed me the wrong way, so I thought I'd check him out. He's looking into the Devon case, the dead guy that washed up in my neighborhood."

"You're kidding. The college guy?"

"The one and only."

"That makes no sense."

"What doesn't?"

"His brother Al, he works security at that university, Ocean Crest. Bill would never be assigned to that case."

My mind started churning. This brotherly connection produced a pungent aroma. My brain still failed to operate, but some kind of skeleton rattled around my attic demanding lots of attention.

Sauers got tired of waiting. "You there, Pierce?"

"Yeah. Sorry. Got too much gobbledygook in my head."

"Yeah, heard you took a serious beating down in Cozumel with two slugs for dessert. By the way, congrats on the blow to the cartel. No one but the likes of you could've forced him out. Sorry about Cecilia. We lost one of the real good ones."

My breath caught when the memory of the three of us celebrating our victory in a cantina in Tijuana took center stage. I heard myself whisper, "She was better than good."

"No kidding. Gutsy, smart, skilled, and gorgeous. A lethal combination our Tijuana bad guys fell for. She sure knew her stuff, man. I learned a lot from her back then. A great loss."

"Yeah, great loss." I shook off the memories and got back to business. "Hey, pal, thanks for the info. I owe you."

"Level with me, Justin. Are you in some kind of trouble?"

I took a deep breath while I decided how to answer that one. "Not yet, Buddy. But I'm working on it."

"Listen to me, Justin." He emphasized the name with a stern tone. "This is my turf, my neighborhood. I know the local rules and the local players a lot better than you do. Use me. Anything you need. I mean it."

I had to smile. Loyalty has gone the way of the dinosaur, and if and when we find it, it's usually by accident. Sauers was my favorite kind of prehistoric.

"Thanks, Marty. I might take you up on that."

"I'll keep my ear to the ground. Good luck."

"Thanks."

As I hung up the phone, a cold shudder made the hairs on my neck and arms stand at attention—my built-in alarm system telling me to shift into overdrive. Time to check for movement in the shadows, glances in a crowd, unusual silences. The list is endless—anything out of the ordinary, anything too ordinary—the familiar and the unfamiliar shift into a different reality. Somewhere in the dustbin of my mind, Marty's info had triggered an alarm. The obvious wrinkle was the two Haskell brothers. Yet that alone was too obvious. There had to be something else bothering me, but I couldn't put my finger on it. Something Marty had said, or perhaps neglected to say, that had left a wake—a tenuous line in a turbulent sea. Invisible, perhaps, but present nonetheless.

I glanced at the clock on the kitchen wall—3:30 in the afternoon. I'd slept almost four hours cocooned under the awning of the deck's lounger. The difference was palpable. My body now demanded that I shock the muscles back into gear. A jog on the beach was the perfect prescription. I slipped on a pair of shorts, a T-shirt, and jogging shoes and hit the sand.

The improved weather brought the sun-bunnies out in droves, the wolves nipping at their heels. There are ever-increasing numbers of almost-topless specimens on the beaches. From a selfish point of view, it's great for uplifting the hapless men of this world, but I'm relieved not to be a father.

The old machinery showed definite signs of rust, so the usual eight-mile jog shriveled to a three-mile trot-and-walk that had me sweating like a racehorse by the time I got back. But the exercise cleared my mind, and since I'd slept through lunch, I was famished.

After gulping down several glasses of water, followed by a quick shower, I made myself a Spanish-style sandwich of French bread, olive oil, and *serrano* ham. I grabbed a beer, stuck the cell phone in my pocket, and ambled out to the deck.

A soft breeze now wafted off the Pacific, and the sun made the sea shine with a silvery glare. I tilted the umbrella enough to provide some shade and took a hearty bite out of my sandwich.

Looking up the beach, one would never picture the gruesome apparition that had drifted into view only three days earlier. The shiny bodies bounced about everywhere, their laughter punctuated by the occasional screech of joy. Lovers shunned the curious eye as they writhed playfully under colorful towels, oblivious to the world around them.

I'd felt that way once, weeks ago, in another life…a life that all of a sudden insisted on playing itself out on a screen hidden somewhere behind my eyes. Cecilia and I had made love and lain side-by-side spent and utterly content. The Caribbean sunset painted golden swaths across the wall in our room. It had been a day of intimacy, interrupted only by the occasional call to room service for the whimsical sensual foods that make the tropics an unending feast for the senses.

For me, that depth of love was a first. Until then, what passed for love in my life had been a series of complicit affairs, affection improvised to fit the occasion, only to be abandoned the moment encroachment set in. The few interactions that lasted at all were more of an exercise in restraint than a fulfillment of closeness. Scratching the surface only enough to feign humanity for a night, a week, maybe a month.

I'd fabricated the best excuse—in my line of work, love is a commodity on loan. At collection time, there's no negotiating. A comfortable shield, a lie as much to myself as to the hapless females I used it on. A concrete way of maintaining distance, creating chasms so wide that, in time, even I couldn't see the other side.

And then Cecilia appeared. Pierce became blunted. Not by clever words or subtle manipulations, but by the unfathomable mystery of love. No good reason for it. If anything, there were countless arguments against it. We worked in the same business, she exclusively for the U.S. and I for both governments—double jeopardy that complicated matters even more. We knew the rules, understood the risks. Despite that, and without hesitation, we fell under each other's spell. We could easily have found ourselves on opposite sides of the same battle and still been unable to avoid betraying our allegiances.

We made no effort to suppress our attraction. It would've been futile, anyway. We simply slipped into each other's arms and, for the first time ever, lived the successive moments to the utmost fulfillment, as if each could be our last.

Without warning, our distorted lives shifted into a new focus. The only discernible meaning of anything at all lay in being together. All else faded into insignificance.

Foolish, irresponsible, and wonderful beyond anything I ever imagined.

Unwise. We were in Cozumel not to search for love, but to find some dangerous vermin that didn't want to be found. Reckless because we lost focus when our very survival depended on our skills and talents to protect not only our teammates, but each other. The price of our folly? Cecilia's life. Followed by my dive into despair and a single-minded desire to die.

Demetrio yanked me out of that pit. My quest now, to never allow the despondent Pierce to rule me again. Cecilia deserved that and more…much more.

A loud pounding from the rising afternoon tide snatched me back. From force of habit, I scanned my surroundings, and my gaze rested on the bodies of two lovely young women as they strolled along the surf, leaving footprints in the wet sand, their limber, sexy shapes artwork in motion. Guilt overcame me, and my eyes quickly strayed toward the hotel.

A shiver blasted along my skin, making every hair stand on end. A man stood on the boardwalk pretending to enjoy the afternoon glare of the Pacific. He looked uncomfortable. Trying too hard to play the part of nature-lover.

I felt more relieved than concerned—it meant my sensors were back online. The discovery made me realize I should call Demetrio and make sure he and Carrie were okay.

Trying not to change my rhythm, I took another bite from my sandwich and a gulp of beer. As insurance, I removed the phone from my pocket and lay it in plain view, next to the sandwich. Clear signs that I intended to return momentarily. I pushed myself stiffly out of the chair and lumbered into the house. I snatched my binoculars from a drawer then slithered into the kitchen searching for an angle to check out the phony nature-lover. He'd disappeared.

I rushed back to my cell phone and called Demetrio. Got his voicemail. I didn't like that one bit.

I punched in Carrie's cell number, knowing full well she'd snap my head off for calling and worrying about her, but the call went directly to voicemail.

I went to the phone file on a desk by the kitchen, dialed Carrie's office, and waited.

After several rings a female voice answered. "Office of Research and Planning. This is Laura. How may I help you?"

I asked her to transfer me to Carrie's extension. More rings. Another female voice. "Dr. Caroline Harding's office."

I told her who I was, and she informed me that Carrie had left an hour and a half earlier with a distinguished visiting scholar from Mexico. No, she had left no message for her brother.

I clicked off. "Where the hell are they?" I muttered.

I decided it might be a good idea to reappear on the deck.

I picked up where I left off, a bite of sandwich and a swig of beer. Part of me wanted to bolt out the front door and find this prowler, but experience told me that this one would come to me sooner or later on his own. I finished my sandwich instead and strolled, beer in hand, to the edge of the deck. Maybe I was overreacting…no. I could feel him watching. I decided to play along.

A beach access zigzags down from the boardwalk at the edge of the public parking to about fifty feet from my house. A professional would know that I'd spotted him, so a natural retreat had to be to a car parked in that lot. I set my drink down on the rail and ambled down the steps onto the beach. Might as well check it out. The shrill buzzer on my cell phone put an end to that plan. I'd left it back on the table next to my lunch. I rushed back onto the deck, expecting it to be Carrie or Demetrio.

"Yeah?"

"Mr. Connors?" It was Mike Marinaro.

An uncomfortable thought crossed my mind. If they had broken into my house and had surveillance on me now, it was also possible my home phone was tapped and my cell phone hacked. "Glad you called."

"My friend would like to talk to you."

"Are you at a public phone?"

"No, I'm at—"

"Shut up! Don't say a word, just listen. Go to a public phone. Get the number for the Pacific Sunset hotel. Call me in exactly five minutes. If you can't get me, call this number again in half an hour, and I'll tell you how to reach me. Is that clear?"

"I don't get it. What are you trying to pull?"

"Do it!" I disconnected, locked the deck door, and dashed up the hill. Three minutes later, I stood panting at the reception desk of the Pacific Sunset Hotel.

Gary Nilles, Mrs. Sandusky's son-in-law, was on duty at the front desk. He confides in me from time to time with the expectation that I might convey some of his needs to the old woman on his behalf.

"Justin, how you doin'? I heard you were back. Be right with you."

He dutifully tended to the needs of a couple checking in.

It gave me a chance to angle over to the phone operator. Angela, a stunning Caribbean beauty who didn't look a day over twenty, glanced through a magazine and spoke occasionally into the almost invisible headset.

"Operator. Can I help you?... Room service is extension 418, I'll connect you...you're welcome, sir."

I reached around into her cubicle and tapped her on the shoulder. She looked up at me with that almost childish look of wonderment that makes her irresistible.

"Mr. Pierce. How are you? Oh, my God, you're bruised and injured."

I kept forgetting that my face nicely exposed remnants of the damage. "Fell down the stairs a few days ago. Distracted. No doubt thinking about you."

"Oh, Mr. Pierce, you certainly know how to make a girl feel good," she said with a coquettish grin.

"Angela, I need to ask you a favor."

"Ask away." She leaned toward me.

I moved into the tiny room and knelt beside her. "Someone will be calling me here in a minute or two asking for a Mr. Connors. Could you patch it into the phone in the hallway between the conference center and the bungalows?"

"Sure." She glanced over her shoulder at the switchboard displays, then back at me. "No one's using that one right now, so I'll keep it clear for you. When you get to it, let me know…Mr. Connors." She winked at me and smiled.

I winked back in appreciation and sauntered down the hall.

This particular phone fit the bill. It sat in an out-of-the-way kind of passage that buzzed with activity when large groups rented the conference rooms to hold their meetings, but otherwise remained completely abandoned. It also stood in the middle of a hallway with a clear view of the entrances at each end. Anyone trying to watch me would have to reveal himself.

I picked up the receiver and told Angela I was in place. While I waited, I re-ran my dash to the hotel over in my mind.

When I'd left the house, I intentionally rushed along the perimeter of the parking lot, keeping an eye out for any cars parked close enough to get a view of my house. Specifically, I looked for silhouettes inside the cars or anyone standing around them. I discovered neither. Whoever it was might be good enough to realize that, having been discovered, the best option to refute my awareness would be to disappear. But I knew what I'd seen.

The phone rang. I let it ring a second time before I picked up. "Connors."

"Here is your call, Mr. Connors," Angela said.

"Thanks." I heard a click. "Hello?"

"Connors?"

"It's me. Are you calling from a public phone?"

"Yes, what—"

"Tell me about your friend."

"I think you'd better tell me first. What the hell is this bullshit?"

I took a quick glance down the hall in both directions. Nothing. "Our phones may be tapped. I don't want to take any risks with your friend. You're sure you're at a public phone?"

"Yeah, yeah. I'm at a public phone."

"Then, talk to me." There were some noises at his end, as if he had passed the receiver from one hand to another. "I'm listening."

"Why didn't you tell me you're Carrie Harding's brother, Mr. Pierce?"

"Who says I am?"

He snickered to impress me. "I have my sources, too. I wouldn't be talking to you if I didn't know more about you."

"Bully for you. Now, tell me about your friend. When can I meet her?"

"When I feel it's safe."

I took another glance down the hall in either direction. "Look, Marinaro, playing games with me can be an expensive proposition for all of us. One person is already dead, another may soon be. I can't wait around. Talk to me or I'll hang up."

"Okay, okay. Are you familiar with the Temecula Creek Inn?"

"Yeah."

"Be there in an hour. Take a table in the restaurant. I'll find you." He hung up.

I stood there pushing back a fervent desire to smash the receiver against the wall. This idiot wanted to play cops and robbers with me, which vastly increased the odds of somebody getting hurt. He wasn't nearly as tough as he envisioned himself to be, but he was vain enough to carry his bluff to the limit. Especially since he fancied himself the clever sleuth saving the damsel in distress. I placed the receiver back in its cradle and attempted to placate my frustration.

Angela was still into her magazine when I sneaked up behind her. "Thanks. I owe you."

"I'll have to collect one of these days." She gave me an impish smile that could have gotten her arrested.

I winked and smiled, then strolled back past the lobby into the perfect Seaview late afternoon.

CHAPTER EIGHT

On my way back to the house, I gave the parking lot another shot, but a party bus had pulled in, and that meant far too much activity to allow my examination to be effective.

I took my phone, beer, and leftovers into the house and changed into more practical clothing. Charcoal gray pants and a black jacket over a black shirt fit the bill nicely. I scribbled a note for Carrie and Demetrio telling them to stay put once they got home. I secured all the doors and windows, turned on the alarm, and headed toward Temecula. If I gunned it, I could make it in time for my rendezvous with Marinaro.

I kept a vigilant eye on the rearview mirror, but spotted no one. Either I was wrong about what I saw or the fact that he'd been discovered scared the spy away. My money was on the latter. There also existed the possibility that he simply couldn't exit the parking lot quickly enough to give pursuit.

The drive inland over the hills turned out to have a soothing effect on me. The adrenaline rush had faded, and I enjoyed the scenery. I'd eaten at the Temecula Creek Inn many times over the years, its three golf courses being among my favorites in the area.

Marinaro's attitude made him unpredictable, so I searched my memory banks for a picture of all the entrances, to avoid any unwelcome surprises. As far as I could remember, the restaurant's entrance stood just off the parking lot and above the pro shop. Inside is a small reception with a hallway to the left that leads to the restrooms and kitchen. The bar is off to the right in what amounts to a separate room with two exits to the outdoor seating area. The restaurant is through the bar and to the left, with access to the kitchen beyond that. I could recall no other way in or out. It was unlikely that the place would be full this early in the week, so we shouldn't have any trouble spotting each other.

The shadows off the hills to the west already engulfed the hotel when, at dusk, I drove into the parking lot outside the restaurant. The diehards were coming off the golf courses and tossing their clubs and shoes into the trunks of their vehicles. I checked once more for a tail, even though I felt certain there was none, and pulled the Explorer into a slot not far from the entrance to the restaurant.

The place was far more crowded than I anticipated, but I managed to secure a table in the dining room that allowed me a straight view of all the entrances. Only the kitchen stood at my back and sitting sideways took care of that. I informed the waitress that I expected two more people and would order when they arrived. She dutifully placed the extra menus across the table from me.

The designated time came and went with no sign of Marinaro and his *friend*. My frustration swelled into anger. But for now, he and Nancy were all I had, so I persuaded myself to be patient.

The maître d' stepped in from the foyer and said something that sounded like a question off to his right, away from me. A second later, he turned in my direction and repeated his query.

"Mr. Pierce? Is there a Mr. Pierce here? Phone call for Mr. Pierce."

I sat there, stunned. No doubt this was Marinaro's idea of being discreet. I considered wringing the bastard's neck if and when I met him again. When the maître d' exited, I made my move. I needed to head him off before he hung up.

When I reached the foyer, I could hear him calling out for "Mr. Pierce." I glanced around as if looking for the men's room until he emerged from the bar.

"I'm Pierce. You have a call for me?" He smiled, relieved to have found me.

"Oh, yes, Mr. Pierce." He picked up the receiver from the phone on the welcome desk. "You can take it on this phone. It's only for use by the restaurant, so please be brief."

I nodded and stepped toward the hallway that led to the kitchen and restrooms. I liked this development less and less.

I stood with my face to the wall. "This is Pierce."

"I see you made it."

"What the hell do you think you're doing?" I was ready to climb through the receiver and choke him. "Where are you?"

"When you exit the restaurant, turn left. Look for the very last building south of the lobby. In front of that building is a red Camaro. Stand next to it, and I'll get you."

"Are you—" He hung up before I could put my foot in my mouth. Had I finished my sentence, chances are he would've called the whole thing off out of fear. I'd come this far, and if there were any chance that Ms. Drier might provide useful information, I'd be a fool to ruin it now. I needed to focus on damage control. If any interested parties found themselves on the premises, they now knew precisely who "Mr. Pierce" was. I might as well have a sign around my neck. Marinaro's antics left me with one choice, select my own route and keep my eyes peeled.

I handed the phone to the maître d'. "Thanks, can't stay for dinner. Sorry."

I crossed the bar and took the exterior stairs down to the pro shop level, then followed the cart path beyond the first tee of the Oaks course for about a hundred plus yards. Once there, I climbed the steep embankment and emerged onto the lower level between a couple of two-story structures, north of the lobby, adjacent to the parking lot. It was almost dark, but anyone crossing the parking lot would be clearly visible. On the other hand, anyone keeping vigil from inside a car would prove almost impossible to spot. Thanks to Marinaro, I found myself at the chiaroscuro time of dusk, when the eyes play tricks and the shadows and shapes take on a life of their own. This kept getting better and better.

If memory served, the structures where I now stood mirrored identical ones on the south side of the lobby. I retraced my steps down the embankment and followed the cart path along the first fairway. The southernmost building stood about sixty feet above a steep climb from the green. Perfect. The only light came courtesy of the few occupied rooms, where the curtains remained open, enough for me to see where I was going.

Several minutes later, I stood at the end of the two-story building searching for the red Camaro. I spotted it about halfway down the length of the building, right beneath one of two spotlights that illuminated the parking lot. Score another one for Marinaro.

I slithered my way along the lower level until I stood a few feet from the Camaro and stopped. The wooden veranda above me creaked—Marinaro, more than likely. I sprinted back to the stairs at the end of the building and made my way up, then glanced along the veranda.

Right again. Marinaro stood with his hands resting on the banister, craning his neck to the right, where he expected me to come from. The evening was relatively quiet, so the odds were against me being able to reach him before the planks underfoot gave me away. I decided to wait. His nervousness increased by the second and, with a little luck, he might make a mistake I could take advantage of.

I heard him mutter from time to time, but he remained at his post. This tactic promised to get me nowhere fast. I'd decided to go for broke and rush at him, when a door flung open on the floor below, and the laughter of a small group of young people gushed out into the darkening shadows, making enough noise to cover my dash along the balcony. My arm locked around Marinaro's neck and my hand clamped over his mouth before he could react.

"It's Pierce. Don't make a sound," I whispered.

He tried to resist me for a few seconds, but tightening my arm around his neck put an end to that.

"Stop playing hero and listen to me. Is Nancy here? Nod." He did. "I'm going to release you. If you even think of making a noise, you'll regret it for a week. Anything you want to say to me you say when we're indoors. Understand?"

He nodded again. I let him go and stepped far enough away to be out of his reach, just in case. He caught himself on the banister and coughed.

"Move! This is the wrong place to be."

"You son of—"

My right hand landed solidly on the side of his ribcage, and I could hear the air as it expelled from his lungs. I twisted his left arm around his back.

"Cut the bullshit, Marinaro." He gasped to pull some air back into his lungs, but he managed to signal his agreement with his right hand. I released him. "Move."

Still struggling to breathe, he turned and nodded toward the door behind me.

"Open it," I said. He wobbled across the veranda and knocked. A rhythmic knock intended as a code. When the door opened, I pushed him through and closed it behind me.

"Oh, my God," Alice screamed, terrified by what she saw. She held her hand over her mouth, appraising Marinaro's condition.

"He'll be all right." I reassured her. "Where's Nancy?"

Alice's eyes flashed toward a closed door at the back of the room. "Are you going to kill us?" she asked, her voice barely audible.

"Don't be ridiculous. I'm here to help. Get yourself some water, Alice. And some for him, too."

My thoughtfulness seemed to have the desired effect. She nodded and moved toward the bathroom door.

It opened as she got to it and a small, exquisite-looking woman in her mid-twenties emerged. She reminded me of Snow White. She glanced at Marinaro, then spotted me and froze.

"Don't panic, Miss Drier. I'm here to help you. I promise. Sorry about him. His antics made things too risky. I needed to quiet him down. He'll be okay in a minute."

She went to Marinaro, put her hand on his shoulder, and helped him sit on the edge of the bed. He nodded his appreciation. She turned to me. "You're Dr. Harding's brother?"

A proud smile overcame me unexpectedly at the sound of Carrie's high-end title. "I am. How did you find out about me?"

"Dr. Harding," Marinaro muttered, "has a photo of you on her credenza."

"A…photo?" I tried to conceal my astonishment, but the words spilled forth without my cooperation.

"Well, it's really more like a framed newspaper clipping of you getting some medal," Marinaro added.

"Mother…" I whispered.

"I beg your pardon?" Alice asked.

"My mother's doing, the framed news article—a memento from my days in the Marine Corps. No idea Carrie had kept it."

"What makes you say you can help me?" Snow White asked.

"Let's say that I have some experience with these kinds of things."

"Are you a cop now, is that it?" Marinaro asked with more than a touch of irony.

I shook my head. "No. Listen," I turned to his pretty little friend. "We don't have time for a detailed resume. Your boyfriend here can vouch for my effectiveness, and under the circumstances, that's all that matters."

Marinaro shot me a dirty look. "I told you, man, I'm not her boyfriend. Cut the crap." He was recovering nicely. "Why would you want to help her?"

"Because someone tried to scare my sister away, and in the process, almost killed someone dear to her. I need to protect her in the same way I can protect Ms. Drier." I stared into Nancy's emerald eyes. "You know who killed Devon, don't you?"

She sat on the edge of the bed next to Marinaro, rolled her head, then peered up at me with doleful eyes. "Not exactly. But…"

Without breaking eye contact, I snagged a chair nestled under a small desk and sat close to her. "But?" I urged.

"I know why and what they want."

"Okay, let's hear it. Why and what?"

She glanced at Marinaro, then Alice. They nodded. "Jeremy compiled some compromising evidence against some people. I think that's why they killed him."

"*They?*"

"Some people that work at the university."

I took a deep breath and shook my head. "Look, Miss Drier. We can't afford to play twenty questions the rest of the night. Tell me what you know in as much detail as you can. Names, dates, anything." I looked over at Alice who still stood frozen by the bathroom door. "Alice, why don't you get some water for all of us?"

She turned and disappeared into the bathroom.

My eyes returned to Nancy. She exuded the kind of beauty that emanates from deep within, a sincere innocence…a naivety that, combined with the perfect balance of her features, exuded irresistible vulnerability. She looked so fragile that I softened my approach. "Okay, let's start over. How did this whole thing begin?"

"Jeremy came to Ocean Crest to take the job of Dean of Enrollment Management four years ago. Doug Morris, the previous Dean, died suddenly and no one on campus understood the system he used for keeping all the student data. Admissions and enrollment records have to be cross-referenced with the research and planning records, the business and payroll records, student fees, and all that stuff. So, Jer had to decipher the whole thing real fast. Turned out to be a gigantic challenge. In the end he discovered that lots of funds had been seriously misused— classes appeared on the rosters that didn't exist on campus, there were lists of non-existing students, fees charged illegally, the works. He discovered that Morris had left behind a real mess."

"On purpose?" I asked.

"We'll never know for sure, will we?" Alice interjected from behind me as she handed water to Nancy and Marinaro.

I glanced at her and nodded, then turned to Nancy, "Go on."

Marinaro stepped in, "After digging through all the data, Devon recommended that we report the misuse to the state. That meant the university would have to return a substantial amount of money, resulting in a huge deficit in the budget."

"Would the state investigate the wrongdoings?"

"Not if we brought it to their attention and told them we were handling it," Alice answered. "They don't have the time or money to investigate, plus, if we did the *mea culpa* and paid back the funds we shouldn't have received from them, all would be forgiven."

I shrugged. "Sorry, but this stuff doesn't sound like a motive for murder."

"Jer," Nancy persisted, "also discovered that two professors had been committing fraud and were still at it. He told their boss, Agnes Braniff, that's the VP of Academic Affairs. She did nothing other than warn Jer to not make any waves."

"Nothing?"

"Exactly," Alice answered. She handed me a glass of water and squeezed onto the bed with the others. "In my mind all this stuff could never have happened in the first place without her knowledge and approval."

"Hm. What did Jeremy do after that?"

Nancy glanced at her friends before answering. "He canceled the fraudulent classes these two professors were pretending to teach, which stopped the extra pay they were getting."

"Extra pay?"

Marinaro explained. "Faculty teach a specific set of classes per quarter, as part of their regular workload and annual salary. After their basic teaching load, they can get paid extra, on an hourly basis, if they teach additional classes."

"These extra classes," I said, "are the ones they were getting paid for, but weren't actually teaching."

"Precisely," a satisfied Alice concluded.

"What happened next?" I asked Nancy.

"Jer told the professors that he was onto them and their shenanigans needed to stop. That should've been the end of it."

"But surprise! They didn't like that one little bit." Alice's sarcasm wasn't lost on any of us.

"It represented a significant cut in their take-home pay." Marinaro's turn. "They tried everything to change Devon's mind. First, they tried the good ol' boy approach. Bought him lunch, invited him for drinks, all that crap. They told him this was the 'Ocean Crest way' and always had been. When that didn't work, the rumors started."

"What kind of rumors?"

"Bullshit. All of it." Marinaro blushed. "Sorry, ladies." They nodded, and he went on. "They filed all sorts of claims against him, from retaliation to unfair labor practices to lying, and even falsifying records."

"They were going after his reputation," Alice added.

"In Enrollment Management, the office Jer headed up," Nancy clarified, "accuracy is critical. Not only at OCU, but statewide, even nationwide. Student records are considered sacrosanct. So, they tried to turn the faculty and administrators against him, saying that he'd fabricated the errors in the records. Then they accused him of making up stories about them in retaliation for speaking their minds."

"One of their claims," Marinaro added, "accused him of abusing female students by exchanging grades for money or sex. In essence, they accused him of doing what they'd been doing themselves for years."

"It got worse from there." Nancy's eyes were watering. "They circulated anonymous letters claiming all sorts of absurd things about him and anyone who supported him. That's how Dr. Harding got in trouble."

"What kind of trouble?"

"After she stood up for him and his integrity, they started rumors about her and Jeremy having an affair." She looked at me then reached to pat my hand. "But it wasn't true. Please don't believe any of that."

I nodded. "What else?"

Nancy retrieved her hand and placed it back on her lap. "After that, Dr. Harding confronted them and they backed off."

"God knows what she said to them," Alice cut in. "You know how frightful she can be when she's pissed off." They chuckled in agreement, then turned to me seeking confirmation, but I didn't indulge them.

"Whatever she said or did, they backed off. And when their bogus claims were denied," Nancy continued, "the threats of physical harm, even death, started to pop up."

"How so?"

"He found notes on his car, in the campus mail, at home, even taped to his computer monitor. They sent letters to his wife, telling her he was sleeping with everybody from the vice-president to the maintenance women. A sick scene."

I squinted. "Wife?"

Quick glances at each other. A thousand-pound gorilla now filled the room.

"They were separated," Alice clarified, but she failed to keep eye contact with me or her companions.

I decided to let the gorilla sit in a corner, for now. "Did Devon threaten to take these people to court?"

"He considered it a couple of times, but once all this started, he couldn't," Nancy answered.

"Why not?"

It was Marinaro's turn to take over. "For the attorneys to step in, he needed the backing of the president and senior staff, not to mention the support of the board of trustees. If they did step in, it could be labeled as retaliation against the employees for bringing up their grievances. Plus, it would damage the university's reputation. Braniff, the VP of Academic Affairs, stood to lose everything if it became clear that she'd allowed or been a participant in their scheme. Or worse, if they found she was in on whatever monkey business Doug Morris had perpetrated with the records before he died."

"Did this Morris guy cook the books?"

"It seems logical, when you consider how long all this crap had been going on."

"What else?"

"Well," Marinaro continued, "the then president didn't want to deal with it. He decided to retire and let someone else deal with the mess."

"The 'then president'?"

"Yeah, we have a new president," Marinaro went on, "Dr. Elizabeth Moore, hired about six months ago. She's been looking into this whole mess, but it'll take time to sort it all out. Especially without Jeremy."

I leaned back and tried to make sense of all this. "If Devon didn't threaten to take these people to court and expose them, why kill him?"

By now I'd observed that the answers from these three came in direct relationship to the jobs they held and their respective expertise. I guessed that this time Alice would be the one with the answer.

"I think," she whispered, "that somebody found out Devon had the records to prove the fraud and the entire scheme, going all the way up to Morris and, in my opinion, Braniff. Maybe even connecting that good-for-nothing past president."

Nancy shook her head. "Alice—"

"I know, Nancy, I shouldn't be so opinionated." She turned to me. "It's a gut feeling. I've got no proof, but maybe Jer did. I believe they decided to steal the records to make sure he could never use them against them. But Jeremy let it be known he'd replaced the originals with photocopies, and made backups of all the computer files. That's when the direct threats started."

"Direct threats?"

Marinaro's turn. "Up until that point all the threats had been anonymous, but we surmised that when they—"

"You keep saying *they*. Who are *they*?"

"We don't know, exactly," Marinaro went on. "We're guessing."

I had to shake my head. "Okay, go on."

"Anyway, *they* sent Al Haskell, one of our security guys, to make their point. He told Devon to hand over the original records, the copies of the computer files, and stay out of their way if he knew what was best for him. He's a piece of work, that guy."

Nancy added, "Jeremy refused, and told him to stop harassing him, and that if they ever bothered him, his family, or friends, he would release the evidence against them. If they left him alone, he agreed to keep it out of sight."

"Did they accept the deal?"

"At first, they did. But things changed a couple of weeks ago. That's when all hell broke loose," Marinaro said as he shot a quick glance at his companions.

"What happened?"

Nancy pressed her lips together and looked away. Then she drained her entire glass of water. Alice handed Nancy her own glass and went off to refill the empty one.

I glanced at Marinaro, who grimaced as he rocked from side to side to alleviate the pain from my blow to his ribs.

"Nancy, what happened two weeks ago?" I asked. She was on the verge of tears.

"Al Haskell attacked…raped a student." Alice whispered from the bathroom door. "She was walking home after one of her evening classes."

This was sounding more and more like a bad soap opera. "What the hell does that have to do with Jeremy?"

Nancy's eyes flooded and she lost her voice to convulsive sobbing, her lustrous blue-black hair bobbing wildly. Alice put her arms around her friend and looked at me with a sorrowful scowl.

"The girl is Nancy's cousin," Marinaro said.

I glanced at Nancy then back at Marinaro and Alice as the picture became clear. "So, Devon told them he'd expose them after the girl's attack because of Nancy?"

"Yes," Alice said as she patted Nancy. "Jer saw the rape as a message to him on account of his rela—I mean—friendship with Nancy. He believed they'd declared war."

The thousand-pound gorilla had just acquired a name—love.

They all looked down.

"What happened then?"

"They found out Devon had hired a high-profile lawyer to take them to court," Marinaro explained. "He'd decided he wasn't going to deal with them through internal procedures anymore. He wanted to destroy them, and rightly so, if you ask me," he concluded with a hint of fury.

"Who told them about Devon's plans?" I asked.

"The lawyer filed a complaint with the Seaview police requesting they conduct an investigation of Al Haskell for threatening Devon."

"You've seen the complaint?"

"No, but Devon did see it," Nancy said. "Before he died, he told me that the police claimed that no such complaint had ever been received."

"No warrant was ever issued for Al's arrest, either." Marinaro glared at me.

"What has the lawyer said about that?"

Nancy cut in. "He's gone. Since Thursday, two weeks ago."

"And Jer was killed the next day, Friday," Marinaro added.

Nancy cried, and Alice consoled her.

"How about the girl? Nancy, what happened to your cousin? Did her parents report the rape to the cops?"

"She is in a safe place far from here. She doesn't want anyone to know. She won't press charges. She's too ashamed and very, very scared." She managed to say between sobs.

"She's young," Alice explained, "and wants to put it all behind her. Plus, no one trusts the Seaview PD with Bill Haskell all over it."

I nodded in agreement. As much as I hated these bastards getting away with the violence they'd inflicted on an innocent young woman, it wasn't my place to avenge her—at least not at the moment.

The time had come, however, to invite the gorilla to join our little gathering. "Do folks at the college know about you and Devon?"

Glances all around, then finally Nancy whispered as she turned bright pink. "I don't think so…maybe…" She dropped her head and stared at fidgeting hands.

I eyed her friends. They shrugged then cocked their heads.

"The rape of her cousin could mean they know," Alice told me. "Or maybe it's a coincidence. The girl has a different last name than Nancy. Devon believed they did know. That's why Nancy's hiding. They may think she has the computer files and the records."

"Do you?"

Nancy nodded and began to cry again. "Yes, but I don't know what to do with them. Should I go to the police?"

"No, Nancy," Marinaro blurted out. "You can't trust them."

I took a calculated risk and placed my hand on Nancy's. She didn't recoil. "I'm afraid Mr. Marinaro is right this time."

The three glanced at each other.

"Who knows about the rape? And who knows she's your cousin?"

"I'm not certain," Nancy said. "Some people may know now. Jer reported the rape to Haskell's supervisor after it happened. But, since it happened off campus, and there's no evidence other than my cousin's word, not only was nothing done, but Jer was ordered not to bring the university into this nasty business."

I turned to Marinaro. Since he wanted to play hero, this would be his chance. "Why are you involved in all of this?"

"Why not? Nancy works directly for me and so does Alice. Devon was simply doing his job. I have a responsibility."

Alice rose defiantly. "He cares. He's one of the few that honestly cares about his employees, about the university, about the students. Don't you dare doubt him."

I had no choice but to laugh. "Okay, okay." I turned back to Marinaro. "Do you think you can hide Miss Drier better than you did tonight?"

He glowered at me with contempt. "What do you mean?"

I turned and faced him squarely. I preferred not to threaten him, but it was indispensable that he set his ego aside and stay focused. "If you play the same stupid games you played with me, Nancy won't live very long. None of you will. These people have to believe that you honestly don't know where she is. It's the only way to keep her safe. Can you handle that?"

He tried to impress me by grinding his teeth to make his jaw muscles tense.

"This macho crap is the first thing that has to go, Marinaro. If you can't hack it, I'll get someone who can."

He slowly softened his attitude and nodded. "I think I can handle it. Tell me what to do."

I turned to Nancy. "A good friend of mine is a professional who can hide you safely. Will you trust me?"

After a consulting look at the others followed by a heartfelt sigh, she turned to me. "Doesn't look like I have much choice, does it?" A wry smile crawled onto her lips. "I don't want to put my friends in danger."

Marinaro stood up, clamped his hand onto my shoulder, and pushed me back. "Pierce, is this really necessary? We need to know where she is and how she is at all times. I don't like this. I don't like it at all."

In one fluid motion, I wrapped my arm under his and locked it under my armpit. The grimace of pain was instantaneous.

"Ugh. You're breaking my arm."

"Heroes get people killed. Miss Drier likes being alive. So do I. If none of us know where she is, it's unlikely that the Haskell brothers can find her. I like her chances better that way." As I released his arm, I gave him a shove and turned to Nancy Drier. "But it's up to you."

Her eyes wandered toward Alice then over my shoulder toward Marinaro. When her beautiful emerald eyes focused on me, she nodded. "I'll do whatever you say, Mr. Pierce."

CHAPTER NINE

Sauers jumped at the prospect of getting involved. He'd met Carrie some time back, and after a brief summary of the story, he understood my need to *unofficially* look into the Devon mess, if only to protect her. Given his resources, I couldn't possibly find a better man to hide Nancy Drier.

I took possession of the box filled with the so-called evidence Devon had gathered and hoped it would shed some light. I felt uneasy about what I'd heard so far, though none of it merited rape or murder. Something had to lock it all together, and I intended to find it.

After hitting Marinaro with a short, albeit intense private sermon on the danger his antics posed to the young woman's safety, and some psycho-babble on the most productive ways to handle his obvious feelings for her, I smuggled Ms. Drier out of the room and into Sauers's capable hands. We agreed it was best if none of us knew where he took her. Not even me, for now, as long as he kept her available in case I needed her.

Marinaro objected to parting company with Nancy, but she persuaded him that she'd rather remain alive and help convict whoever killed Devon. Alice readily concocted a story to tell at work of how she'd spent most of the night helping Nancy pack to go visit her aunt, who had suddenly taken ill in Wisconsin and was in imminent danger of dying. A clever pack of lies that the Haskell team couldn't unscramble. Marinaro had approved

Nancy's leave without pay, and no, Alice didn't know when, or even if, Nancy would be back.

Before going our separate ways, I impressed upon Marinaro and Alice how their relationship with Nancy Drier meant that they might be in significant danger themselves. I listed a few basic precautions, such as keeping an eye on each other when possible, and instructing their trusted coworkers to accompany them when leaving the office late at night. Alice agreed readily, but Marinaro wanted to play tough guy. He changed his tune once I provided a gruesome description of his possible fate at the hands of the Haskell duo.

I'd ascertained the name of Devon's missing lawyer, Roger Paxton, and Sauers offered to look into his disappearance.

By 10:20 I drove back home. Called the house phone and got my monotone voicemail message. Tried Demetrio and Carrie. Their voicemail picked up. It unnerved me.

When I pulled into my driveway, I found my house in complete darkness. I tapped the remote, the garage door raised, and the light flickered on. Demetrio's rental Mustang wasn't parked in front of the house or in the garage. The Pierce distress system snapped to full alert. From now on, I'd take nothing for granted. I removed the Baby from my ankle holster and reached for the flashlight in the glove compartment. Before I exited the Explorer, I closed the garage door, got my phone, and disarmed the house alarm. The garage light shone bright enough to keep me from bumping into anything solid, but not enough to spot anyone hiding. I made my way to the back door of the house. Slid the key into the lock, entered quietly, then shined the flashlight into the hall that led to the front door.

I could see straight across one side of the living room all the way to the glass door that opened onto the deck. Nothing. That left the stairs, bar, and the kitchen as possible hiding places. I dowsed the flashlight and resolved to make do with the light from external sources. It leveled the playing field only slightly because I knew the layout.

I removed my shoes and I pushed my brain to search for some viable plan to secure the rest of the house. In an effort to slow down my pulse and make as little noise as possible, I stood motionless in the foyer next to the stairwell, taking in gradual, deliberate breaths. In a matter of seconds, my ears had tuned into even the dimmest noises in the house—the hum of the refrigerator, the ticking clock on the kitchen wall, the soft sound of waves breaking below the deck. Otherwise, the house seemed still.

I resolved to remain motionless for as long as it took to force any intruder to move first and give himself away. Turned out to be a long wait.

The prolonged silence indicated that the house was most likely free of prowlers, but I opted for caution, so I crouched down and peered up the stairwell. The lights from the parking lot next to the hotel bled through the windows enough for me to confirm an empty staircase. I peeked around the corner into the living room and evaluated shadows both there and in the dining room. All clear. Using those same shadows for concealment, I eased my way toward the kitchen. Nothing, save for the flickering light on the phone indicating at least one message—it would have to wait.

I carefully climbed the stairs and methodically checked rooms, closets, and bathrooms.

Satisfied that I represented the only living threat in the house, I flicked on the lights, made my way to the phone, and hit the *messages* button.

"You have four new messages. First message, playback," said the indifferent voice and a dial tone played on. When it stopped, the second message played. "*Hola, gabacho,*" Demetrio's voice. "Are you there? *Bueno,* I'll try later. *Nos vemos.*"

The next two messages were dial tones, probably Demetrio checking to see if I was back yet.

"End of final message," concluded the machine.

I glanced around the room as if in some magical way I might find a clue as to what to do next. Demetrio's message held no information at all. It had to be for a good reason. I stood there in a kind of limbo without a solitary useful idea on how to proceed.

The phone rang. I let it ring twice more before I answered.

"Hello?"

"*Vaya, camarada. Al fin.* I called several times. Did you forget we had a date?"

He remembered my fears about bugged phones.

"No, had to take care of some business. Sorry."

"The bar is open for another hour. You still want to come?"

"Sure, I'm on my way." I had no clue where I was supposed to be on my way to, but I trusted Demetrio to give me a hint.

"Ethel already left. She got tired of waiting. But there is another girl here who is dying to meet you, so hurry up, okay?"

The reference to Ethel meant Ethel Sandusky, the manager of the neighboring hotel. That indicated he was in the hotel keeping an eye out, waiting for the lights to flick on at the house.

"Okay, I'm on my way, keep your shirt on."

The shortest way there was my usual route up the boardwalk and over to the hotel's side entrance. But that made it challenging to spot anyone following me. The main street route, with its open spaces, made concealment far more difficult. I checked the Baby once more and slid it back into my ankle holster. I activated the alarm and locked the front door behind me.

If there was anyone on the street, I failed to spot them. When I got to Beachside Ave., I turned left in the direction opposite the hotel and picked up my pace. California being a state where people drive to get from the bedroom to the bathroom, few pedestrians used the sidewalk, especially at such a late hour. So far, just me, myself, and I.

Three hundred yards later, I stopped and feigned interest in an imaginary event down on the beach, chuckled to myself, then glanced around as if seeking someone with whom to share my amusement. No one. I walked another fifty feet to a crosswalk and pressed the signal button. As I waited, I peered casually up and down the street. Nothing.

Between detours, stops and improvisations, it took me some twenty minutes to reach the Pacific Sunset. I crossed the lobby and headed to a phone that allowed a clear view of the entire reception and hotel entrance, and waited. No one entered looking for me.

I made my way to the bar and looked around, not expecting to find Demetrio there, but making sure nonetheless. I sidled up to the bar and onto a stool. The mirror along the back of the bar gave me a complete view of the room behind me. There were two other guys staring over the bar at a poker tournament playing on the TV, and two couples huddled in a booth laughing far too loud to be sober.

Dennis, the bartender, spotted me and sauntered over.

"Hiya, Mr. Pierce. Somebody's been calling you but won't leave a message. Keeps sayin' he'll call again. What'll ya have?

I slipped him a five-dollar bill. "Hi, some water and the phone when it rings again."

"Will do."

He scooped up some ice with a glass and shot some water into it. It all took no more than ten seconds.

I realized then how thirsty I really was. It had been an intense day and an even more stressful evening. I gulped the liquid down. Dennis swooped over to retrieve my glass as the phone rang. He shot me a "this could be it" kind of look and answered.

"This is the bar. Dennis speaking, how can I help you?" He listened for a moment while he looked at me, and nodded. "Hold on, I'll see if he's here." He placed his hand over the mouthpiece and held out the phone.

I signaled for him to hold for a moment while I made another quick evaluation of my surroundings. Satisfied, I nodded, and he handed me the receiver then shuffled off to the other end of the bar.

"Yeah," I said in a soft voice.

"We have to stop meeting this way."

"*¿Dónde estás?*"

"*Habitación 322.*"

"Okay."

I waved the receiver at Dennis. He hurried over to retrieve it and placed it back on its base. I thanked him, then made my way out to the lobby and toward the bank of elevators.

I got to the third floor and was about to knock on the door of room 322 when a familiar voice down the hall whispered, "*Acá.*"

Demetrio's inventiveness made me smile. The number on his door was 326. An automatic check down the hall confirmed that there was no one about, so I stepped in and closed the door behind me.

Carrie's absence was obvious. Demetrio anticipated my question.

"Next door." He nodded toward the connecting door. "She's asleep—tough day."

"Why did you come here?" I asked.

"I spotted your unpleasant friend outside the house."

"Haskell?"

Demetrio nodded. "He did not see us. I thought this was the next best place to go. What do you think?"

I smiled and patted him on the shoulder. "Where the hell have you been?

"Running around San Diego—touristy stuff."

"Why didn't you call? Got a problem with cell phones?"

"We left her office in a rush, I left mine on top of her desk. Carrie forgot to charge hers, so it went dead. I did not think it to be a good idea to reach you on your cell. What if you were in the middle of something?"

"Why the rush to leave her office?"

"A really big, ugly-looking son of a bitch that looked very much like Haskell was walking around outside her office, eying it. He looked like he was waiting to pounce. We rushed out the back, left her car in the lot, and took mine."

"Did she give you any grief?" I asked, nodding in Carrie's direction.

"She didn't want to believe he was after her. His name is Al, she said, 'a crude guy that works security.' I would not have used the word *crude* to describe him. Foul is more precise, I told her. I insisted that we use my car and that I would not take no for an answer, so she finally agreed to leave. She got angry when I made her hide in the back seat. But seeing Bill Haskell hanging around your house made the danger much more real for her. I would say she is much more scared now."

"Maybe she'll tell me what I want to know."

"Let us hope. She is not easy to crack."

He poured a couple of drinks from the mini bar. While we enjoyed them, I related how things had gone with me.

"Other than the documents, what do you think they want with Carrie?" he asked.

"I suspect she knows the answer to that one. Whether she'll give it up is another question entirely. Did she tell you anything useful?"

He shook his head. "*No soltó prenda*. She is no dummy. She knows I would tell you."

"She sure seemed cozy with you back at the house. When did that start?"

"Years ago, *amigo*. She came to a lecture I gave on the differences between the various Proto-Mayan languages at UC San Diego. She insisted we have dinner because she had a long list of questions for me. We sat up talking in my hotel room the entire night."

I squinted inquisitively at him. "Just 'talking'?"

"As you have witnessed, my gray cells are irresistible. Yes, exclusively talking."

I smiled at the image of Carrie's infatuation with the gray cells of my buddy the scholar. "I never realized you'd become so close."

"You were not interested. I became an admirer of her intellect after that, and we have stayed in touch. She is brilliant. I like challenging her, and she loves arguing with me."

I resisted the urge to ask if she ever mentioned me. More pressing matters such as the Haskell brothers took precedence. "Okay, Mr. Scholar, think you can persuade her not to go back to that university of hers? She's bound to have some vacation time due, and I'll need her help and yours to get a better handle on this mess."

"I can try."

"The hardest part will be to keep her hidden. She's way too neurotic to stay put for long."

"We can hide without having to stay locked up here. I can think of many things we can do undetected. As far as getting her to agree not to go to work, that will be a bit more difficult. You know how she is about lying. I will have to come out with something she can use with honesty."

"I don't doubt you'll come up with—"

"Come *up*, not come *out*. I will remember this one."

I didn't doubt he'd convince her. Demetrio's powers of persuasion are nothing to sneeze at. Years ago, I tagged along on an archeological dig of his as cover for one of my ops and got to witness his gift first hand. He talked down an antigovernment guerrilla leader in Oaxaca who threatened to kill me and Demetrio's team of archeologists as they prepared to dig into some ruins high in the mountains. He saw us as weapons of the corrupt regime. Demetrio, however, managed to deescalate tensions almost immediately, and by the end of their *conversation*, the *comandante* sat down to share his *aguardiente* with Demetrio, while his men stood guard along the perimeter to protect all of us from bandits. No idea what he said, and he's refused to divulge his strategy. The next day, the head honcho actually sent six men to help clear away jungle debris and assist in the dig. Nothing short of amazing.

"I'll pack a change of clothes and toiletries for you both. Anything special for you?"

His eyebrows went up and he gave me a look of *are you kidding? What do I care?*

"See you at dawn, then."

"*¡Ay! ¿Por qué tan temprano?*"

"The Haskell brothers won't expect us to be up that early."

I followed my regular route back to the house. The lighting that illuminated the boardwalk and the parking lot during the night shone like midday sunshine. A couple of assaults over the years had made its installation inevitable. Three floodlights lit up the beach to discourage any illicit use of that expanse as well. No surprise to find the area deserted.

CHAPTER TEN

I forced myself up a little past 4:30 in the morning after a torturous night where events, both real and imaginary, mixed incoherently to assure that total rest was never achieved.

Coffee in hand, I called the hospital to inquire about Paul's condition. Unchanged, except for having brought the hemorrhage in his brain under control. Great news by my standards. Carrie would be relieved.

When I opened the fridge, the sight of the various supplies purchased for the heart-to-heart sessions with Demetrio produced an unexpected pang of regret. The entire purpose of his visit had been to help me smooth over my unbearable loss. At that moment, I realized that Cecilia's death had slipped away from the forefront of my consciousness. An excruciating pain of betrayal darted through me and threatened to derail my purpose. I forced it into submission—no time for self-recrimination. No matter the pain, the past needed to take a back seat to the present threat. Distraction meant that Carrie, Demetrio, and I, not to mention Nancy Drier and friends, stood a good chance of falling victim to whoever had put Paul in a coma and Devon in the morgue.

I fried a couple of sausages, sat at the counter with my coffee, and fingered through the box of evidence Devon had gathered. Data sheets, as far as I could tell, folders with correspondence or copies of e-mails, and a bunch of CDs. Carrie and Demetrio would do a far better job of sifting through this academic stuff than I.

I scarfed down the sausages, showered, dressed, camouflaged my remaining scars, and picked a couple of my favorite disguises. As I packed two duffle bags with Demetrio and Carrie's belongings, I came across her laptop. I snagged my own laptop and Demetrio's and crammed them into the bags.

Laden with computers, files, and clothes, I drove south, away from the hotel, checking frequently to make sure I didn't have a tail. I spotted no one. After a few blocks, I made a U-turn, and ten minutes later I knocked on room 326.

Demetrio opened the door attired in a Pacific Sunset terry robe that almost reached his ankles, coffee cup in hand. His eyes widened when he saw all the gear I had. "You did not have to bring the entire house."

"Work for you both," I said as I lugged my load into the room. I placed the box on the bed. "Where is she?"

He nodded toward the door that connected to the neighboring room. "Doing the freshing up."

I chuckled at his attempt to *speak American*, as he calls it. In his book only the Brits speak proper English.

I slipped the bag with his clothes off my shoulder. "This is your gear. Brought your laptop and mine for safekeeping." I ambled toward my sister's room and knocked on the door. "Carrie? I brought some of your things."

"Come in," she answered.

Also wearing a terry hotel robe, she sat facing the mirror on the vanity, drying her hair. Without the layers of makeup and her customary condescending mask, she looked spectacular. "You look great this morning," I said sincerely.

She turned off the hair drier and stared at me, not knowing how to react. A good sign. "I called the hospital," I added. "Paul's hemorrhage is under control. They're keeping him in a coma, but things are looking up."

She smiled. "Thanks."

I had no number for this particular smile. It conveyed a sincere sense of relief and gratitude unfamiliar to me. More and more, Carrie's shortcomings were proving to be a product of my own prejudices. *As you judge, so shall you be judged.*

I placed her duffle bag on the bed. "If you need anything else, make a list, and I'll bring them later."

"How long do you plan to keep me captive in this horrid hotel?"

"Not long. I brought work for you."

"Work?"

"Come on, I'll explain."

Without protest, she followed me into the next room.

Demetrio welcomed her with a kiss on the cheek and a hot cup of coffee. *"Buenos días, niña hermosa."*

She smiled and kissed him back, then took a sip of her coffee. "Mm," she purred.

"What about me?" I pouted. "Where's my kiss and coffee?"

Demetrio tilted his head toward the table with the coffee. "Coffee's there, but you will have to survive without the kiss. You're not my type."

Carrie approached the box on the bed. "What's this?"

"Devon's evidence."

They both studied me, then stared down at the box.

Carrie recoiled, as if somehow it might contain the corpse of her former colleague. "Where'd you get this?" she whispered.

"I can't tell you for now, but I need you guys to sift through it and tell me what it all means."

After a deep breath, she approached the box and peered into it. She pulled a file and fingered through it. "Oh, my God. These are original records."

"Devon's copies are at the college. Can you decipher its contents?"

She nodded. "For the most part, yes. Can't tell what's on the CDs."

"You need to go through it all and tell me exactly what type of evidence he collected."

"Justin, this is university property. Who knows you have this?"

"The persons who gave it to me and now the two of you."

"But—"

I approached her and placed my hand on her shoulder, hoping she wouldn't slap it away. "Carrie, people have been hurt and died over this stuff. I need to know what's in it if I'm to protect you. Will you help me?"

She blushed.

I'd never seen her blush before. Demetrio also noticed and eyed me in acknowledgment.

"Carrie, is there anything you need to tell me? Something you haven't… shared?" I asked her. "It's important you fill me in."

The barrier shot up, and the cool and calculating Carrie stepped on stage. "For crying out loud, Justin, don't be so melodramatic. I'll look into this and tell you what I find."

She turned away from me and sat on one of the chairs by the table, scowl number five, *don't bother me with your crap*, in plain view. It dawned on me that her protective mechanisms were so second nature that the walls materialized without any conscious effort on her part. That box frightened her. Instead of my customary annoyance with her attitude, a surge of love washed over me, and produced an almost overwhelming desire to embrace her. The emotion took me entirely by surprise, and I liked it.

"I will help," Demetrio added, breaking the awkward silence.

"No need to!" she blurted out. "I can handle it."

"No, *chiquita*, I want to help, and I insist. Do not be so possessive." He paused for a moment. When she remained silent, he sauntered over to her. "Unless, of course, you are afraid this old archeologist might discover something you missed and make you look bad." He placed his hand on her shoulder. "I have an idea. We will compare notes at the end and find out who did the good job." His raised eyebrows implied a personal challenge. "Loser buys dinner and an expensive bottle of wine."

Her eyes narrowed and a fierce look came upon her, but she thought better of it, simply smiled, and patted his hand.

He winked.

I stood in awe of Demetrio's manipulative genius. In one fell swoop, he'd deflected her reluctance, or perhaps insecurity, and cornered her into doing what needed to be done. He'd turned an unsettling task into a game.

"That's settled, then," I broke in. "I got a charger for your laptop and one that should work with your phone. I'll be picking up Demetrio's cell from your office when I go to the college and—"

"Why would you go to OCU?" Carrie clearly didn't want me there.

"Need to chat with some folks. Don't fret, I'll behave."

"Who are you going to see?" she insisted.

"The muckety-mucks—VPs, you call them, and—"

"Whatever for?"

"To sort a few things out."

"You don't—"

"Stop. I'm going because that's where I'll find the answers to Devon's death and Paul's injury. To understand how and why Devon died, I need to understand his environment. I'm going because I don't want anyone else to get hurt. Especially you. In a nutshell, I'm going because I have to, and that's that." She shook her head and averted her eyes. I realized a softer tone might be more effective. "Don't argue with me, Carrie. Please. But I don't want to go in blind. It would be helpful if you could fill me in on these people. Start with the guy in charge of students."

She looked up at me and sighed, then crossed her arms and legs ready to hold court. "Have it your way." She took a second to compose herself. "Dixon's the guy you mean. Gossipy type, can't keep his mouth shut, tells anyone who'll listen all the so-called secrets and rumors."

"For what purpose?"

"Mostly to feel important or to get what he wants."

"Such as?"

"Gossip breeds gossip. He's a backstabber who pretends to be chummy by spreading any nasty rumors he picks up, regardless of who they might hurt. He shares confidential things and his buddies share secrets with him. Problem is, most of what he shares is either a lie or a distortion. I swear he makes up stories just to feel important."

"I know the type. What about Braniff?"

She produced a grimace of utter disgust. "Ugh! Nasty bitch of a woman, to put it mildly. Got where she is by sleeping with anything that moved. With nothing more than a masters, she went from faculty to VP thanks to the president she was fu— screwing some twenty years ago."

"Got to the top by sleeping with the boss? Common as white bread. I thought you guys went through some big elaborate interviews before you hire someone. Aren't there some rigorous laws that—" I never finished my speech. The look on Carrie's face, condescending stare number two—*you can't be that naïve or stupid, oh brother mine*, stopped me cold.

"Yes, Justin. There are very strict laws and regulations about hiring," she said at a snail's pace, as if by slowing down I'd be able to catch on more easily. "And yes, there's a complex selection process academics must go through to be hired. But," she added with a smirk, "the president can bypass all that, especially if no one complains about it. In Braniff's case, the selection committee rejected her for the VP job, but the president chose her anyway, and not a single person objected…publicly, anyway. *Fait accompli.*"

"She must be really good in the sack," I chuckled.

"Once, maybe. Wait till you see her. She's a grotesque, vulgar troll." Unable to disguise her disdain, Carrie added, "And a viper. She's gathered muck on everybody, and that gives her power. If she doesn't have any filth, she makes some up. Dixon is useful for that. She uses people as puppets, and destroys anyone who stands in her way." She turned to me, anger oozing from every pore. "It's all about control. For years she's been the *de facto* president. Everyone, and I mean everyone, is afraid of her. She's mean and vengeful. Don't believe a word she says."

"*Dios mío*. This is like a *telenovela*," Demetrio said. "How does anything ever get done at that place? Why do you work there?"

Carrie smiled sarcastically. "I often ask myself that."

"And?" he insisted. "What do you answer to yourself?"

She shrugged. "Habit. Plus, a damn good salary. Besides, I'm good at what I do, so I get very lucrative speaking engagements all over the country and abroad. Adds up to what we call 'golden handcuffs.'"

"Ah, *claro*. The old security curse," Demetrio said with a sarcastic lilt.

"You wouldn't understand," she retorted, as she stood and condescendingly caressed his cheek on the way to pouring herself another cup of coffee. "You're wealthy and—"

"Ah, ah, ah," he interrupted. "So are you."

"I had to work for mine." She stirred cream into her coffee, then waved the spoon. "You were silver-spooned into it."

Fascinated by this exchange, I realized the true comfort of their friendship. I'd never seen Carrie so at ease. With me, the multiple facades and the fuck-you attitude invariably kicked in. With Demetrio, she was simply herself. As I studied her now, I perceived glimpses of what had kept Paul at her side all this time.

"Three marriages do not qualify as hard work," Demetrio countered.

"Oh, yeah? You try it, you coward." She winked at him and returned to her spot. "Look at you, a middle-aged, single, lonely—"

"Happy man, with no attachments or responsibilities I do not choose to have. It is called freedom, *cariño*."

Their conversation had turned so personal, I felt like an intruder.

Demetrio pressed on. "You did not answer me. Why do you remain there?"

"I could ask you the same. You don't need to work. Why do you still teach at the university? Why do you continue to traipse through the jungle to all those mosquito-infested digs?"

He shrugged. "Because I love it."

"Well, so do I…love it."

He shook his head. "No, you do not. And it is not the money. *Papá* Demetrio knows you too well. Tell me the truth."

"Well," she shrugged, "maybe I don't 'love' it. But I can't leave, I can't—" She suddenly realized I was still in the room. "Justin—" She seemed confused. The conversation had taken an uncomfortable turn.

"Don't worry," I said, coming to her rescue. "I get the picture." I could tell a deep fear had grabbed hold of my sister. She remained at that college out of fear. Fear of what? I knew that pushing her now would get me nowhere.

"What picture?" she asked nervously.

"Those two VPs," I answered lamely. "Tell me about the third one?"

She sighed, relieved I had steered the topic in a different direction. "Oh. Well, Lawrence, the VP of Administrative Affairs is a good guy. Inept with a capital I, but a kindhearted man."

"Is there anyone of quality at that dump, Carrie?" Demetrio's turn to speak slowly, "*Por favor*, you cannot be the only person there who is worth their salt and pepper."

She laughed. She looked delightful when she laughed. I realized, much to my surprise, how much I enjoyed seeing my sister in a whole new light.

"No, *cariño*," she said, "there isn't. Not at the top level. I'm the only good salt there is. The only pepper too," she chuckled. "Except," she waggled her finger emphatically, "except for the new president, Elizabeth Moore. She's got what it takes. But I bet Braniff and her cohorts are already gunning for her."

"Elizabeth, a good strong name." Demetrio winked at Carrie coquettishly. "I'm interested. Can you introduce us?"

"Sorry to rain on this little tête-à-tête," I interjected, "but it's time for me to hit the road. Demetrio, whatever you do, don't let her go anywhere or talk to anyone until I get back. I don't care if you have to tie her down and gag her."

"*Ya lo sé, hombre.*"

"Justin, for God's sake. You're insufferable."

I walked over to her. "I know. But for now, you'll have to put up with me." I leaned down and kissed her cheek—might as well go all the way with this new-found relationship. I nodded toward the files. "Get to work, you two. See you later." I couldn't swear to it, but I think Carrie smiled as she touched her cheek where I'd planted the brotherly kiss.

CHAPTER ELEVEN

From Carrie's comments, the most promising VP had to be Robert Dixon, the backstabbing gossip monger. People like him tend to be unmitigated cowards who'll kiss anybody's ass to get ahead and sell their own mothers to benefit themselves. Spineless, egotistical people who will use their power to get what they want, but crumble under the tiniest pressure. Weasels like Dixon are snack food for the Martin Sauerses and Justin Pierces of this world.

I parked in the visitors' lot. Before exiting the car, I donned my favorite disguise—a black pork pie hat, a thin mustache, and large round black-rimmed glasses, black pants, white shirt, baby-blue jacket, and bowtie—my Wilbur costume. I like it not just for its simplicity, but mostly because I enjoy playing the part.

On my way toward Matheus Hall, where the student services were located, I encountered a handful of students. A good opportunity to practice my nasal voice. "Excuse me, do you know where I can find VP Dixon?"

First, they glanced around the grounds as if looking for something, then one of them answered, "Yeah, he hangs around the quad a lot, but I don't see him. His office is in the student complex." He pointed toward a large building behind the quad as an effeminate man in his late fifties exited. "Hey, man, there he is. That's Dixon."

I thanked them and headed in pursuit of Mr. VP.

"Excuse me."

He stopped and peered over his shoulder at me.

"Are you Vice President Dixon?"

He must've decided I was harmless. "Yes, what can I do for you?"

"Wow! Hi." I shook his hand vigorously. "I'm very pleased to meet you. I've read so much about you."

His ego embraced my enthusiasm. "You have? Where?" he asked with a self-satisfied grin.

"Oh, in the data we're collecting for the investigation."

All color drained from his face, and the corners of his mouth sagged.

"You're with the McIntire firm?"

"That's the one."

"What do you want, Mr. …"

"Walters, Wilbur Walters, WW if you like. Most everyone calls me WW."

"What can I do for you?" he asked, a nervous tremor in his voice.

I placed my arm around his shoulder and eased him to one side of the building. "I need to hear it from the horse's mouth instead of reading about it. Know what I mean?" I winked and laughed, adding a loud snort at the end.

"What?"

"All that stuff about Braniff and her schemes." I winked again and snorted with a muffled laugh. "Is it all true?"

His knees wobbled and he propped himself up against the building.

"Why are you asking me? I know nothing about Braniff." His voice strained with panic.

I chortled, snorted, chuckled, and added a bit of spit to close the effect. "Oh, you're funny, really funny." I slapped his back a couple of times.

"What do you mean?"

"I can read between the lines, clear as day. Everyone says you know it all. You're the man of the year, as far as we're concerned. Impressive. Whole office is abuzz about you."

"What—"

I leaned in to whisper, "I appreciate that you're the soul of discretion. But, no need to play coy with me, Mr. Dixon. We're aware—excuse me—we have the evidence that you have all the info, and I want you to rest assured that we've got you covered. You're safe. I just need to hear it all from you to confirm we've got it right."

"Info? What info?"

"Oh, my gosh, all of it." I winked again and licked my lips, smacking them with satisfaction. "Braniff's dealings, you know, with the likes of Ruthskin, Hanley, and the other guys. Oh! And the ring leader, you know, uh… what's his name?" I pretended to search my memory banks.

"Sheridan?"

I snapped my fingers and pointed at his chest. "Yeah, that's the guy. Sheridan. He's the one that… well, other than the fake classes scheme of Ruthskin and Hanley, he's the one that, you know…" I paused and smiled to give Dixon time to tell me the part this guy played. It worked, because he suddenly loosened up.

"Yeah," he whispered with clear resentment. "He gets what he wants no matter what. Even money." He glanced around to make sure no one could hear him. "A real shit. Don't you agree?"

"Oh, absolutely. What a piece of work, huh?" Mr. Know-It-All-Tell-It-All was mine to toy with. He fell for it so fast, I felt cheated.

"Hmm. So, you're the ones that have Devon's evidence," Dixon whispered as if he'd discovered a new planet.

I nodded in all seriousness, my lips tightly pressed as if to stifle a smile. "Mm hm."

"You mean Devon included my stuff in his evidence?"

I shrugged, this time with a serious wink for encouragement.

"You guys sure work fast. You've just started investigating and already—well, that's why you're the pros, right?"

I nodded with a condescending smile. "My boss is a stickler for detail and wants me to tie up a couple of loose ends. He says you're the man, so—I'm all-ears. Let's start at the beginning, shall we?"

He glanced about to reconfirm that no one was within earshot, then leaned toward me. "Sheridan's a piece of shit, I tell you. Always harassing the female staff, and that really awful habit he has of humiliating students who contradict him in class. And constantly insinuating himself on the female students.

It's disgusting. I'm telling you, I get complaints all the time about that." He leaned closer to me so only I could hear him. "When he encouraged Al Haskell, with Braniff's blessing, mind you, to strong-arm those two young women and hush them up, I decided I'd had enough." He struck a pose of righteous indignation followed by a quick nod to emphasize his point. "A decent man can look the other way for so long. Not me. No sirree. That was the last straw. I said to myself, 'Bob, enough's enough.' That's when I started keeping records of what she was up to with Sheridan."

"Very smart of you. We're glad you did." I patted his arm. That's why you're our main guy."

"I mean, Leonard was not only the worst professor you could ever come across, but also a sex-crazed little shit."

"Was?" I lowered my glasses to make sure he could see my inscrutable look.

He looked at me a bit puzzled. "Well, he's retired now." Then a realization made him smile. "Oh, how silly of me. Of course. You're right, the creep still teaches part time. Anyway, over the years several students brought allegations against him. Braniff always derailed them and used the Haskell brothers to put the fear of God into any of the women who threatened to make any noise."

"Right. I read about him." I looked down and shook my head. "But this is where it gets interesting. You all were well aware of what was going on and did nothing. Hard to believe."

"Oh, it's true enough. And I'm not proud of it. Want to hear the best part, though?"

I nodded vigorously.

He got really close to me. "Braniff asked Sheridan to do a workshop on sexual harassment."

When I didn't react, he decided Wilbur required an in-depth explanation. "Don't you see? Braniff figured it would help deflect any future allegations. Talk about putting the fox in charge of the chicken coop," he added with a sarcastic chuckle.

"So, you decided to…" I looked at him over the rim of my glasses.

He scanned our surroundings apprehensively. "I'll tell you, but let's go somewhere a little less… exposed. How about a cup of coffee?"

I smiled, and this time, he hooked his arm in mine as we walked around the building towards the R. R. Wallen Dining Commons building. WW and Dixon, best pals ever. Two heroic paladins committed to the righting of all evils.

"Anyway, Braniff irks me, and I couldn't—"

I stopped him. "Let's talk when we're sitting. Don't want others to hear our conversation."

"Yeah, right. I'm not used to investigations. Come on, you'll love our coffee."

He relished playing the big important guy, greeting everyone we came across, expertly projecting that he actually knew who they were. It's the kind of talent the more successful politicians have. It's an acquired skill that necessitates the ability to deceive without hesitation or remorse.

After several dozen hellos, we arrived at the coffee stall. He flashed smiles all round and greeted every employee by name. Another well-honed skill. When at last we'd poured our coffee, we walked past the cashier without paying.

"No need to pay?" I asked

"I'm their supervisor, so I get perks here and there. Look, there's a table in that back corner. No one'll bother us there."

We made our way to the table.

He started talking before our butts hit the seats. "Anyway, I couldn't figure out what was going on with Sheridan and Braniff, see? So, I spied on them." He couldn't suppress a sheepish grin.

Wilbur was duly impressed. "Wow, spying…that takes stones, man."

He leaned back with an air of unqualified superiority. "Hey, what the hell? I figured, why should a bitch like that be the only one with the power to blackmail people into submission?"

"Why, indeed."

"I already knew they'd slept together. Hell, everybody did. But I knew there had to be more. I mean, why go out on a limb for the guy time and time again, right? And then there's the Haskell brothers, they're deep into it too, somehow."

"As far as we can tell from our evidence, she uses them a lot." I sniffled, just for effect.

"Hell, everybody is well aware of that tidbit. Bullies, those two, real bullies. She lets them get away with anything because they're cops. I stay out of their way. You're checking them out, too?"

I threw him a blank stare as I tilted my head. "Mr. VP…"

"Doctor."

Time to look impressed. "Wow! Doctor! That's impressive. I knew that, of course, but didn't want to embarrass you. Silly of me." I snorted loudly. "Go on then, Doctor VP."

He beamed, then leaned next to me and whispered. "The money from Sheridan, I can't figure that out."

I wrinkled my brow and nodded. "Yes, the money. That has me stumped, too." I had no clue what he was talking about, but he felt the need to share. Oh, the delights of doing business with a blabbermouth.

"You already know from the evidence that she's been on the take from the faculty who get cash from students or fake classes."

"Yep, the likes of Ruthskin and Hanley."

"Yeah. Can you believe they've been running that private fitness business for years right under our noses?"

"Pretty amazing, I'd say…I mean, the fact that nobody knew."

"Yeah, well, we did, but Braniff…well, you know."

I nodded.

"They've taken in big, I mean BIG, money with their 'how to become a professional trainer' program and shit like that. I can only imagine what she's pocketed."

"But frankly, you and I know they weren't the only ones. Right?" I winked.

"No. You know about the guys in the automobile engineering program." He leaned close to me again and whispered. "I bet you she's cashed-in big time with them, too. What with their profits from that huge private car repair business they run on campus—" He paused and looked around, "I get my own car serviced there and the bill's pretty hefty given all the technology cars use nowadays." He cleared his throat nervously. "Don't get me wrong, I only do it for the students. They need the experience. If working on my car helps, I'm all for it."

"Yeah, that one caught our eye right away. Fixing cars for cash using free student labor. And university facilities and equipment, don't forget. Brilliant idea. Nice profits with no overhead."

"Yeah, yeah, but of course, you already have that evidence. What puzzles me, what I can't figure out, is why Braniff gives money—I'm talking cash, mind you—to Sheridan. I mean, you've read in the stuff I gave to Devon that I actually saw her doing it. But, why? Braniff takes. She never gives. She takes, takes, takes. Bitch." He huffed with frustration.

"Yeah, I get that. But you're a real smart guy, so why haven't you found out? You've spied on them long enough. What's stopping you? You've been really awesome with everything else."

He rolled his head from side to side. "Well, when Devon went public, which I didn't expect him to do, all hell broke loose. They pulled back. Stopped everything. It got really hard to spy on them. Pissed me off. I was this close to controlling her and it all fell apart."

"So, what did you do?"

"Hell, I figured it's best to back off," he snickered. "I told Braniff that Devon had collected all this evidence against her, that it could end her career and maybe send her to jail. I used some examples of what I knew so she'd believe me. Told her it would be *our little secret*. She got the point. I'm so fuckin' tired of being Braniff's puppet."

I gave him a snigger of encouragement. "You kick ass, man. Keep up the good work. Oh, and this meeting, just between us. Understand?"

He made a zipping motion across his lips. "Mum's the word."

"I got to go, but you carry on like nothing's happened. Don't forget, you're our ace in the hole, so keep your ears open and your eyes peeled."

He beamed and gave me a thumbs up.

I rose and leaned toward him. "You're a champ. See you around." I winked and fled out into the fresh air.

$$\textbf{——— • ◆ • ———}$$

CHAPTER TWELVE

Worms like Dixon always make me want to take a shower after an encounter with them, as if I've dragged myself through the city dump and burrowed deep into all the rotten, maggot-infested trash. But no time for purification. I had to make contact with Braniff and get the hell out of Dodge to avoid the Haskell duo spotting me on campus.

I made a quick detour to Carrie's office to retrieve Demetrio's phone. I lowered the hat to cover most of my hair and push my ears forward, then I slumped enough to decrease my height. The effect, coupled with the large glasses and a Mexican accent inspired by Demetrio, proved enough to avoid being recognized as Carrie's brother. The receptionist expected me because Dr. Harding had called to inform them she was taking a few days off to host a distinguished scholar from Mexico, and that one of his assistants would be by to collect the phone he'd left behind.

My geek disguise wouldn't work with Braniff, though. She needed to be awed. So, I decided to play the FBI card. My bureau agent look—black suit, aviator sunglasses, and slicked-back hair—always impresses a lioness on the prowl. From all accounts, Braniff fit the bill. I returned to my car, drove around the campus to make sure no one tailed me, parked in a different visitors' lot, and swapped costumes. I dashed toward the nearest classroom building and headed to the restroom, where I slicked back my hair, touched up any visible scars, and stepped into the role of Agent Dorset.

After parking in yet another guest slot, I made my way toward the Academic Affairs offices. I entered at the exact time that Braniff did, although at that precise moment I had no idea who she was. I opened the door for a short, middle-aged, heavily pregnant woman with thinning hair, a pale complexion, and a permanent scowl of revulsion etched onto her face. She carried a large ratty notebook that rested on her protruding belly. A purse the size of a backpack dangled from her shoulder down to her sizable rump.

I opened the door and ushered her through. "After you, ma'am," I said with a nice southern twang. I have found that most women like the melody of the south, particularly in tall, handsome, FBI types.

She waddled through the door huffing and puffing. She oozed an odor of cheap perfume mingled with sweat.

She blushed and nodded her thanks. "May I help you? I'm Agnes Braniff."

Carrie's description fit her to a T. I acted fittingly impressed to cover an unrepressed chuckle. "Well, I'll be damned. How lucky can a man be? Ms. Braniff, you're the very person I'm looking for. What an honor, ma'am."

She blushed even more and regaled me with a coquettish smile that resembled a scary Halloween mask. "You're lucky indeed. I happen to have a few minutes between meetings. Come with me, please."

I followed her into her office. The clutter of papers, files, and books strewn over every surface was such that I had to sidestep to squeeze in. The mess didn't faze her one bit. She shuffled over the mounds of paper, tossing her notebook onto myriad files that cluttered her desk, and sagged into her chair. I realized she wasn't pregnant at all, just grotesquely overweight and disproportionate. I wondered what sexual exploits she could possibly perform to merit any promotion. I fought back my revulsion and forced a professional smile upon my lips.

"What can I do for you, Mr. …?

"Dorset, ma'am. Duran Dorset." I looked for a place to sit, but even the guest chairs had stacks of materials on them.

"Toss those papers on the floor," she said as she pointed to a chair across her desk.

I did as directed.

"Well?" she said as she leaned back in her chair. The belly became far more evident as a result.

The sarcastic part of me was tempted to ask her when she was due, but I contained myself and got back into my role. "FBI, ma'am, Special Agent Dorset." I flashed her my Dorset ID.

That one took her aback for a moment. She recovered nicely then leaned forward, slid on her glasses, and read the badge. Satisfied, she removed the glasses, and slumped back into her chair. Her coquettish charm had transformed into full frontal attack. "And?"

"We're looking into the death of a Mr. Jeremy Devon."

The color drained from her already pale face. "The FBI? Whatever for? Didn't he drown?"

I smiled from ear to ear. "Not exactly, ma'am." I wiped the smile off my face and gave her my somber FBI agent leer. She swallowed hard. "After a closer look, we discovered a big gash on his head. That's what killed 'im, I'm afraid. Poor fella."

Pearls of sweat formed above her lip. "Well, that certainly has nothing to do with me. Why are you here?"

"I understand that you're the boss around here, if you know what I mean?" I winked.

She blushed. "I'm one of the VPs. The president is in charge."

"C'mon now, honey… you don't mind if I call you that, do you, sweetie?"

She shook her head.

"You're a peach." I flashed a condescending smile. "Where was I? Oh, yeah. Anyhow, the word on campus is that you're the person everyone looks up to around this place. So don't be modest."

She couldn't conceal her satisfaction. "Well, I've been here over thirty years, so—"

"It can't be. No, it can't. Thirty? Really? Darlin', you must've started working here when you were a mere child."

More blushing, now accompanied by a flirtatious little smile.

"Please, I need to know how you do it." I couldn't resist pushing on.

She was utterly perplexed. "Do what?"

"Stay so young and beautiful."

"Oh, c'mon, you're putting me on. I'm old and fat."

I laughed. "Honey, I'm from the south. I love me a full-figured woman. Skin and bones might be good for makin' soup, but not for makin' whoopee." I winked. "Nothin' whatsoever wrong with you, sugar, believe me." Ever so slowly, I licked my lips.

"Mr. Dorset—"

"Agent."

"Sorry. Agent Dorset, you don't need to play this game with me to get the information you're seeking."

"Game?" I became officiously serious. "Oh, darlin', this ain't no game. But you're right. I apologize. I should control myself, hard as that might be. It's just that there's a certain *je ne sais quoi* about you that drives me to distraction. I'm sure you've been told that before."

A blush, a coquettish look, and a shrug of the shoulders coupled with a nod. The ugly caterpillar was striving to become a beautiful butterfly.

"It's true, ain't it?" I exclaimed with a nice long drawl followed by a full guffaw. I pretended to recover. "But, you're right, business comes first, honey pie." I feigned a shift into officialdom. "You know about the McIntire business."

She grimaced. "Yeah."

"What d'ya think?"

"I don't see why Elizabeth went out and hired an investigating firm."

I sucked air in between clenched teeth. "Just between us, me neither. But there you have it. Now they've dumped this can of worms on me. Whatcha you think about that?"

"A waste of public money, if you ask me."

I nodded. "Ain't that the truth? But they do have a nasty habit of finding things, don't they, these private investigators?"

Her eyes opened wide and she wrung her hands. "What do you mean? What have they found?"

"Oh, nothin' I can talk about. Little peccadillos here and there."

She nodded with pursed lips. "And only the president knows, right?" She said sarcastically. "It really irks me that I can't be told."

"And rightly so, hon. Seems kinda disrespectful to me... given your position and all."

She nodded effusively.

"Well, you see, that's why I'm here to look into a Mr.—" I pretended to consult my notebook. "Leonard Sheridan. Do you know him?"

She surged forward, her face flushed with color. I'd hit the jackpot.

"He's retired. Why the hell would you be looking at him?"

"Oh." I glanced at the notebook again. "Hm." I shot her my best suspicious squint. "He's still teaching for you, darlin', isn't he?"

She searched for a plausible answer. "Well, yes, part-time. But why are you looking at him? He had nothing to do with Devon's death."

"Well, that's for me to find out and for your pretty little head not to worry about."

"Why ask me, then?"

"Oh, I want your opinion. Need to get the skinny on him, find out all I can. You're the boss lady, and by God, what a lady you are." I slowly licked my lips as if savoring the most delicious morsel. "Anything you can share about Mr. Sheridan?"

She stared at my tongue as it made its way across my lips. The mental wheels spun into overdrive. She was worried.

I leaned forward and whispered, "Ma'am? Your opinion?"

She snapped out of her bewilderment and forced a smile. "Oh, yeah. Well, he's a professor."

"Honey, you're smart enough—" I winked, "not to deny that you and him…well…now, c'mon, don't be bashful."

"Oh, for Christ's sake! That was years ago."

I gave her my best coy smile. "Who are we kiddin', sweetie? With someone like you, once the fire's lit, it never stops burning."

She blushed.

"You think he could've killed Devon?"

She bolted upright, and braced herself against the desk. "No! Of course not. Why would you think that? He had nothing to do with Devon."

I tilted my head and sighed. "You're not being truthful with me, dear heart." I turned deadly serious and lowered my voice. "You know what happens to naughty girls who lie to the FBI?"

She swallowed hard then shook her head. Deep breaths came in rapid succession. The Big Bad Wolf was knocking, and she had nowhere to hide.

I raised my eyebrows and shrugged. "Obstruction of justice to begin with… assuming you refuse to cooperate with my little old investigation."

"I'm not—"

"Oh, but you are, honey bunch." I oozed with so much sappiness I almost gagged. "Now, please, sweetheart. Your honest opinion, please, of this sex maniac called Leonard Sheridan."

"Sex maniac?"

"We know that you've covered up his many indiscretions. He must've been quite the sex machine for you to go out on a limb for a pervert like that." I feigned a eureka moment. "Unless…"

"Unless what?"

I sensed the panic in her voice. I tilted my head with disappointment. "Unless there's something else between you two." I smiled suggestively.

"What?"

"Tell me about the money."

"How…?"

I winked. "It's my job. Don't lie to me, now."

Her panic shifted into full-fledged aggression. "We're done. I need my lawyer."

"Oh, don't be a spoiler," I said sarcastically. "We were startin' to have fun."

"Please leave, Mr. Dorset." Her rage was intended to camouflage her fear.

I tilted my head and smiled. "And I had all these expectations that we—"

"Just leave."

"Not even a—"

"Leave."

"Okay, be that way. It'll be harder if you choose to follow this path."

"Harder?"

I stood up and walked toward the door.

"Harder?" she asked again. "How? What do you mean, 'harder'?"

"I gave you a chance to come clean, and you turned me down. My boss hates that. It won't be fun when we drag you down to headquarters. You know how people are when they see their boss handcuffed and hauled away by federal agents. Not a pretty sight. Oh, and the gossip."

"You're going to handcuff me?"

I turned to her with the most appealing smile I could muster. "No, no, darlin', not right now. Not me. I don't concern myself with stuff like that. They'll be sending some boys in blue to take care of that. My boss loves to make a statement. My guess it'll be two or three SUVs and a couple of squad cars, lights flashing, sirens blaring. It's quite a show."

"But, you can't."

"Oh? Why's that, honey?"

"I mean, I've done nothing wrong."

I leaned against the door. "Other than to cover up for Sheridan's—what do we call them—misdeeds? And, refuse to help with our investi—"

Someone knocked on the door behind me, and I stepped aside.

A young woman entered Braniff's office. She nodded at me, then looked at the bewildered woman behind the desk. "I'm sorry Ms. Braniff, but your next appointment is waiting."

Braniff stood petrified.

I smiled at the secretary. "I'm done here, anyway. Thanks for your time, Ms. Braniff. We'll be in touch."

"But, wait."

I shrugged and left.

I shed the last of Special Agent Dorset and drove away. Now, more than ever, I longed for a shower, but it would have to wait. First, I had to talk to this McIntire character, and see what light he might shed on things. I needed an introduction to help cut to the chase.

I stopped at the Fish Shack by the beach, scarfed down a squid sandwich, then connected with Sauers to ask if he knew McIntire.

"Hell, yeah. He worked with us some time back. As straight a shooter as you'll ever find. Don't tell me he's involved in this."

"Sounds like it. I'm not sure."

"I'll give him a call, but don't expect much. If they've hired him, mum's the word."

"Got it, but I have to try."

"Call you back in ten."

For a moment, I succumbed to the rhythmic pounding of the waves—*the gentle beating of the earth's heart*—I thought. I cracked a smile at my musings, aware that my senses had reawakened to the world of the living. As I enjoyed my sandwich, I replayed the information Dixon had spewed. Whatever had prompted them to kill Devon ran much deeper than the fake classes. This Sheridan fellow sounded like the kind of guy who thought of himself as the untouchable ringleader. Prying anything out of him would require a bit of leverage, which at present I lacked.

Time to check in with Carrie and Demetrio. I called the hotel. "Hi, Angela, hope all is well with you this beautiful morning."

"I'm doing fine…Mr. Connors," she said with a smile in her voice.

I chuckled. "Good. You're priceless. Can you connect me with room 326?"

"The guests in room 326 have moved to the grand suite. You know, the private cabin. I'll put you through. Have a good one."

"*Hola*," Demetrio answered.

"The grand suite? Really?"

"Our prisoner wanted more room, and I wanted a view. By the way, have you noticed that bikinis are getting smaller and smaller? Some don't even have a top."

"How's she doing?

"Both of us are making good progress. We'll have plenty for you. When can we expect you?"

"Later this evening. Don't wait for dinner, you guys go ahead."

"Okay. Anything useful?"

"Yeah, I'll fill you in later. Don't let her out of the room. No beach escapades."

"*Ya lo sé, ya lo sé*. She's not into the sun, anyway—I got a lecture earlier on the effect those evil sunrays can have on my baby-soft skin. Anyway, she is knee-deep into unwrapping the gift you left behind, and she is eating it up. I am, too, as well, with the occasional therapeutic distraction of beach-bikini-watching. Did you know that the grand suite comes with binoculars?"

"Got a call coming in, see you later."

It was Sauers. "He'll see you at 3:30. Can you make it?"

That left me with about 35 minutes to get to downtown San Diego. "Unless I get stopped for speeding."

"He asked me to remind you that he may not be able to give you anything you can use."

"I know the drill."

"This case reeks of fraud. That's his firm's specialty. This is getting more and more interesting. Let me know how it goes."

"Will do. Any news on Devon's attorney?"

"No leads yet. But folks at his office are worried about him. Not like the guy to disappear without a word."

"How's the girl?"

"I think she's okay, given she's cooped up. You know how hard that can be. You should visit her. Ready to know her whereabouts now that her companions are not around?"

"Sure."

"She's where Turin spent time. Remember?"

"Yeah."

"The code is south, eight, east."

I chuckled. "Sweet."

"Thought you'd like it."

The law offices of McIntire and Associates occupied the entire sixth floor of a modern building in downtown San Diego on C Street, a few blocks from the pier where the cruise ships dock, and next to the train station and trolley stop.

Marty had managed to set up the appointment with the man himself, John McIntire, and even though traffic forced me to turn up twenty minutes later than expected, the receptionist ushered me into his office almost before I finished saying my name.

She told me to sit in front of a large desk that was buried in foot-high stacks of papers, some in folders, some loose. She offered me a cup of coffee, but I refused.

"Mr. McIntire won't be long, Mr. Pierce. He's meeting with a client, but he will be here momentarily."

With this outpour of attentiveness, I found myself at a loss to say anything other than, "Thank you."

She shot me a perfunctory smile and waggled her way back toward reception.

I felt awkward. To allow a stranger into an investigator's office when he isn't around is not a policy I would advocate. True that most investigations are tedious, extensive, and monotonous, but there can be some juicy morsels from time to time and, had I possessed ulterior motives for being there, I could've helped myself to any of the documents piled on McIntire's desk.

Instead, I busied myself examining some of the diplomas and acknowledgments that adorned the walls. They displayed the usual recognitions and whereases from this group, or that city, or charitable organization. On a bookcase under the window with a sweeping view of the waterfront stood a row of photographs of a man and wife, a mother and two boys, one of the boys in a baseball uniform with the word "Yankees" splashed across the chest, the other boy with a set of golf clubs standing before a sign that read "Southern California Junior Golf Association."

Across the desk from me stood a deep brown leather executive chair, backed by a row of bookcases that were as cluttered as the desk. A variety of large legal tomes rested on the shelves, crammed behind other books, along with papers, boxes, assorted statuettes, and knickknacks.

A man's voice emanated from somewhere down the hall, and moments later a distinguished-looking man, in his late fifties, glided through the door, his right hand outstretched toward me.

"Mr. Pierce. John McIntire. Heard interesting things about you."

I shook his hand and found myself towering above him. "Thanks for seeing me on such short notice."

He smiled and took his seat behind the desk and, for a second, I thought he might vanish from sight. "I'm not sure I'll be able to help you much. My investigation into the Ocean Crest University matter is confidential. At least for now. I can only share what's public information."

"How about who hired you?"

He nodded. "Since that's public information, I can tell you we were retained by the new president, Dr. Elizabeth Moore."

"To do what?"

"Also, public information. She asked us to look into some alleged irregularities in class rosters and record keeping."

"The professors Ruthskin and Hanley?"

"That, too, is public information. As you know, they'd been filing grievances and claims against the now-deceased Mr. Devon, who supposedly uncovered their alleged scheme."

"Why hire a private firm to investigate university business?"

"This very question has been publicly debated by the Board of Trustees before they issued my contract, therefore I'm at liberty to tell you how that came about. Shortly after Dr. Moore was hired, she received a whistleblower complaint about a private business being run out of the automobile engineering department. This complaint necessitated an expert not connected with the institution to investigate. Their security force doesn't have the expertise to look into claims of fraud, and the Seaview PD doesn't have the manpower."

"The whistleblower, an employee?"

"Yes."

"In the auto shop?"

"Yes."

"Disgruntled?"

"So I'm told."

"Reliable?"

"We're looking into that. Can't tell you any details on employee records. Sorry."

"I understand. Thing is, if there's any chance that you can shed some light on a few things, some lives might be spared." A bit melodramatic, but nonetheless, the truth.

"Explain, please."

"I thought Marty briefed you on the situation."

"In general. I'd like to hear what you've uncovered. It might help us."

"Okay." I outlined the events up to that point—Devon's death and his lawyer Paxton's disappearance, the attacks on Paul, and Carrie's relationship to both me and Devon. I didn't mention Nancy Drier or the box of evidence. But I did give him a breakdown of what I had learned so far and the possibility that further evidence might be acquired.

When I finished, he interlaced his fingers, forming a small steeple with his two forefingers, and placed them across his lips. He rocked back and forth for a moment then leaned across the desk.

"Not bad, Mr. Pierce. You've done a very thorough job in a short time. I'm impressed."

"Enough to help me out?"

"This character, Leonard Sheridan, surfaced for us as well. Has a nice lifestyle."

"Unaccounted money?"

"That's what we're looking into. I can tell you that his IRS records do not match his lifestyle. I can't give you any specifics."

"Is there anything you *can* give me?"

He thought it over for a moment and stared at me. Finally, after a very deep sigh, he said, "Tell you what I'll do. Ask me anything you want, conjecture or otherwise. If your assumption or your information is wrong, I will tell you so. Fair enough?"

I had to smile. "More than fair."

CHAPTER THIRTEEN

Although I'd learned nothing beyond what I already knew, McIntire had confirmed my suspicions that Sheridan, Braniff, and the Haskell duo were into something bigger than merely defrauding the university and students. Pocketing money from fake classes and fees and profiting from illicit businesses, although illegal and corrupt, didn't warrant murder. The fact that McIntire's firm had expanded their investigation to include Sheridan's activities was significant. We agreed to keep in touch and assist each other when possible.

By the time I hit the road, rush-hour traffic was in full swing. Since my drive to North County would be unbearable, I decided to visit Nancy Drier.

The safe house stood in a neighborhood no more than ten miles from downtown. I'd provided safe houses for witnesses over the years, and the recurring themes of the occupants always came down to unbearable boredom and claustrophobia. To be locked up with oneself for hours and sometimes days without the possibility of human contact, beyond the occasional agent or interrogator, can wear a person down very fast. In Nancy's case, she was also mourning the loss of the man she loved, a tough burden to carry in complete solitude, as I knew only too well.

During an international stakeout some time back, Sauers and I had spent a few months in the house Nancy now occupied. Our surveillance centered on a shady businessman whose enterprise met a sudden death when we busted his place and confiscated his property—some twenty young Mexican girls he intended to sell to local pimps—along with all his ill-gained possessions, which included priceless art, two Ferraris, and millions in gems and jewelry. One of our most satisfying joint ops.

I drove down the ramp to the gated underground parking lot located some fifty feet from the actual house, camouflaged under a nearby apartment building, and entered the same code we'd used during that stakeout. The alarm system activated, opening the gate and emitting the familiar five short beeps followed by two long ones. If the beeps varied, it meant some unwelcome visitor had entered or attempted to. I parked near the secret entrance to the house and locked the car. At a steel door labeled DANGER! DO NOT ENTER, I punched in the same code again. The beeping sequence confirmed there were no intruders. I emerged into the lower level and made my way up the stairs to the first floor of the house. I announced my presence to avoid unnecessary alarm. "Hello, Nancy, it's Justin Pierce. All, okay?"

A barefoot Nancy came bouncing down the stairs, clad in a simple summer dress, and flashing an irresistible smile. "Mr. Pierce, how great to see you." She shook my hand effusively.

"Thought I might join you for dinner if that's okay. There should be good food here, but if you prefer, I can go get something."

"Wow, I've been munching chips and watching TV all afternoon. I didn't expect any visitors."

"Not hungry then?"

"Yes, for sure. But I'm up for something healthy. That's what I meant."

"C'mon, let's see what we can find, then." I made my way to the kitchen with her in tow.

"Is this your house?"

"No, no. Nice, isn't it?

"Beautiful. Is it your friend's?"

"You can say that."

I opened the fridge and found it loaded with food. Obviously, Nancy hadn't been eating much. "You don't like what's here?"

"Oh, I do. But it's not mine."

I burst out laughing. "Oh, dear girl, it's all for you. You're the guest in this house, and everything in here is yours to use, eat, and have while you're a resident. Didn't he tell you?"

She turned pink with a look of utter innocence. "He did, but I… well, why would he do that? I'm not that kind of woman, you know."

I reached over and patted her bare shoulder. "Nancy, he's not that kind of man, either. He's a good guy with a house he uses to help those who need it. I've stayed here myself at times. He doesn't expect anything from you whatsoever. C'mon, let's fix dinner while we chat. Do you like wine?"

"Love it."

She smiled, then dove into the fridge. Before I'd finished opening the wine, Nancy had dinner well in hand. She'd gotten out lettuce and vegetables to make a nice salad and placed four chicken thighs to grill on the stove.

"Boy, that was fast."

"Truth is, I'm really starving. I left little notes in the cupboards each time I took what I thought were nonessential foods. Silly, huh? If only I'd been sure there were no strings attached, I'd have enjoyed my stay a lot more."

"Hope you like red wine," I said as I handed her a glass.

She took a sip and graced me with another charming smile. "Delicious. Tell me, Mr. Pierce—"

"Call me Justin, please. Let me help you with that. How about I chop the celery?" I took a knife from a drawer, ran some water to rinse the stalks, then started chopping.

"Okay," she said as she tossed some peeled and sliced cucumbers into a bowl. She paused for a moment and stared at me. "Justin, if you don't mind my asking, what exactly do you do?"

"I'm in industrial insulation, working in Latin America mostly. But I had… an accident down in Mexico some weeks back, and I decided to retire from that business."

"Oh, gosh, what happened to you?"

Hoping to distract her while I thought of the answer, I smiled and took a long sip of my wine. "Got hit by a truck."

"Oh, my God. Must've really hurt."

"Yes, it did." My face contorted with the sudden pain brought on by the memory of Cecilia's limp body in my arms.

Next thing I knew, Nancy stood by my side, one hand placed gently on my shoulder. "I'm sorry. You lost someone dear to you in that accident, I can tell."

A couple of rogue tears showed up as I nodded. "How—"

"I'm in the same place you are. I lost my Jeremy." Her eyes reflected sincere compassion.

"Yes, of course," I managed to say, then turned back to the celery and continued chopping in silence.

Nancy returned to her side of the table to slice some tomatoes and tossed them into the bowl with the cucumbers. As I observed her, it became apparent that this diminutive, sweet young woman possessed far more strength of character than I'd given her credit for.

"Tell me, Nancy, how did you and Devon hook up? Is it okay to talk about him?"

She smiled and nodded. I noticed that she'd shed a couple of tears.

"Well," she shrugged, "to tell you the truth, it was love at first sight." She moved to the stove and sprinkled salt and pepper on the chicken thighs, then flipped them over.

Before I could stop myself, I blurted out, "You're kidding."

She giggled. "I know, he didn't look like…well, like you, tall and handsome, but to me he was perfect. His eyes hooked me. When he looked at me, I could see the gentle, loving, and honest man he was, and I melted inside every time."

I decided to ask the uncomfortable question. "The fact that he was married didn't bother you? You're so wholesome."

She smiled. "Oh, thanks, Justin. It did at first, to be honest. But he was separated. She walked out on him four years ago. They only remained married on account of Alex." She finished tossing the salad and expertly drizzled in some olive oil, rice vinegar, and a dash of soy sauce.

"Alex?"

"His son. He's autistic, and Blanche—that's his wife—faults Jer for the bad sperm that created Alex. Can you imagine how horrible that must've been for him?"

I nodded.

"Broke his heart." She placed the chicken thighs on a platter and sprinkled them with chopped parsley. "To make matters worse, Blanche blames Jeremy for Alex not becoming more normal as he grew up, which is ridiculous. Autism isn't a disease that suddenly gets cured in adulthood. It isn't a disease at all." She took the chicken platter and the salad to the dining room and placed them in the middle of the table.

"You get the plates. I'll get forks, knives, and napkins." She left the room but continued. "Blanche claims it all happened because Jer smoked and drank too much. He quit the smoking part, but she kept attacking him more and more viciously over the boy's condition, until he couldn't take it any longer. Small wonder the poor man drank. He tried to correct that as well, drank a lot less in the last year or so." Nancy came back and handed me the utensils and a napkin. "Blanche refused to give Jer a divorce because she feared the court would give Alex to his father because she's got no job or prospects. Besides, she'd lose her medical coverage, which Jer had through his work. Truth is, she used Alex as an excuse to avoid working and exploit Jer as much as possible. He supported both so that she could take care of Alex full time. But if you ask me, Alex doesn't need full-time care."

We sat down at the table without missing a beat—an old married couple relating the events of the day over a comfortable dinner.

"Jer got a place near the campus," she went on, "and only saw Alex on weekends. Two homes, three people to support, one of them disabled. It gets really expensive. Thank God for OCU. We're all paid well, so he managed okay. That's why he put up with all that mess. He didn't want to leave. The money's too good, and those jerks weren't going to ruin it for him."

She looked up at me, and for an instant, I felt I could plunge deep into the lovely emerald green pools of her eyes. She was bewitching, and I now understood how a man of Devon's size had managed to persuade such a divine little thing to share his bed—compassion. Plain and simple—he needed rescuing, and she'd answered the call.

"Tell me about the threats to his family."

"Why don't you tell me about the woman you lost in Mexico?" she asked. "It's only fair."

I didn't want to talk about her, but Nancy deserved an honest answer. "Her name was Cecilia, and she was in the same line of work as me."

"Like me and Jeremy."

I nodded. "Exactly, we were both unattached, with jobs that didn't let us indulge in relationships. We'd just gotten together when she died. Not much more to tell really. Let's get back to Devon. After all, we're trying to find out who killed him, aren't we? Tell me about the death threats."

"They sent him photos of Blanche and Alex doing everyday things. At school, at the store, outside their house, things like that. It sent the message that they could harm them whenever they wanted. Then they sent nasty letters to Blanche about Jeremy, telling her he was a fraud, that he slept with this one or that one."

"How did she take it? Do you know?"

"Jeremy said she enjoyed them, and she'd use the stuff in court if he ever tried to divorce her. Sick, don't you think?"

"Did Devon have any money set aside? What about his will?"

A couple of tears rolled down her rosy cheeks. "Yes. He got a life insurance policy that is now worth over three million. I have a copy of his will. The original is in his safe deposit box in the bank."

"You have access to that box?"

She nodded. "I have the key. He made me a signatory so I could access it."

"Who benefits?"

"Jer set up a trust for Alex so he can be taken care of. He also made arrangements with his attorney that, if both Alex's parents died —"

"Go on."

Her cheeks turned crimson red. "I should be appointed as his guardian. He wanted his son to be sent to a special private residential school. He'd made all the arrangements with the school as well."

"What's in the safe deposit box?"

"His will, the life insurance paperwork, the instructions and agreement with his attorney about Alex and his guardianship, the trust documents, and the papers regarding the special school."

"Nothing else?"

"Nothing."

"What about you? Did he make arrangements for you?"

She lowered her eyes. "He made me the executor of his will along with his attorney. He also set up a trust for me."

I reached over and patted her hand. "I'm glad he took care of you."

"He was a wonderful man." She bolted from her chair, rushed to the kitchen, and ran the water.

I waited till she'd composed herself and returned to the table. After she sat down, I changed the topic. "What were you supposed to do with the box of evidence he gave you?"

"Keep it. That's it."

"Do you know what's in it?

Nancy lowered her head and nodded, a pink hue covering her neck and face. "So do Alice and Mike. I report to them. Well, to Alice, who reports to Mike. They're good people."

Not what I wanted to hear. "You guys didn't remove anything, did you?"

"Oh, no, no! Please believe me, we didn't."

"Who else knows what's in the box?"

"I think Jer showed it to President Moore. He said she knew he had it, and told him to keep it safe. I don't think he had permission to give it to me, though. Do you think I'll be put in jail for this? I mean, for keeping all these original records? They're the property of the university. It's like stealing."

The idea of this beautiful, petite flower being interrogated at the Seaview police station by Haskell or one of his clones irked me, but she didn't need to know that. "No, don't worry about that. I have the evidence now, anyway. I'll let Ms. Moore know."

"Doctor."

"What?"

"Dr. Moore, the president."

"Oh, yeah, I forget that you college types love titles."

"Well, they do. I just have a bachelors, but if I'd put the time and money into getting such a degree, I'd love for people to call me doctor. Wouldn't you?"

I had to smile. "Makes sense. Tell me something. Does Devon's wife know about you? Can she tell people about your relationship?"

"I don't know. I don't think so. She told him he was too fat and ugly for anyone to love him. He didn't argue. Said it was better for me that way."

"That may be true, as far as his wife is concerned, but there might be enough people out there who do know about the two of you or believe the gossip. Given that some real bad guys are after the evidence, I think it's safer for you to stay put for now. Don't leave this house under any circumstance. I know it's boring and tiresome, but you must stay hidden."

"Can my friends visit me?"

"No, sorry, and you are not to call a soul. No one can know where you are. Understand? My friend took your cell, right?"

"Yes."

"Good. It's vital that you do as I say. It's the only way I can protect you. Okay?"

She nodded.

"I'll try to visit you at least every other day."

She looked up with a heartbroken puppy look. "How long will I have to stay here?"

"A few days. Not long. Try to think of it as a nice indoor vacation."

"You're sure Mr. Jones won't try—"

"Jones?"

"Your friend. Isn't his name Jones?"

I bit my lip not to laugh. "Oh, that Jones. No, he's not going to try anything. He's not that kind of man. I swear. Trust me. Enjoy the great comfort of this house and don't go out, peek out, or let anyone see you or hear from you in the next few days. You promise?"

She tried to smile. "I promise."

"Good. Do you happen to know President Moore's home address?"

"No, but Mike can get it for you."

I handed Nancy my cell. "Dial his home number, please."

She did and handed me the phone.

The moment Marinaro answered, I said, "This is Connors."

"Hello, Mr. Connors. It's late. Anything wrong?"

"No, not at all. Our little bird is doing well, so nice of you to care. I'm supposed to meet Dr. Moore at her home, but I misplaced her address. Can you give it to me?"

"Oh, no, we're not allowed to—"

"Just do it."

"But—"

"I'm waiting."

I heard papers shuffling, as he whispered, "If you ever let anyone know that—"

"No need to whisper, Mr. Marinaro, and no need to chitchat. Give me her address. That's all."

He whispered her address, and I hung up before he had time to protest or issue more warnings.

"Alright, I need to go, Nancy. Thanks for dinner. Let me help you with the dishes."

"No, please don't. You've done enough already. Besides, it'll give me something to do."

"Okay," I said as I took my plate to the kitchen. "I'll see you soon."

I said goodbye, left through the door that led to the underground parking lot, and reset the alarm.

My GPS indicated that Elizabeth Moore's residence stood a little over ten miles from my house, and I thought it might be better if I spoke to her away from her office. She lived on the southwestern side of the hills overlooking the lagoon.

Dona Margarita Road wound tortuously up the hillside. The houses on the west side of the road framed wonderful glimpses of the ocean, and the moon reflected off the water through the miniscule spaces between them. On the opposite side, the hill shot up almost perpendicular to the road, the occasional shrub or bush visible in the glare of my headlights.

The curves followed one after the other with dizzying frequency and became tighter the higher I climbed.

On approach to yet another right-hand curve, I glimpsed a flash of reflected light on the white façade of one of the houses. I assumed it to be a vehicle coming down the hill and decided to slow down.

Moments later, a large truck with lights ablaze shot by me and sped off down the hill after missing my car by no more than a few inches. As my adrenaline shot up, I imagined that if the driver eventually hit something, he would probably not be the one to suffer the consequences. It's a disturbing trait of mine to fantasize about removing people that are a senseless threat to the rest of us, but I've come to terms with the fact that I'm unlikely to ever act on such notions.

People who live on these winding hillsides have the annoying tendency to see these curvy streets as their own private Daytona and resent anyone else who dares to drive them.

Several deep breaths and three curves later, I came upon number 14087, Elizabeth Moore's residence. A late model Mercedes sat in the carport, a white mailbox with the name Moore in black letters stood by the curb. No porch light and no lights inside that I could see.

I slowed to a crawl and stole furtive glances as I made my way around the curve and looked for a place to turn around. After negotiating two more curves, I found a house with an empty carport and pulled in. I turned around and made my way back down the hill.

Some hundred yards from Moore's house I found enough space by the road to park. Something bothered me, but I couldn't put my finger on it. After all, I'd come up here at a late hour of the night, so why be surprised if the house appeared to be in darkness? I sat in the car for a few minutes with the vague hope that I might glimpse some sign of life that would justify ringing the bell.

As my eyes adapted to the limited light, I determined that it was a two-story house, one at street level, the other beneath that. There appeared to be a wraparound deck along the upper level facing down the hill toward the Pacific. Nice view, probably. Maybe Moore was downstairs.

Instinct compelled me to check it out.

I peered along one side of the house, then strolled across the front to the other side and gave it the once-over. Nothing. Futile to hang around. For all I knew she could be out on a date, or at some political fundraiser, or simply asleep.

A mild breeze rustled the leaves as I headed back to the car. When I crossed the front of the house, I heard a slight clicking noise. I froze and listened. The noise came again.

I headed toward the front door. Another click. I realized I had left my flashlight in the car. *Dumb, Justin, real dumb.*

I sauntered up to the door as silently as possible. It was unlatched and shifted slightly as the wind blew across the porch causing the latch to tap on the frame. An all-too-familiar image came to mind. No choice but to take the bull by the horns.

"Hello," I called. No answer. "Anybody here?" Nothing.

I removed the Baby from my ankle holster and chambered a round, then nudged the door open with my foot. It swung silently open.

The interior of the house stood in complete darkness, but I could make out the silhouettes of living room furniture against the relative light from outside windows.

"Dr. Moore?" No answer. "Elizabeth Moore, are you here?"

Silence, except for the occasional rustling of leaves in the wind. I eased further into the house and tried to get a feel for my surroundings. The moon chose that moment to hide behind a cloud, greatly reducing visibility.

"Dr. Moore?" I repeated.

Still no reply.

I stood in a small foyer that presented a door on either side, perhaps a closet and a small bathroom. Beyond the foyer to the left was an open doorway, while ahead and to the right stood the living room.

I remained motionless and listened. I knew that if my sudden arrival had caught anyone in flagrante, their reaction would most likely be heavy breathing. If I waited long enough, they'd give themselves away sooner or later. After a prudent lapse of time, I eased to where I could get a look—limited though it was—into the living room area. By now my eyes had adjusted to the darkness inside the house, revealing my surroundings far more clearly. The moon decided to reemerge and lend a hand.

As I edged out into the larger space of the living room, a painful groan floated toward me from my far right. I dropped to one knee and aimed the Baby. Peering into the darkness, I could make out a hallway. There was no one in my immediate vicinity. As a second groan floated my way, I could tell it came from one of the rooms along the hallway.

I followed the sounds until I reached an open door to the room from where they emanated. After doing my drop-to-the-knee-whirl-and-aim routine, I found myself in an in-home office illuminated by a computer screen playing a screen-saver, one of those endless spheres of different sizes and colors that pop endlessly into view. I scanned the office. It had the typical stuff—computer, phones, file cabinet, a built-in desk along two of the walls, a bookcase, and assorted awards and recognitions covering the available wall space. Then, lying across the floor, I spotted a body, the source of the groaning that had guided me there.

I flicked on the light switch activating a couple of lamps, one on a desk and the other a floor lamp in the corner. Elizabeth Moore lay in the center of the room, sprawled in an unnatural position. Some splattering of blood speckled the light-colored carpet and her face. She emitted the now-familiar groans from time to time. As far as I could tell, she'd been beaten about the head with something blunt enough to break bone, but not sharp enough to break the skin. Blood flowed from her mouth and nose, and her eyes wobbled about under nearly closed lids. A very bad sign.

Self-preservation screamed for me to high-tail it out of there, but this woman needed someone to keep her in the fight, and Pierce was the only available cheerleader. Using her home phone, I dialed 9-1-1, then took a place beside her on the floor and tried to coax her into remaining alive. She was far beyond my measly expertise, so I stepped away from her. No sense in causing more injury with good but ill-advised intentions.

I made a cursory examination of the rest of the house, then called Sauers and told him the situation—needed him in the loop in case this Good Samaritan act of mine went south. The house had been trashed. Someone had thoroughly searched every inch of the place, yet all the obviously valuable objects appeared untouched. Either the culprits had found something very valuable and easy to transport, or they'd been after something specific. It brought Carrie's condo to mind.

I returned to Moore, knelt next to her, and encouraged her to fight for life. I wondered if I'd been the indirect cause of her injuries. Maybe I'd pushed Braniff too far. What if she'd acted on my comments that Moore possessed the evidence that connected her to Sheridan? Could Marinaro's phone be tapped? Did the Haskell goons do this on account of me? I hoped not, but a bad taste in my mouth screamed otherwise.

When the paramedics removed her from the house, I asked, "Think she'll be alright?"

"Hard to tell right now," was the noncommittal answer. They loaded her into the ambulance and rushed her off to an uncertain future.

Carrie's description of Paul lying in the middle of her apartment flashed in my brain.

A tall, Hispanic-looking fellow about forty had made his way through the hall and into the living room, where the cops had ordered me to wait. He seemed familiar to me, but I couldn't place him. Despite the fact that I'd already told the uniforms what had happened, I knew the detective in charge would want to grill me personally. He signaled one of the officers near me with a waggle of his index finger, and the cop sauntered over to him. They spoke in hushed tones that I didn't attempt to overhear. The detective glanced at me for a moment then had the officer return to my side.

Where the heck have I seen you?

He kept me waiting for another five minutes before he decided to give me a try.

"Mr. Pierce?"

"Yeah."

"I'm Detective Casillas, Seaview PD." He took a seat a few feet from me and leaned forward. "How do you know the victim?"

"Frankly, I don't," I said. "I was coming here to meet her and found her lying in there. Called it in and waited. End of story."

I retold every detail I could conjure, and he jotted down one or two.

"What was the meeting about?"

I'd anticipated that this would be the sticking point in this Pierce-to-the-rescue saga and had scoured my brain to come up with a plausible story that contained enough truth to be viable. "My sister works for the college, and a colleague of hers was found dead on the beach in Seaview a couple of days ago. Then, my sister's ex was attacked. I don't know what to do to protect my sister other than to ask around. I ran into President Moore on campus, but she was in a hurry and asked me to call on her at home later. That's when I found her."

"What makes you think she'd know anything about the other two victims?"

"I assumed a president would know more than others. Plus, she's got an investigator, McIntire, looking into whistleblower complaints. I don't know, detective, just grasping at straws."

"Mr. Pierce, why did you stick around instead of taking off? Most people would've."

"I could tell she was still alive and figured I was the only one available to get her some help."

Detective Casillas stared right into my eyes for a few seconds. He was evaluating this Pierce guy and trying to determine if it would be more advisable to make me a guest of the SPD for the night or cut me some slack for being a Good Samaritan.

"We have your address and phone number. We'll be in touch. You planning any trips in the near future?"

"Not until I feel that my sister is safe, detective."

"Okay, you can go. We'll talk again. Give my best to Sauers."

That wasn't too bad…the favors on Sauers's account were adding up.

I nodded and walked to my car, grateful that I'd had the presence of mind to call my friend.

CHAPTER FOURTEEN

I raced back to the Pacific Sunset Hotel as fast as ten miles over the speed limit could get me there. The attack on Elizabeth Moore added a serious wrinkle, and I needed to prod Carrie into talking before the night was over.

My cell phone rang… *At this hour?* "Yes?"

"Sauers here. Are you free or in handcuffs? Can you talk?"

"Free, thanks, man. In my car driving home. What's up?"

"Bad shit. And you didn't hear this from me. Casillas would throw a fit, but—"

"Is it Carrie? Something happened to her? Demetrio?"

"No, no. Calm down. Devon's wife's been murdered. She didn't pick up her disabled son from school this afternoon. Unusual for her not to show up. When she didn't answer her phone, they sent someone to her home and found her beaten to death, house in shambles."

"What about the boy?"

"In protective care with social services. He's okay. This is getting uglier by the second."

"Why did Casillas call you?"

"He isn't too keen on you snooping around and compromising his investigation. Wants you out of the picture. I vouched for you, but he keeps his own counsel, so watch your back. He's uncomfortable with all this agency involvement."

"Got it. Owe you one more. Your chips are piling up."

"Just stay clear of any more bodies. Take care. Bye."

I couldn't shake Casillas from my mind. The more I tried to remember where I'd seen him, the more Devon's floating body kept popping up, peppered with flashes of Bill Haskell. To rein in my mind, I forced it to replay the view from my deck on that late afternoon when Devon's body drifted onto the beach. After I visualized all the events, a figure milling around the background came into focus…*I'll be damned, Casillas*. No doubt about it. But if Haskell supposedly had no part in the official investigation and had acted solo, did he slide under Casillas's radar?

Maybe, maybe not.

The stakes suddenly went through the roof, but the real motive behind the killings and assaults still eluded me.

Carrie troubled me most. She persisted in hiding something, and our long history of remoteness added to the struggle of prying it out of her. Guilt stood front and center, given her reaction to Paul's predicament and how readily she'd accepted the responsibility for what had happened to him. Guilt is a funny beast. People will go to any lengths to deny having engaged in bad acts, even when confronted with irrefutable evidence. My sister fits into that category, hands down. Shame rested squarely on her shoulders, coupled with the possibility that she could join him in a similar condition. These bits gave me some leverage. No doubt this scenario loomed in her mind and should help me siphon something out of her.

Her dogged refusal to acknowledge what tied her to this job, given her pedigree, poked sharply at me. I'd never been able to figure that one out, and now that she'd snubbed Demetrio with a nothing excuse for her continued presence there, it worried me even more. She didn't even need to work. Between the tidy inheritance our parents passed on to us, plus three handsome divorce settlements, she could afford to travel around the world in luxury and add to her collection of rich husbands for the rest of her life. Something tied her to this place. Something, or perhaps someone, she couldn't escape from.

If she was as frightened as Demetrio had intimated, maybe the violent events of this day would force her to open up. I had to capitalize on the moment before she could erect one of her *go fuck yourself* attitudes.

I parked three blocks south of the Pacific Sunset and walked the rest of the way, keeping a sharp eye out for anything or anyone that might hint at the Haskells' presence. Half a block from the hotel, I phoned Demetrio.

"¿*Qué pasa, gabacho?* Where are you? Are you okay? We've been worried." There was genuine concern in his voice.

"I'm fine. How are things with your ward?"

"She's perfect."

"Any sign of our friends?"

"*Nada.* It is so quiet I can hardly stay awake."

"Yeah, that's the hardest part. Things have gotten complicated, though. Stay alert."

"What do you mean?"

"See you soon." I cut the connection.

The attack on Devon's wife, Blanche, added an alarming new layer of danger. It meant that whoever was carrying out these assaults, and my money was on the Haskell brothers, had upped the ante and was playing for keeps. Alice and Marinaro, not to mention my sister, now stood in imminent jeopardy. Nothing I could do at the moment about Nancy's friends, but I sure as hell didn't intend to allow Carrie to be their next victim. No doubt they had me in their crosshairs as well.

I stood in the shadows across from the Pacific Sunset long enough to ascertain my prospects of reaching the grand suite unnoticed. I darted alongside the hotel gardens and slinked along the path that led to the cabin at the edge of the property. Too isolated for my taste. Too vulnerable. I could only hope that Demetrio's good intentions didn't backfire.

After a quick wrap, I positioned myself directly in front of the peephole to allow Demetrio a clear view.

"*Ya era hora,*" Demetrio whispered, as he opened the door wide allowing me to slide past him. He shut the door behind me.

I handed him his cell phone while I scanned the room. "*¿Dónde está mi hermana?*"

He nodded toward the bedroom.

"All's well?"

He nodded. "*Tu hermanito* is here," he called out.

She burst out of the room and threw her arms around me. For an instant, I wondered if she'd ever hugged me before. I had no clue how to react, so I simply embraced her back. It felt good.

She sobbed as she struggled to form words. "Oh, my God. You're okay."

I patted her shoulder in a vain effort to separate from her. She was locked on. I glanced inquisitively at Demetrio, who responded with a shrug.

"I'm alright, Carrie. Calm down."

Her sobs reached a crescendo before they began to subside. Once they did, she released me and stood there, staring at me through water-filled eyes.

"Jesus, Justin! Where have you been all day? It's so late! What—"

"I'm okay, but I don't have time to get into that right now. I need some answers from you, and I need them fast. Do you understand?"

"You mean about what we've found?"

"No, we'll come to that later."

She cocked her head. "Then, what are you talking about?" I could see the barrier beginning to form.

"I'm talking about Devon, Paul, Bill Haskell and little brother Al, Ruthskin, Henley Sheridan, Braniff...and you."

My aggressive barrage so dumbfounded her that her jaw dropped in a way that gave her the stunned look of someone who's been shot but doesn't quite grasp what's happened.

"I can't waste time sparring with you, Carrie. I'm trying to save your life and Paul's, and catch some very bad people who are on a rampage. So, talk to me. What ties you to this college?"

She glanced at Demetrio for support, but he shrugged. She turned away. "I have no clue what you mean."

"Cut the crap!" I caught her arm and spun her around. "Look around you. What do you see, Carrie?"

She looked at me, bewildered. "What?"

"You and my best friend are hiding out in a hotel room because neither of you can go home without risking your lives. People are dead and more may be dead soon, including the three of us. Their latest victim, Devon's wife, beaten to death this afternoon." I paused briefly to let her digest the information.

"Oh, my God," she whispered.

"Elizabeth Moore, rushed to the hospital unconscious from a serious blow to the head. She might not make it."

"What?" She bolted up. "That can't be!"

"It is. You're in deep shit, Carrie. If you think this is a nightmare that's going to go away when you click your heels, then you are far stupider than I ever imagined. So, drop the act and tell me what you know about whatever the hell's going on here!"

She glared at me in a way that told me she was seriously considering scratching my eyes out. I glared back.

After several intense seconds, the harshness gave way to resignation, and she rocked her head, searching for a place to begin.

"I need to sit down," she whispered.

"No," I answered firmly. "We don't have time for you to sit back and relax."

She shot me an incredulous glance, sagged on the edge of the bed, and lowered her gaze. "Okay, okay. Where do you want me to start?"

"Braniff."

"Hah. What a piece of work that bitch is."

"So you've said. Cut to the chase."

"I told you, she's a third-rate teacher who shacked up with the president twenty-plus years ago. He promoted her to VP. People soon learned that if they kissed her ass and did as she said, they got promoted or were given perks."

"You've covered that already, get—"

"No ass-kissing, no promotion." She went on as if she hadn't heard me. So, I cut her some slack. "No obedience, no perks. Those who went against her were shunned and their lives became a living hell."

When she stopped, I allowed the silence to linger. Then I said, "What does she have on you?"

She jumped up, her hands defiantly clasped about her waist. "What makes you think she—"

"Carrie, I don't have time for your holier-than-thou crap. What does she have on you?"

She slumped back onto the bed, her eyes fixed on her lap. "I had a little…indiscretion," she said in a small voice.

Jackpot. "What kind of indiscretion? What the hell did you do?"

She looked at Demetrio for help, her eyes now filled with tears.

"It is okay, *mi niña*. Tell him."

I turned to him, stunned. "You know what it is?"

"We have been locked up here for hours and have gone through this entire mountain of evidence. What she did is nothing in comparison, but you know how hard she is on herself."

"Demetrio," she protested, "you know it's not that, and—"

"Cough it up, Carrie." I pressed on.

"Okay, okay." She took several deep breaths while she summoned the courage to continue. "Years ago, while finishing my doctorate, the chair of my dissertation committee decided I needed to get some 'on the job experience' since I'd never worked before. Sounded logical, so I agreed. He knew the VP of Institutional Effectiveness and Strategic Planning at OCU, pulled some strings, and I got hired part-time as the man's personal assistant, his de facto second-in-command. This happened before our parents died and—"

"Cut to the chase, Carrie."

"She's getting there," Demetrio chimed in.

He made me realize how difficult this was for her, so I forced myself to wait.

She lowered her eyes. "I made the mistake of…dating one of the board members of the university's foundation."

She looked up to see if I knew what that meant. I shook my head and shrugged.

"The foundation," she went on, "is the branch of the college that raises private funds. The board members are wealthy for the most part, politicians, business owners, CEOs of corporations, and so on. They give money and help fundraise as well. They're members of the community, people with influence, not employees." She paused to see if I'd understood.

I wasn't in the mood for her condescension and needed to push her before she had time to adopt a pose. "Got it. Get on with it." I lied.

"Give her time," Demetrio mumbled. "It is hard for her to tell you she made a mistake."

"Why? That's absurd. Cut the hysterics, Carrie, and tell me what you did."

She bolted up and glared at me. I'd pushed her too far. "It's not hysterics, you moron, and how would you know what matters to me?" With each word she got closer and closer, ready to punch me in the nose. "Do you have any idea what my reputation means to me? Can you even imagine what damage it would do to my career if people knew what I did? Let alone other, more serious, consequences?"

We were nose-to-nose. It reminded me of when we were children and she'd beat the snot out of me. Now, I'd be the one to flatten her.

Calmly, I placed my hands on her shoulders and separated her from me. "I didn't mean to be…insensitive." That's as far as I could go on the apology. "Please tell me what you did, and what it means to you. Help me understand."

That last part sounded good enough to earn me a flicker of a smile. She eased back onto the bed and sighed. "I told this guy—the foundation board member I was…dating—"

"Having sex with?"

She glared up at me. "If you must be crass about it."

"Okay, go on."

"I mentioned the amount of money the college anticipated the lowest acceptable bid would be for the design of a couple of new buildings."

"So?" I couldn't disguise my incredulity.

"He owned a large architectural firm." She rose and paced uncomfortably back and forth in front of the bed. "I don't know what possessed me. We'd gone to dinner, drank only a couple of glasses of wine, and were chatting when I blurted it out."

"Is that it? What's so wrong with that? Hardly a life-changing mistake."

"It is, Justin, it is." She spun around to face me. "Don't you get it? God, you're dense! That information isn't public. Only a few people knew about it. I was privy to it because I'd filled in for my boss who was ill, and I'd prepared some of the paperwork. Not that it matters to you, but at the time I was starting my career, and all of a sudden, I found myself representing upper management, albeit temporarily. I didn't know the first thing about protocol in the upper echelons. For a month or so, I performed at the level of a VP—one step down from the president. It gave me access to confidential and sensitive information. The amount of the lowest bid is kept confidential until all the bids are in, and the winning bid is awarded the project. The guy used the information I gave him to alter his bid and—"

"That still doesn't—"

"Oh, for crying out loud, Justin." She grew increasingly irritated with my dimness.

"I don't get why—"

"Then shut up and listen!" She rolled her eyes in exasperation, then went on as if addressing a child. "We should accept the lowest bid when awarding large contracts. The guy had inside information obtained from me and used it to put in the lowest bid. He won the contract. Several million dollars' worth. All because of me."

"Insider trading," Demetrio offered.

"Ah." I'd finally caught on. "How did Braniff find out you were the one who told him?"

"The asshole bragged to her about dating me at some university function. She put two and two together. When she sent Bill Haskell to question him, he got scared, and fessed up. He's paid Braniff and Haskell handsomely for their silence ever since." She lowered her head and slumped down on the edge of the bed. "My boss never returned from illness leave. His heart gave out. Braniff persuaded the president to hire me in his place since I'd done such a good job in his absence. Believe me when

I tell you that I didn't want to work for this college. By then, I'd finished my dissertation, had applied and been interviewed by various universities and—"

"She had offers," Demetrio interrupted, "from Princeton and Harvard."

"Braniff left me no choice but to apply here, or she'd turn me over to the authorities. When the president offered me the job, I had no choice but to accept the damned post. If I'd refused, she would have blasted me publicly and I'd be arrested. "Felony charges," she said. I'd be sent to prison—conspiracy to commit fraud—plain and simple. Even if they didn't file criminal charges against me, my reputation would've been shot. I'd never get a job in a reputable university if my actions became known. Braniff had me under her thumb."

"Shit, Carrie, why didn't you—" This time, I had enough sense to stop before I stuck my foot into a deep pile of hurtful recriminations. Instead, I lifted her from the bed and hugged her. "I understand. I'm sorry. I really am."

At first, she stiffened and looked to Demetrio for help, but all he did was shrug and smile. She tried to break off the embrace, but I refused to let go. In the end, she gave into it and allowed the anguish to surface. She sobbed in my arms for a long while, allowing the years of reproach, guilt, and shame to wash away. A healing moment for us both.

When she regained her composure, I eased her onto a chair. "Want a drink?"

"Here," Demetrio had already poured a glass of cognac and handed it to her.

"*Gracias*," she whispered and took a sip.

"All is well, *cariño*," he said as he caressed her hair.

She nodded and sipped her cognac.

After an uncomfortable silence, she found her voice. "Years and years of lies, of fear of exposure, of denial and looking the other way, of knowing the crap these people are into and doing nothing about it. Justin, I'm so ashamed."

I knelt down beside her and cradled her hand. "C'mon, no more of that. Granted," I paused for a moment and looked into her swollen eyes, "you should've spoken up and done something about it. But—"

"Yeah, I've heard the lecture from Demetrio already," she said softly.

"No lecture. I'm trying to say that I understand the pressure you've been under, particularly because you knew what you ought to have done. But all that's in the past now, over and done with."

"What about prison?"

"Don't worry about that. Let's focus on the present and what we can do about it. Okay?"

She smiled, then caressed my cheek. "You are a good guy after all, little bro."

I stood up, and in turn caressed her hair. An odd feeling, to discover how much we cared for one another after all.

"Okay, then, let's move on." I needed to bring our focus back to the motive for all the violence. "What did you guys find in Devon's stuff?"

The shift brought her back to the now. "These are actual documents that Devon collected," she said, her voice recovering some of its luster, "and all of them have been copied onto CDs and flash drives for backup."

"Can you give me specifics?"

File by file, Carrie and Demetrio walked me through the contents and explained what they knew of each.

Several things stood out, such as the Haskell brothers doing the heavy lifting over the years, mostly as intimidators and enforcers. Harassment by Braniff explicitly documented. A systematic, multifaceted effort to defraud the university described and presented with crystal clarity. All of it with the knowledge of the previous two presidents.

The dark side of Braniff exposed in detail. The stranglehold this woman had on different people plain as day. An entire file devoted to the first president, a married man with children and preeminent roles in his church, whom she blackmailed with their sexual affair and his compulsion for nudity, gambling, and sexual escapades. The file, complete with copies of photos of him nude on Seaview's clothing-optional beach, with none other than Robert Dixon, the gossipy VP. In a couple of the photographs, the two guys were kissing.

"Where did Devon get all this stuff?" I asked.

"I surmise he downloaded it from Braniff's computer." Carrie shrugged. "Where else? Jer knew his way around computers and servers and all our computers are connected to the in-house servers. Piece of cake for him."

Another extensive file Braniff created for the subsequent president, where the blackmail zeroed on his incompetence, coupled with his inability to make decisions, all of which had resulted in Braniff becoming the pseudo president. The master puppeteer and her dummy.

Devon had compiled rosters of non-existent classes for which teachers got paid. He'd gone so far as to log the hours that these guys were actually teaching and compared them to the hours they'd been paid for.

He'd also assembled personnel files of the complaints from students regarding the abuse by Ruthskin, Hanley, and Sheridan. He'd gathered original copies of personnel files with grievances against our pack of culprits, plus whistleblower complaints that had been hidden or swept under the rug.

"Look at this." Demetrio handed me a letter. "Two of the female students who decided to take the matter of Ruthskin's molestation to the police fell into Bill Haskell's hands. The girls were attacked, one raped by 'unidentified' ruffians, and ended up in the hospital. They left as soon as they were well enough. This letter to the college describing the events is from the mother of one of the girls." He went to the table and grabbed a folder. "This is Ruthskin's personnel file."

"Clean as a whistle," Carrie added. "The copy of the mother's letter describing what he did is not in it, nor any mention of what, if anything, the administration did about it. Nothing. As if it never happened."

"It is obvious that someone in the personnel office kept an unofficial file of these nasty things, and Devon got a hold of it, or else that person gave it to him," Demetrio surmised.

"I'd say so," Carrie confirmed. "These are original documents. Either Jer broke into the different offices to swipe them, which I doubt, or whoever gathered these files passed them to him in hopes he'd use them to stop all this crap."

"Years of corruption from the look of things," Demetrio added. "These men should have been fired and prosecuted, but their misconduct was ignored and even rewarded."

I glanced from one to the other and chuckled. "Wow, I'm impressed with what you two have done."

"Don't be. Devon put all that together. Demetrio and I did nothing but read."

"And Moore is aware of what he'd collected," I added.

Carrie's eyes popped wide open. "She is? How do you know?"

"It's not important how I know. The fact is that she authorized Devon to have it and hide it."

"That clarifies a lot," Carrie said. "Elizabeth hired an outside investigator to look into some wrongdoings in the automobile engineering department, and—"

"The whistleblower. Wait," Demetrio interrupted as he went to the table, grabbed a folder, and handed it to me. "Here is the formal complaint."

"Anyway," Carrie went on as I glanced through the file, "right after that, Elizabeth and the members of the board who supported her decision to pursue the investigation by an outside firm, all got death threats. More than once and—"

"Death threats? Did she report them to the police?"

"Yes, the FBI investigated, but nothing concrete turned up. That's when she must've authorized Devon to hide this stuff and give it to the investigator."

"But before he could hand it over, he ended up dead on your beach," Demetrio concluded.

"Possibly, but we don't know for sure that's the motive," I objected.

"Braniff is certainly capable of using Haskell to do something like that, believe me," said Carrie.

"That's the stuff of TV shows, not real life."

"Think about it," Carrie insisted. "I thought I knew how evil she was, but never imagined the extent she'd gone to defraud the university, pocket ill-gotten profits, and blackmail so many of us. She's got too much to lose if this becomes public."

"Anything else?" I asked to avoid a debate with Carrie.

"Isn't all this enough?"

"Ay, *compadre,* you know how it goes," Demetrio said. "If people get away with one little violation, they try something bigger. If you complain about it, you get flushed down the toilet. If you play along, you move up in the world."

"How much are we talking about?"

"A lot." Carrie grabbed a file and it tossed to me, "Devon documented exactly how much." She flipped through the pages in the file on my lap and pulled out a spreadsheet. She almost pasted it to my nose to demonstrate her point. "How about working twenty hours a week and getting paid for forty, plus hefty bonuses if you take your students on a field trip or do something special for your class? It practically doubled their base salary! How about getting university employees and students to do work for your private business, where you take in all the profits, while the college pays for the labor, facilities, and utilities? They pocketed all this money! Add it over several years, and you tell me if it's worth it or not. Six-figure salaries. Six-figure profits for private enterprises. These totals are insane!"

I stared at the spreadsheet in awe of the enormity of the fraud.

"It's insidious," Demetrio offered. "A little here, a little there. You don't notice the bits or the crumbs until you pile them up and realize you have a mountain of cookies."

I smiled at his childish metaphor. I placed the spreadsheet back in the file, closed it, and sauntered over to the mini-bar in search of something to perk me up. "How come the auditors never caught any of this? And why did it suddenly become such a big deal after so long?"

"Auditors never saw these documents. They were compiled by Devon. Braniff and company made sure that all the 'extras' didn't appear in the official records, so they couldn't follow-up. The profits from the businesses were not reported. Unless you have the correct data that shows the actual numbers, this stuff goes undetected." Carrie slumped down. "I should've caught it, had I not been such a—"

"That's not important now, *mi niña*. Think about it, Justino, the answer is simple. The whistleblower—" Demetrio smiled. "I love that word—*whistleblower*—it has a great sound."

"Well…?" I asked impatiently.

"Okay, hold on to your horses." Demetrio laughed, "Another expression I like…*hold on to your horses.*"

Before I could berate Demetrio, Carrie stepped in. "Whistleblower complaints had been filed in the past, but nothing came of them."

I picked a couple of miniature bottles of whiskey, unscrewed the tops, and poured the contents into two glasses. "What's different with the current whistleblower?"

"Ah-hah, a fly that's in the ointment." Demetrio chuckled. "Another expression—"

He was on a roll with Americanisms. "Demetrio, enough with the—"

"Yes, yes, I will stop. The answer is obvious, *amigo*. Think!

I appraised him, then glanced at Carrie. I began to shake my head when my dim brain suddenly lit up. "The university acquired a new president. Elizabeth Moore." I handed a glass of whiskey to Demetrio.

"That's it! *Salud.*" He shot me a wide smile and raised his glass.

"She was hired," Carrie explained, "with specific instructions to clean up the mess left by her predecessor. Braniff and cohorts have nothing on Moore, so—"

"This time the whistleblower complaint gets investigated by an external party and people panic," I concluded.

"Bingo," Carrie exclaimed.

"Where does Devon fit into this bigger picture?"

"That's what I've been trying to tell you, but you keep interrupting," Carrie scolded me, and continued before I could object. "When you said that Elizabeth knew Devon had these files in his possession, it all fell into place for me. I suspected she'd asked Devon to work with the investigator and turn over the files. I had no concrete evidence to prove my suspicion nor that she knew the content of the documents. But here you are, little brother, corroborating my conclusions."

"I'm impressed, Madam Investigator."

She winked and blew me a kiss.

"What about Sheridan? Anything in there about him and Braniff?"

"We found nothing other than what we've told you. What are you looking for? Specifically."

"Motive for murder and assault. If Al and Bill Haskell beat some people up, and one or both, are guilty of rape, I can see them getting heavy-handed to save their asses. But this other stuff with Sheridan, Braniff, and company, doesn't add up to motive for murder."

"Why are you so dense? The evidence Devon collected proves that fraud was rampant among those protected by Braniff," Carrie protested. "The proof shows they—senior management—knew about it for years and did nothing. It even shows that Braniff and the presidents helped some of these people conceal their schemes!"

"Yeah, I get that. But murder?"

"Justin, really." Carrie's patience was evaporating. "We're talking years of theft, fraud, and conspiracy to defraud. Add to that the knowledge of, and encouragement of, the Haskells' activities by Braniff and the previous presidents. When, and if, the evidence stood up in court, they would lose their jobs, be convicted, get significant jail time, probably forfeit their extremely generous retirements, not to mention the public humiliation. As for the Haskell brothers, police corruption and collusion are serious matters. These people are not going to roll over."

Carrie did offer a compelling argument. I glanced at Demetrio, and he gave me a nod that confirmed that he bought her line of reasoning as well.

"Justino, do you think the evidence will support those kinds of charges in the U.S.?" he asked me.

"In the right hands. But I'm still not convinced."

Carrie threw up her arms and Demetrio shook his head.

They had a point. Folks whose reputations could be destroyed by otherwise insignificant actions would go to unspeakable lengths to prevent those facts from becoming public. But my gut told me something far more sinister had yet to surface. Something serious enough that it could only be concealed through murder.

The overload of information had left us all exhausted and hungry for a midnight snack. We decided to carry on the following day and give ourselves a respite. A few drinks, followed by room service, fit the bill nicely. It also provided the chance to simply sit around and shoot the breeze, which we all needed.

After the perfunctory goodnights, I left my charges at the hotel and headed home. I left the Explorer where I'd parked and opted to walk the main thoroughfare. The cool breeze off the Pacific Ocean presented an irresistible invitation that might also serve to clear the mind. I reached the far end of the lot where it slopes down in the direction of Starview Lane—the small street that ends at my house. I treaded softly down the slope and inched my way towards home. Everything appeared to be in order. Given the late hour, I surmised that if the Haskell duo had been there at all, they'd probably gotten bored and headed off to bed or to bully someone else. Feeling at ease, I reached the front door.

The back of my head exploded in a flash of pain. An instant later the world plummeted into blackness.

CHAPTER FIFTEEN

The splitting headache throbbed with enough intensity to warp everything into a mass of confusion. I grunted in a futile attempt to make the pain vanish. A wasted effort. When I attempted to raise a hand to touch the source of the pain at the back of my head, it refused to move. Pain increased when I rolled my head around and tried to open my eyes. The darkness failed to abate.

Laughter and some incoherent voices seeped through the haze that muddled my mind, and I strained to make sense of it. Impossible.

I ran a systematic physical check of myself and reality became obvious. I was tied, or more likely taped, to what felt like a wooden chair. Tape had been applied to my mouth and eyes as well as my legs and arms. Something confined my chest, making breathing a painful affair.

The fog in my head dissipated, and the voices became more identifiable. Someone was watching TV—a game show.

One by one, my body parts managed to check in for duty, which allowed me to better ascertain the full extent of my situation. My first impressions proved accurate. Duct tape kept my chest and waist tightly strapped to the back of the chair and also sealed my mouth and eyes. My feet were secured to the front legs of the chair, and each of my wrists affixed to the arms. The only thing I could move was my head.

From the slight echo, I surmised that I must be in some sort of warehouse or storage room. The tape over my eyes prevented even a hint of light from entering. As for the blow to my head, the main source of pain, it produced a throbbing point a couple of inches above and behind my right ear. I couldn't tell for sure, but it felt intense enough to suggest that blood had to be all over my hair and neck.

I felt parched and a slight tremor in my left hand suggested a nervous system reaction—shock.

Whoever had me in this condition, and I had a pretty good idea who that might be, left nothing to chance. It took several minutes to assess it all, but in the end, I had a clear picture of my physical condition.

I might acquire a sharper understanding of my surroundings if I pretended to be unconscious for a while. I let my head hang limply to one side hoping that my captors hadn't noticed my return to the real world just yet.

"Not that one, asshole, the other one," said a gravelly male voice located some twenty feet away and off to the right.

"Pick the other one, you moron," said Gravel Voice, followed by the sound of a can of something fizzy being opened. The TV show clearly more interesting than me.

I decided to press my luck a bit by testing the extent of my immobility one extremity at a time. The ligature that pinned my chest to the chair felt solid enough to prevent me from inhaling fully. Of my two wrists, only the left had a slight bit of play. My left ankle also felt freer than my right. I pressed my toes slowly against the floor and found that I could raise the chair.

The sound of a heavy door sliding open brought a momentary halt to my experiments. The TV went silent as the door slid closed again.

"It's okay, it's me," yelled the familiar voice. Bill Haskell had made his entrance. "Anything goin' on with smartass over there?"

"Nah," said Gravel Voice, "I musta smacked him harder than I thought."

"Grab some ice water from the cooler. Let's see what we can get," Haskell said as he moved towards Gravel Voice's location.

I heard the shuffle of footsteps and the thud of the cooler lid being slammed shut. The footsteps moved in my direction.

I could feel my heart picking up speed as I struggled to remain motionless. I knew what was coming.

"Gimme that and take the tape off his mouth," Haskell commanded with evident superiority.

In one excruciating yank, the tape left my face. It felt like half of my mouth had been removed along with it. Less than a second later, the cold water hit me. Gravel Voice had been kind enough to leave several pieces of ice in the water, one of which hit me squarely on the tape over my right eye. It stung like a son-of-a-bitch.

I did my best to seem shocked and bewildered, which I really was, anyway, and sputtered and gasped. After a second, I shook my head, and yanked at my restraints, testing their actual effectiveness in the process. The binds to my left wrist and ankle gave way a bit. I stopped struggling with those so as not to reveal their possible weakness. I grunted and groaned with each movement to enhance the effect of panic.

"What the fuck is this?" I growled.

An awkward silence followed until Gravel Voice whispered, "What?" I heard clothes rustle. "Oh, okay," came a second whisper from Gravel Voice.

"Who the fuck are you?" I pleaded.

"We don't matter. Who are you?"

"I'm a salesman. My name is Pierce," I said, injecting even more panic into my voice. "If you want money, I don't really have any," I lied.

A stinging slap came across my left cheek from a hand the size of a baseball mitt.

"Don't get smart, asshole."

"Okay, okay," I whimpered. "What do you want?"

"How come you been snoopin' around OCU?"

"I was trying to find my sister. She works there."

"Bullshit!" Another slap.

"I swear to God, she works there. Her name is Carrie Harding. Ask them if you want," I pleaded in my most whimpering cowardly tone. I figured that if they were convinced that I was a frightened weasel, they might also believe me to be less of a threat.

There came more rustling of clothes as the pair moved several yards away, followed by some angry whispering. They shuffled back my way.

"What about that guy on the beach?" Gravel Voice asked as he brought his face close to my left ear.

The interrogation plan was in play—Billy Boy didn't want me to recognize his voice, so he cued Gravel Voice—none other than little bro Al—as to what to ask. Only he hadn't caught on to the plan fast enough.

"The beach? You mean the dead guy?" I said, acting calmer. "He worked at the college, I think. Yeah, I remember reading that in the paper. That's all I know about him."

"Does your sister know him?"

"I don't know. I guess so."

"What did she tell you about 'im?"

"Nothing, I swear. She said that the police had questioned people from the college. That's it."

"Cut the bullshit, pretty boy. She gave you something to hide, didn't she?"

"Hide? No. Like what?"

"Like maybe a computer disc, or a file."

"No. Why would she? We don't even get along."

"That guy was her friend, right?"

"I would imagine she knew him from work. I don't know, I swear." Even I felt pity for me.

"Why did she come to your house, then?"

"What?"

He slapped me again to reiterate his dominance.

"She came to your house to give you something to hide, didn't she?"

"No, no, no. Someone broke into her house, so she's staying at my place till they clean up the mess."

"Where is she now?"

"At work, I guess. How the hell should I know?"

Another slap.

"Don't fuck with me, asshole. I wanna know where she is."

I increased the whimpering to the pathetic level. "I don't know, I swear. Oh, God, I don't know. I really don't. I'd tell you if I did. I swear to God, I'd tell you."

The rustling and shuffling moved away again. More whispering. Bill was sounding extremely upset while Al's tone sounded apologetic. Footsteps shuffled off in the direction from where Bill Haskell had arrived, followed by the sound of the large door sliding open then shut.

Al sighed a couple of times, then uttered, "Shit," as he came closer.

After pausing next to me for a moment he leaned into my ear and did his utmost to sound threatening. "I'm gonna need better answers even if it takes all day."

I heard him straighten up before a solid blow landed on my right eye and cheek, followed by another blow above my right eye almost squarely on the forehead. The blows rattled the wound in my head, sending shock waves through my brain to the degree that I almost lost consciousness.

"Got anything to say, pretty boy?"

I wondered how much of this I could take, and how much Haskell had ordered brother Al to dish out. "I don't know anything. Please, let me go," I whimpered. "I don't know anything."

Two more blows even harder than before to the opposite side of the face. At least I'd look evenly smashed up when the coroner laid me out on his table.

"Please stop!" I pleaded.

Personal experience dictated that this kind of violent agitation can get out of hand in a heartbeat. Once the fiend is unleashed, the human animal loses control quickly and escalates to deadly levels in seconds. The "Monster Mash" reputation of Bill and Al made it clear what lay in store for me.

I heard him shuffle away, open the cooler, grab and open what sounded like a can, followed by a loud gulp. "Son of a bitch!" Another loud swig. "I'm getting fed up! Why do I have to do all the shitty jobs?"

My training had turned me into what is considered to be an above average specimen as relates to strength and stamina. However, the experiences in Cozumel had eroded considerable amounts of that conditioning and, at present, I was nowhere near my normal self. Plus, Al possessed none of the sophistication of the trained interrogator who finesses the physical torture to obtain a desired effect. My captor, incapable of the distinction between obtaining information and causing death, needed to unleash his pent-up violence for the mere pleasure of it.

Things didn't bode well for Justin Pierce.

Between the smacks and punches, I saw only two viable options; pretend to have lost consciousness again and see what played out, or offer to find the information he sought, and pretend to betray my sister. My pain threshold already stood on the verge of being breached, so I determined to try option one first. I figured, what the hell, there would always be time for option two, providing I remained alive.

"Talk to me, asshole, or I'll beat your fuckin' brains out."

That was my cue. As soon as the blow that coincided with "brains" struck my face, I let my jaw go slack and dropped my head onto my chest causing his subsequent punch to glance off the top of my head. I let my entire body go limp hoping the deception would work.

"Hey," he shouted, "hey!" He yanked my head back by the hair. "Hey!" My non-reaction pissed him off. He stomped off to the cooler and got some more ice water. He trudged back to me and threw it at my face.

I did nothing.

He tried it again.

Nothing.

"Shit, what a wuss."

When his third attempt to wake me failed, he stood there for a moment, heaving sigh after sigh, mulling over his options.

Finally, he stormed away, and I heard the beeping sounds of cell phone dialing—then a pause.

"It's me," he said. "Maybe you better get back here, I think he's dead… I didn't…. No, Bill, I swear I slapped him a couple of… yes, I'm sure… I tried it already, he's hardly breathing… Where?... Yeah, I remember where that is… okay… yeah, okay… yeah, I'll call you." I heard Al shuffle back to me.

He shook my shoulders as he yelled, "Hey! Hey, wake up." He shook me again. "Goddammit." He slapped me as hard as he could. Stars flashed in my head. "Wake up, you piece o' shit! Wake up!" Another slap.

He stood there in silence for a moment, then I heard the jingling of keys as he fingered them in his pocket. A moment later he tore away and opened the sliding door. A car door slammed shut and seconds later the ignition kicked in. A large vehicle, I imagined either an SUV or a truck, stopped a few feet from me.

The vehicle door opened then slammed shut, followed by his footsteps back to the sliding door, which he closed. He headed back to me.

Another slap. "Hey!" He moved away briefly to rummage through what sounded like a toolbox before coming back.

I felt something, probably a knife of some sort, cut through the tape around my ankles, first the right then the left. There was the sound of duct tape being unfurled before my feet were thrust together and re-taped.

Throughout the process he muttered under his breath, "Fucking pain in the ass. He should do this shit himself. I'm not his goddam slave."

He released whatever bound my chest to the chair, a wide belt, it seemed. The one restraint that had me seriously worried because it prevented me from breathing properly. A huge relief.

He cut the tape on my right wrist, then the one on my left.

He stepped away, no doubt to get the duct tape. My chance had come. I kicked out with my bound feet while at the same time peeling the tape from my eyes.

The light blinded me for a moment, but I could make out his body falling back as my feet slammed into his face. I rose to my feet, and clamped my right hand onto the arm of the chair that restrained me.

A look of utter stupidity and incomprehension flashed across Al's face as I brought the chair down with all the strength I could muster. Unfortunately for him, the chair was a solid piece of furniture that didn't shatter or even crack. Instead, it came down with the unyielding thud of a baseball bat, cracked open his forehead, and caused him to slump to the floor.

I brought the chair down again onto his back with more force than before. He lay motionless on the floor.

I reached for the knife, cut the tape binding my ankles, and ripped it off.

Before I could straighten up, I felt a blow to my feet that brought me unceremoniously to the floor.

Al had recovered quickly, thank you very much.

I landed with a painful thud on my right elbow and instinctively rolled away from Al and onto my feet.

He'd become vertical himself, and before he could pounce on me, an odd look came over him. He stopped.

That's when I saw it. His left arm dangled across his chest at a bizarre angle. Dislocated. He shot me a glare of rage and hatred that telegraphed his intentions. But I now had the advantage. Nonetheless, he stood to his full height—at least three inches above mine—determined to have it out.

The chair lay sideways on the floor almost exactly between us. He glanced at it, trying to ascertain his chances of getting his hands on it before I did. The odds were against him, but he went for it, anyway. So did I.

We claimed it simultaneously, I by the back, Al by one of the legs. Both of us were in serious pain and far from being at full strength. My advantage was having the use of both hands and being in far better physical shape. His was in his prodigious strength and size along with hands bigger than dinner plates.

I twisted the chair until he could no longer hold on to it. In seconds, his grip gave way.

After a slight hesitation, he came at me, fist clenched and meaning business. I stepped to one side as I swung the chair into his right leg. He winced but maintained his footing. He turned and came at me again more quickly than I would've expected from a man his size.

This time I took a shot at his dislocated left arm. He emitted an agonizing roar as I landed the blow, and his legs gave out. His knees hit the concrete floor with a bone-shattering crack. He'd not be getting up again anytime soon, and he knew it. He slumped to the floor and rolled onto his right side, one arm cradling the other, then onto his back.

"Goddamned son of a bitch," he managed through a painful moan. "I'm gonna kill ya. And that bitch sister of yours."

I raised the chair as if to slam it down on his stupid head and put his lame brain out of its misery. He didn't cower at all.

"Never threaten the guy who's got your life in his hands, Al. You're big enough to know that."

"Fuck you."

I brought the chair down close enough to make him wonder for a moment whether or not he might live to see another day, but instead I placed it on the floor. I parked my exhausted ass on top of it and sat glaring at Al. He glowered back.

When I had enough of his face, I snatched up the roll of duct tape.

"Let's start with your feet."

CHAPTER SIXTEEN

With Al immobilized, I inspected the place from top to bottom. Dry blood splatter covered one entire corner of the warehouse near four iron rings set into concrete. No doubt restraints used for the brothers' victims. Shoved against the wall sat a large metal table covered in disgusting stains and equipped with leather straps to restrain their hostages—the fate that awaited me had things gone differently. The building consisted of four cinderblock walls some twenty feet in height, roughly insulated in an ineffective effort to dampen sound. A rail-mounted hoist with chain pulleys and a hook dangled from the rafters near the center of the warehouse.

Aside from the chair used to restrain me, a clutter of furniture at the opposite end of the room consisted of a soiled threadbare rollaway bed, a small desk, and a beat-up TV with a missing knob. I riffled through the desk in search of my watch, cell phone, and gun, to no avail. At least my wallet remained in my back pocket—a serious oversight by the pair of dim-witted pseudo-cops.

A rusty door led to a bathroom that hadn't been cleaned in years. The filthy mirror, minus the upper half, reflected a nauseating image. My right eye, a narrow slit due to massive swelling, adorned a grotesque face that resembled mine, decorated with bruises, cuts, and uneven bulges. Dried blood stuck my shirt to my neck and matted my hair. A black and blue stripe had emerged across my chest.

The rusted faucet produced a trickle of questionable purity, but sufficient for me to clean up a bit. I felt tempted to embellish Al's face with the same colorful display, but the pain from his shoulder coupled with the possibly cracked kneecaps, would remind him of me for the foreseeable future. Besides, I wanted to save the best for Bill Haskell—he deserved it.

Al's watch read 7:25. I'd left Carrie and Demetrio around two in the morning. That meant I'd been out for about four hours before regaining consciousness in this makeshift torture chamber. Billy Boy would be checking in, so I needed to extract information from Al as quickly as possible.

I had to move him to another location that would render him more vulnerable to interrogation, while at the same time placing more distance between his brother and us. I picked up Al's cell phone and stepped outside to call Sauers.

"Sauers," came the terse voice at the other end.

"It's Pierce."

"Where are you? I've been calling you."

"I'm at the firm of Haskell and Haskell."

"Hold on."

I heard him cover the mouthpiece.

"Okay," he said when he returned. "What's up?"

"They paid me a visit last night. I've been passed out for a few hours."

"You okay?" he asked with honest concern.

"I've been better. I'll give you a rundown later. For now, I need protection for my sister and my friend Demetrio. Any chance you could do that?"

"You got it. Is this the Demetrio I met in Mexico City?"

"The one and only. They're at the Pacific Sunset—the hotel near my place—hiding in the grand suite at the end of the property. They've got the evidence box that Devon gathered. Fraud's the least of what's documented."

"Fraud?"

"Same reaction from me. I've got Al Haskell under control, but Bill is on a rampage and I'm worried that—"

"I'll take care of it."

"Great. How well do you know Casillas? Can he be trusted?"

"He'd love to put away Al and Bill, if that's what you mean. That's why I tried to reach you and tell you he's put a team on the older Haskell since yesterday."

"Billy Boy found a way to lose them."

"How?"

"He's versed in their ways. That's the rub. We need to come at him sideways."

"What do you have in mind?"

I asked Sauers to determine my location by zeroing in on Al's cell phone. Once he set that in motion, I laid out my half-baked plan to provoke Bill Haskell—once he realized his little brother's predicament—into saying things that could be used against him. Sauers surmised it promised to be a nasty scene, and that without an official presence, I might disappear permanently.

"How much time do you think you have?"

"Zero to none," I said. "Billy Boy's bound to call to find out what's holding up Al, and when I answer, he'll be back here in a flash. Assuming he isn't on his way already. I need a place to store Al, and pronto."

"You sure manage to get yourself into some sticky spots, don't you?" he chuckled. "I'll see what I can do, but you better get yourself a backup plan."

"I'm working on it. But I need to find the motive for all this violence other than what's in Devon's box of evidence. If I'm right, the information Devon gathered is only the tip of a very large, very nasty iceberg."

"Hold on a sec."

While I waited, I went back to check on Al, who was making a token struggle against his ligatures, despite the obvious pain.

Sauers came back on the line. "You there?"

"Yeah." I stepped out of the warehouse.

"We've tracked you down."

My exact location turned out to be in a small desert community east of I-15 somewhere out by Palomar Mountain. He also provided me with the perfect alternative for my tête-à-tête with Al Haskell.

"I owe you big time, pal. Thanks," I said with heartfelt gratitude.

"And I intend to collect, so stay alive, Pierce."

"I'll do my best. Thanks, again."

I slipped the phone into my pocket and searched Al's vehicle for my gun and phone. Nothing. The interior of the van—a Ford E-series with windows only in the front doors—made me want to puke. Filth, grime, and muck made the ideal transport for my crude cargo.

The rail-mounted hoist was perfect for lifting the lump of meat named Al into the van. I moved it into position below the hook.

Al resisted when I dragged him to the hoist. With more than a little satisfaction, I bashed him over the head with his own gun to render him unconscious. The hoist worked flawlessly. Once loaded into the van, I taped him into complete immobility. He had a dislocated shoulder that I didn't bother to fix, and I could hear one of his knees crackle as I folded his legs and taped them to his hands. He'd fractured his kneecap when he'd dropped to the floor. He'd walk with a limp for the rest of his life, and the pain would predict the weather with uncomfortable regularity.

I pulled out the van, locked the warehouse, and drove off.

I decided to head in a southwesterly direction until I came across something familiar. Before long, I found myself driving northeast on Highway 76.

Al's phone rang as I reached I-15 heading north toward Murrieta and the rendezvous Sauers had arranged for me. I opted to leave it unanswered for now. Bill would call again soon enough. I realized that Al's phone could become a potential problem, so I reversed direction and headed south towards San Diego. The phone rang again, and I ignored it. When it rang for a third time, I answered. My position was a good five miles south of my original location. If Bill tracked the GPS, he'd follow the wrong scent.

"Al's warehouse."

There was a brief silence at the other end followed by, "Who the hell is this?"

"Let's say that I'm your brother's keeper."

"Pierce?" He couldn't disguise his amazement.

"No, sorry. This is Al's warehouse. To whom do you wish to speak?"

"Where the fuck is my brother?"

"He's fine. For now. He'll stay that way as long as you don't do anything stupid. Are we clear on that?"

I could hear him breathe heavily into the phone.

"I'll rip your throat out, you piece o' shit."

"Like I said, Billy, Al depends on you."

I terminated the call.

Now that Billy Boy had been taken care of, I called directory assistance and got connected to the Pacific Sunset. Demetrio answered.

"*¿Cómo van las cosas?* I asked.

"*Bien.*"

"Carrie?"

"Still asleep. She is very afraid for Paul, and has not slept well for the last couple of nights. She is dying to see him, but understands the risk is too great to go there. She is good. How about you?"

I gave him the abridged version of my situation, and warned him that Haskell would almost certainly make a concerted effort to find him and Carrie.

"I've arranged protection for you. Remember Sauers?"

"Yes, your buddy agent from the U.S. We sure partied that night."

"He'll be calling you."

"He already did. He is on his way to pick up the bundle."

"Good. Keep your eyes and ears wide open, Demetrio. And thanks for looking after Carrie." I emphasized that Haskell was not to be trifled with, but Demetrio had gotten the point.

"*No hay problema, compadre.* You be careful."

"*Gracias...*" That's all I could think to say.

I memorized the number Bill had called from, then turned the cell phone completely off to neutralize the GPS. I reversed course again and headed north on I-15 toward my original destination.

Sauers had an older brother who owned a spread out in the desert. Bret Sauers, a former Marine with a penchant for solitude and a visceral dislike for dishonest cops, had welcomed the chance to help bring down the Haskell brothers.

I followed Marty's directions, got off on Old Highway 395, and soon found myself bouncing along a dirt road into arid and desolate environs.

I'm not a desert person, and it's always puzzled me why someone would choose to live in a place that scorches in the summer, freezes in the winter, and swarms with creatures that you don't want to run into on a dark night. Then again, who am I to talk about dangerous creatures?

In the middle of nowhere, Bret Sauers leaned against his rusting pick-up truck. Big, burly, and rugged, he seemed the opposite of his brother. As I pulled up, I signaled him to stay put, then I took a quick peek at my hostage before exiting the van, and approached Bret.

"Pierce?" he asked, squinting in the bright desert sun.

"Guilty as charged."

"Looks like you been hit by a truck. Should get that looked at."

"It'll have to wait, but if you have some alcohol and bandages, I'd appreciate it."

"Done deal," he said.

I nodded toward the van. "The guy's in the back, and I need to take care of him, too."

"I'll get you settled in and go get whatever you need."

"I can't thank you enough for doing this."

He smiled. "Happy to do it. It'll be more fun than I've had in years. I hear you're a Marine."

"A few years back."

"Same here. Glad to help."

"Thanks, man. Some things you need to be aware of, though," I said, and gave him for-instances of the Haskell brothers MO, and underscored the danger.

"They'll never figure out where this is. And if they do, hey, I'm a big boy."

My turn to smile. "Guess you're right."

"Follow me," he said as he climbed into his truck.

I made my way back to the van. Bret made a U-turn and sped off in a cloud of desert dust with me in pursuit about a hundred feet behind.

After countless turns, sometimes onto roads invisible to me, he pulled up in front of an old adobe hut that sat deep in a gully under the shadow of two large trees.

He jumped out of his truck and gave a nod toward the structure. I parked in the shade and climbed out of the vehicle.

I followed him into the hut as he kicked a few items out of his way.

The hut couldn't be better for what I had in mind. The only furniture was an old table and three rickety chairs not far from disintegration. The area that served as a kitchen had no running water, and the cooking space was a simple grate over a cavity for wood or coal. A dilapidated outhouse stood at the rear of the hut.

"Just as I found it when I bought the ranch and surrounding land back in the nineties. I'll get you some water, food, and medical supplies. No electricity. We've got to run a line from the light pole twenty feet from here."

"This fits the bill. Can you get me some recording equipment? I need to capture the song from my canary."

"I've got some beauties you can use. Ran some undercover work while in the corps. Got hooked on electronics."

"Perfect. But after you get those supplies, you might want to stay away until Marty tells you it's safe to come back here."

"What if you need something?"

An honest concern, and he did have a point.

"Listen," he went on, "It'll be hard for you to do both. I can set up the mechanics and run the bugs. Your bird won't smell it and might give you more."

"But—"

"Don't sweat it. Here," he handed me a nylon rope. "Thought this might come in handy. What else can I get you?"

"Actually, I need a phone."

"You'll have to come to the house for that. I don't carry a cell phone. Don't like being tied down to a machine."

"I'll need to get one. Any chance of a decent sized town out here?"

"This ain't the Sahara. What do you need?"

"Any cell phone would do with a couple of chargers, one that you can plug into the lighter of the van. Think you can pick one up for me?"

"Do rattlesnakes play the maracas? Consider it done. Anything else?"

"I'm certain I'll think of something once you've gone, but that should do it for now." I took out my wallet and handed him a couple of hundreds.

"This is too much," he protested.

"Give me the change when all's done."

"Okay. I'll help you get that guy inside and take off."

"I can handle him."

Bret nodded and headed toward his truck. "See ya."

I opened the back of the van and pulled on Al's foot. He emitted a deep-felt moan. I cut the tape that connected his feet and hands, and took a quick step back in case he tried anything. He didn't. I sat him down, legs dangling off the back.

It required considerable effort for him to limp his way into the hut. I shoved him toward the table, coaxed him onto it, and laid him down belly up. He gave me no trouble as I secured him to the tabletop with the nylon rope.

I camouflaged the vehicle as well as possible with the scant shrubbery scattered about, then returned to work on Al.

With the tension fading away, my own aches and pains were making themselves known, and I was utterly exhausted.

Not the ideal condition for the effort required to interrogate my captive. Al had been secured, and over the next few hours the pain from his injuries would certainly intensify, which might render him more cooperative without too much prodding on my part. Time to give myself a break.

I rechecked Al's bindings, and confirmed that he wasn't going anywhere for now. Next, I picked the stronger of the chairs and placed it near a wall with another chair facing me. I reclined the former against a wall and placed my feet up on the latter. It wasn't home, but it would do.

The clatter of Bret's truck as it bounced along the road woke me. Al had passed out.

Bret exceeded my expectations. Not only did he bring the essentials, like water, food, more nylon rope and duct tape, but also the cell phone with its chargers, strong pain meds, and a brand-new first aid kit. He'd picked up a new shirt and a pair of pants so I could shed my bloody ones, a cooler full of ice, some firewood, and a few other sundries.

He'd contacted his brother to let him know how things stood, and Sauers confirmed that all was well with Carrie and Demetrio.

Bret went about connecting the electricity and setting up the recording equipment as I washed, tended to my wounds, changed clothes, and wolfed down the food he'd brought.

When we were set, I roused Al by simply trickling some ice water on his face. No need to slap him around yet. That would be the extent of my courtesies, however. I needed him as uncomfortable and scared as possible.

I'd secured his right hand to his waist and placed a tight noose around his neck. A simple yank on the rope would end any attempt to come at me.

"Ready for a little chit chat, Al?"

He rolled his head toward me with a wry smile, "Fuck you."

Compared to my aches and pains, he had to be in agony, although he did his best to conceal it. "Let's start with how you and Billy use that warehouse."

"What warehouse?"

I squeezed his knee, eliciting an explosive yelp on his part. "What the fuck do you care?" he yelped.

"You the one who ransacked my sister's place, or Billy?"

"Screw you."

This time I slammed my hand down on his knee, and the pain brought tears to his eyes.

"You're a dead man," he growled.

"Threatening me isn't going to work in your favor. At best, it'll guarantee that you'll never leave this place alive." I clamped my hand around his wrist at the end of his dislocated arm. I could see the sweat beads on his forehead. "Now, let's try again." I squeezed.

"Shit! Yes, I did your sister's house. That handyman guy showed up outta nowhere, and I did him too. Happy?"

"He may die. That's called murder, Al. How about the rest of it?" I squeezed tighter.

He screamed. "Stop! What do you wanna know?"

"Everything. Let's start with the whys and the whos. Why did you kill Devon, and who told you to do it?"

"I don't know what you're talking about."

A yank on the arm knocked the wind out of his lungs.

"Last chance."

After several gasps for air, he managed to speak. "I don't know anything about that."

"Okay," I said calmly. I walked over to the flimsier of the chairs, smashed it against the wall, and wrenched off one of the legs. I returned to the table and tapped Al's shinbone below his broken kneecap.

"I can't waste time with you, Al. This is the last call." I banged his leg a little harder and a little higher. His entire body tensed with anticipation.

"Fuck you. I don't know nothin.'"

I hit his knee hard enough to make the pain resonate all the way to his head, but not so hard as to make him pass out. I needed information, not a complete dimwit.

"Okay, okay," he screamed in a raspy voice. "Give me a sec."

"No, I don't think so," I said and I tapped his knee again. He gasped.

"I do what Bill tells me."

"And what is that?"

"He's got some scams going with some folks at the college."

"What kinds of scams?"

"Petty shit. Getting paid for doing favors for them. He squeezes them."

"That's not worth killing for," I volunteered.

"It is if they get caught. They go to jail, lose their jobs, shit like that."

"Give me some names."

"I don't know them all."

"Give me what you got."

"There's a guy in the auto shop who runs a scam charging cash for repairs and pocketing it. Gets cash from students for supplies and shit like that. Been doing it for years. Bill gets a cut, and I sort of help. Some shit-ass wrote about it to the new president. Bill had to clean it up."

"What's this teacher's name?"

Al groaned a couple of times as he tried in vain to shift his leg. "Madison. Karl Madison."

"Is that when you went for Devon?"

"No, that was later." The pain was really getting to him. He tried to conceal it with limited success.

"Don't stop now. You're on a roll."

He took a deep breath before continuing. "Madison didn't want to share his profits with the snitch, so he fired him. The stoolie threatened to tell all. The VP contacted Bill, and he sent me to convince the shit-ass to shut up and get a job somewhere else."

"Which VP?"

"Braniff, who do you think?"

"Then what?"

"The dickhead wouldn't budge. We took him to the warehouse to talk. It didn't work."

"Why?"

A few more deep breaths. "Too late. He'd already sent the damn complaint to the new prez, Braniff, tried to stall it, but the Moore dame, she wouldn't let it go. That's when all hell broke loose."

"What happened?"

"All I know is the college hired some hotshot investigator to look into it, and everyone got real scared he'd find all the stuff they'd been doin'." He was almost panting now. "Can I get some water here?"

I picked up one of the bottles of water Bret had brought and twisted the cap off. I trickled some into Al's mouth, causing him to choke for a moment. When he recovered, I carried on.

"I'm listening. Get to Devon."

He glared at me for a second before continuing. "Devon's been diggin' shit up, so Bill and I went to scare him off before he could talk to the investigator. But the shit-head threatened us. He'd hidden all the stuff away and wanted to make a deal with us."

"What kind of deal?"

"He'd keep the crap from showing up if we made the folks who were after him stop."

"Did you?"

"Yeah, but the son of a bitch went and got himself a lawyer who spilled the beans to the Seaview PD."

Finally, we were getting somewhere. "And?"

"Can I have more water?"

I offered a trickle. "Go on," I said as I put the bottle away.

"He made up some crazy story about a rape. Something about retaliation for him having evidence."

"That's odd, because as I heard it, you raped Nancy Drier's cousin. Did you?"

He looked at me as if I'd suddenly become an alien from outer space. First, I let him wonder how the hell I knew, then I whacked him on the shin for good measure.

"Shit, man! Why'd you do that? I've been talking."

"Answer my question. Did you?"

"I didn't know who she was, okay? Bill went crazy and beat the shit out of me, but I didn't understand why he got pissed off like that. It's not as if it was the first time I'd done one of them bitches."

"What bitches?"

"You know, girls at the college. They ask for it, struttin' around with their tight pants or short skirts at night after their classes. I didn't know she was Nancy's cousin. She didn't look like her."

"A random rape?"

"No, man. I told you she asked for it."

I smacked him across the face even though I really wanted to kill him. "You raped her, asshole! You raped her!"

I punched his stomach so hard his body trembled with pain. He passed out.

It took a superhuman effort not to bash his head in.

⟢ • ◆ • ⟣

CHAPTER SEVENTEEN

I paced around the shack to cool my temper and release the energy generated by my rage. It took a while. I coaxed Al back to life to unravel what sounded more and more like a bad melodrama, but with real villains, genuine victims, and actual damsels in distress.

I supplied Al with enough water to keep him going. Once he recovered enough to produce coherent answers, I continued our chat. "Who killed Devon?" I asked.

He glared into my eyes with such intensity that he didn't even blink. I let him enjoy his moment before I placed my hand on his knee and gave it a little squeeze. Not in the mood for games.

Al's body tensed, his head strained back. He took a deep breath then rolled his eyes in my direction. "Not me."

"Help me believe you."

"Can I sit up? My back…is…going spaz on me."

"We're here as long as it takes. Your call."

He glowered at me, rolled his head, sighed, and groaned. Anything to give himself time to think. I eased my hand close to his knee again.

"Shit, shit, shit! Take your hand away."

I lifted my hand so he could see it, but left it hanging in midair ready to come down hard. "Don't let me get tired."

"It was Braniff's idea."

"How do you know?"

"Bill told me that she'd said they knew too much, especially Moore. Best scare them off."

"So, you killed Devon and went after Moore."

He took yet another deep breath before answering, "I did Moore. The bitch surprised me and I hit her. I didn't kill her."

"Devon?"

"Bill took out Devon and the lawyer guy. Okay? Move your hand, man!"

I didn't budge. "Devon's lawyer?"

"Yeah."

"Where's the body?"

"We dumped it a couple o' miles from the warehouse."

"Where, exactly?"

"I don't know. Bill made it look like some kind of accident on a dirt road off of I-76 down some ravine."

"What's Sheridan's role?"

"Don't know."

My hand dropped on his knee.

He squealed in pain. "Fuck! Stop! He handles the dope."

At last. The motive for murder. "Where, how?" I left my hand on his knee.

"Stop the squeezing! Please! I'm not in on that one. Bill kept that for himself. Fucking bastard! I get pot or mushrooms sometimes, but Bill's the one that handles that score. I swear to God, man!"

I believed him. He definitely didn't have the smarts to be reliable in that racket, and big brother Bill wouldn't risk it.

"Why go after my sister?"

"Devon collected a lot of shit on all these guys. We didn't know what or how much. When it went missing, we went after it. Bill figured she worked close to Devon, so—"

"How did Bill kill Devon?"

"Bill set out to scare the shit out of him. Found him in the head takin' a piss, and after a few blows, he fell and hit his head."

"You want me to believe it was an accident?" I raised my hand again.

"No, no. Bill figured he'd kill him and had to get rid of the body. Got Sheridan to help toss him overboard."

I lowered my hand.

"How about Devon's wife?"

"Wanted to get dirt on her fatso husband. The bitch came at me! I had no choice! Couldn't figure out why she got so full of herself and thought she could take me down."

"You killed her."

"No, I just beat her up."

"She died, you idiot!"

He looked at me in total disbelief. I walked away and let him be for a moment while he came to terms with what he'd done.

"You're a murderer, Al." I growled as I approached him. "Can't deny it. You're an animal. Now, tell me, who else is involved in this mess?"

"I didn't mean to kill her."

"Doesn't matter. She's dead. Now, answer my question."

"A shit load of assholes. Bill knows 'em all."

"How come he knows so much?"

"Braniff. The fat troll turns him on."

My mouth dropped—not a smart thing to do in the middle of an interrogation.

He cracked a sarcastic smile. "Yeah, piece of garbage," he went on without prompting. "He's been fucking her for years. I wouldn't be caught dead with that whale, but he digs her. Almost as weird as pretty doll Nancy shacking up with fatso Devon," he chuckled. "Go figure."

"Yeah," I chuckled back. "Go figure."

We were becoming buddies now…at least he thought so. Time to shift tactics. I untied the nylon rope, sat him up, opened the bottle of water, and helped him drink it. I eased him into a chair and tied him to it.

Admitting to rape, drug trafficking, assaulting Paul and Elizabeth Moore, plus killing Devon's wife and lawyer, should put the fear of God into him. He also realized that with me in the picture, they were up against more than they'd bargained for. Whether my next step would be to kill him to prevent him from coming after me once he healed also had to loom as a very real possibility.

I needed a break myself to check with Bret and regroup. My own aches and pains had sapped most of my energy. I stepped outside the shack and walked over to the paltry shade of the nearby trees where Bret had set up post.

When he saw me coming, he shook his head. "You've got a hell of a mess, man. With Al boy hostage, this Bill character presents an imminent threat."

I nodded. "He's motivated enough to try something reckless, and angry enough to pull it off."

"I'll clean up the tape. I can give you one without his whining. That'll give you a tidy confession."

"Thanks, man. Can you ship a copy to Marty?"

Bret agreed, packed up, and took off.

I sat under the measly shade of the tree and pondered my next move. The picture established with Devon's evidence and Al's tale implicated folks that justified their criminal behavior with a refrain: *Everyone else is doing it. Why shouldn't I?* They conjure all manner of pretext to convince themselves that there's nothing wrong with stealing or looking the other way. In particular, when there's significant profit to be had. I've dealt with my share of institutional corruption over my checkered career. Once it becomes part of the culture, it's a bitch to eradicate.

Drug trafficking colored another story entirely. Except for Al's word, a third party's hearsay, I had no hard evidence on that score. I needed solid facts.

The fraud had been well documented by Devon, and on that front, we stood on solid ground in relation to criminal prosecution. But Carrie was right—this bunch didn't perceive themselves as crooks. Everything flowed along uneventfully year after profitable year, until, out of the blue, a Jeremy Devon showed up. An incorruptible guy with an autistic kid, and too much to lose to be persuaded to join them. Couple that with the arrival of Elizabeth Moore, a no nonsense-hold-them-accountable kind of gal, and all of a sudden, a spotlight is cast upon their schemes. The fear of prosecution makes ordinary people become desperate, and desperate people often resort to extreme measures to save their necks. Panic sets in. I've seen it firsthand. Even counted on it. They become irrational, grow bolder and bolder, until it all goes to hell and spirals out of control. And the shit hits the fan.

It's easy to imagine the moment Braniff had panicked when gossipmonger Dixon, in a bid to gain the upper hand, stupidly threatened her with Devon's evidence. Her fear drove her to suspect that someone had spilled the beans on their trafficking scheme, causing the trio of the Haskell boys and Sheridan to jump into action. Fraud on campus they could fight off, but drugs brought in a new and far more dangerous set of problems—especially, since they usually come tied to some very nasty people from down south.

Time to send in the cavalry.

"Sauers," came the brusque answer from the other end.

"Pierce."

"Now what?" He sounded impatient.

"Caught you at a bad time?"

"No, no. I get pissed at bureaucracy sometimes. This is one of those times. What's up?"

"We've got Al on tape—"

"We?"

"Bret's editing the tape. He'll send you a copy. For your ears only, buddy."

"Justin—"

"Please, just give me a day with it. Do you have any idea where Bill Haskell is right now."

"No, but I can find out. I got all the stuff from your sister. OCU is in deep shit."

"And it's going to get deeper. Al admits to beating Devon's wife to death, and Bill killing Devon and Paxton, his lawyer."

"Damn!"

"Paxton's body is somewhere in a ravine off of a dirt road alongside I-76, a couple of miles from the Haskell warehouse. Al admits that he raped Nancy Drier's niece. He confesses to Paul's and Moore's assaults because they surprised him while searching their places. He could've worn gloves at Carrie's and Moore's, but not with Devon's wife. He went to talk to her, not search the place."

"Casillas might have his prints."

"But the best part is…wait for it…big bro Bill is running drugs."

"Holy hell. No wonder things have gotten ugly so fast. Best reason to be worried about your sister and her babysitter. By the way, I moved them both to the safe house. They're welcome company for Ms. Drier. Covertly, I left Demetrio his cell so you can connect, but confiscated Carrie's. She didn't like that one bit."

"Good. Thanks, man. Here's what I'm thinking, I'm going to check with my guys in Mexico to see who's in the racket from down there. I'll get back to you with what I find. But we need to fish out Billy Boy, and in some way tie him to Braniff—the VP from—"

"I know who she is."

"And Sheridan—"

"Who's he?"

"Leonard Sheridan, a retired professor who's connected to them somehow. He dangles around the periphery of this whole thing. Could even be the ringleader."

"His name hasn't surfaced."

"I suspect he might be the link to the drugs. McIntire has him on his radar and may have more. I've got no evidence other than Al's word. We need to fish that out, too."

"I'm all ears."

"I'm thinking a sting at the Haskell warehouse. Do you think Casillas will go for it?"

"He might. I'll brief him when I turn the copies of Devon's evidence box over to him. He'll be here pretty soon. I imagine he'll need a few days to set it up."

"Why in hell are you going to turn the evidence over to him with Haskell on the payroll?"

"You get how officialdom works. Think about it, if I turn it over to the DA or the feds, a shitload of explanations as to how I got it have to go along with it. Casillas is already in the loop, he looks good, and it's less crap to deal with. I'll ship a copy to McIntire."

"I don't like it."

"Ditto, but that's the drill. What are you going to do with little Haskell?"

"Leave him here for now, if Bret can keep an eye on him. I'm off to gather the others. The sting needs to happen no later than tomorrow. Can't give them time to catch a whiff."

"I'll work on it. Call you back in ten."

"Ten it is." I knew Marty needed to make sure his brother was on board. Friendship or not, Bret wasn't part of our racket and shouldn't be too involved, in case this whole mess went south.

While I waited to hear back from Marty, I contacted Luis Murillo, a special agent with the Mexican Federal Ministerial Police, and longtime collaborator and friend. The names Leonard Sheridan or Bill Haskell didn't ring a bell for him, but he agreed to look into it and ring me back.

Then I dialed Demetrio's cell.

He answered in the middle of a yawn. "*Diga.*"

"*Despierta, compadre,*" I said. "Are you alone?"

"Yes."

"How's everything?" We had a spotty connection. I imagined from interference with the alarm systems in the safe house.

"*Carajo, gabacho*, tell me this is all going to be over soon."

"I'm working on it, can't make any promises. *¿Cómo está mi hermana?*"

"Carrie is fine. *¿Cómo estás tú?*"

"Exhausted. But I may have caught a break. *Ya veremos.*"

"This place Marty found for us is all right. We can wait here for a while," he said with resignation.

"Yeah, sorry, old friend. I'll make it up to you, somehow."

"I think you said you'll make it up to me, the connection cracked. If you did, the beauty you have hidden here, she—"

"Hands off, she's in mourning. She was Devon's girl." I heard loud crackling, but wasn't sure if it had come from the line or Demetrio.

"No, no, no," he said as if trying to convince himself. "This connection must be very, very bad. I did not hear you well. The big man that washed up? This little precious—"

"Yes. She's a good kid. I mean it, hands off."

"All right. You can buy me a new driver, then."

I chuckled. "You can have a whole set of clubs."

"*Ah*, tempting, but no need. I have enjoyed spending time with Carrie. She's quite a woman. You would like her if you spent more time with her." He spoke away from the phone. "In a moment." He returned to me. "The girls in the other room need me."

"Demetrio, I mean it, hands off—"

"You have such a dirty mind. Not everything is about sex. Although it should be."

"*Nos vemos pronto.*"

"*Suerte*, Justino."

As silence set in, I glanced up at the sky and, for an instant, I reveled in the awesome beauty of stars strewn across the heavens in encroaching dusk. A poignant contrast to the day I'd spent in the pursuit of a despicable truth.

The sight overwhelmed my senses. I felt an urge to pray. Not for myself—God has better things to do—but for Demetrio and my sister. And for Nancy Drier. Intellectually, I'd been aware that they were in imminent danger. Emotionally, I hadn't allowed myself to indulge what losing Carrie or my best friend could mean to me. Nancy's blind love for Devon reminded me of Cecilia and what could've been.

The pale stars blurred as tears welled in my eyes.

CHAPTER EIGHTEEN

Sauers agreed to keep Al's confession under wraps and for his brother to babysit him. However, he lectured me on the risks my plan presented not only for me, but also for whatever agencies ended up involved in the sting. He ran through some unpleasant scenarios for the sake of bureaucracy, investigative regulations, and to cover our asses, as he indelicately put it. I offered no resistance and thanked him.

Bret helped me take Al to the outhouse. We fed him, dressed his wounds the best we could, tied him up, and put him to sleep with a strong sedative. Bret set up camp right outside the hut.

I needed to rest and tend to my own wounds before I jumped into what might turn out to be the end of the line. I couldn't go back home, and Bret's place didn't seem appropriate given he'd be roughing it. I craved the comforts of ready service, so after a quick stop at the drugstore for some painkillers and sundries, I treated myself to an upscale room at the Temecula Creek Inn.

After a warm shower, I ordered room service, poured myself a couple of whiskeys from the mini-bar, and downed the meds. I looked like hell and felt even worse. Propped up several pillows and nestled onto the bed to enjoy the rest of my drink. I woke startled by the ring of my new cell phone. For a second, I didn't know where I was. I grabbed the phone.

"Yeah," my voice crackled.

"Sauers here, with Casillas. You're on speaker phone."

"You shouldn't have taken Al Haskell, Mr. Pierce," Casillas wasted no time putting me in my place.

"He shouldn't have beaten the crap out of me, either. Let's move on."

I heard him grumble something to Sauers, and I heard Marty mutter something back. Best to be patient.

Casillas came back on the line. "Okay, Mr. Pierce, on account of you're part of the service and already inserted, we'll play it your way, but only up to the hook, then you get the hell out of our way."

"Done."

"Turns out," Sauers said, "that my little old company, along with the DEA and the feds, will be in on it as well."

I didn't like where this was headed. "Sounds peachy," I said sarcastically. "At least we won't be short on dicks."

Casillas muttered something that resembled *asshole*.

Marty and I had worked together enough that we'd developed our own internal language. He'd alerted me that something deeper was at play, and not only did I need to fish it out, but the multiple agency involvement could muddle our private sting.

"Yeah, can't tell you any more, you know, on account of your status."

"My what?"

"Mr. Pierce, you're on medical leave. We can't disclose. That's the drill." Casillas enjoyed—at least it felt as if he did—making sure I knew who was the boss.

"Cozumel *and* Tijuana, Buddy," Sauers added, "That's the drill. You know what I mean, right? It's about your vacation once you give us Al Haskell back."

Fuck! This was even bigger than I'd imagined. Sauers meant that we were dealing not only with drugs, but also with human trafficking.

"I get it. Sounds good," I answered, "but don't jump the gun and send me off to suntan yet, Marty. I need to make sure my sister's safe. That's the only reason I got involved in this mess and brought you in on it. That's my entire focus."

"Yeah, I'm there." He'd understood I intended to fly solo with only him in the loop and to hell with this multi-agency crap and Casillas riding shotgun.

"Mr. Pierce," Casillas said just as I heard a knock on the door. "It's—"

"Hold on a sec, captain. Dinner's here." I could almost feel Casillas smoldering.

I went to the door and took the tray from the waiter, signed the bill, and shut the door behind him. I placed the tray on the bed, sat back, and picked up the cell phone. "I'm back. Sorry for the interruption."

"It's vital," Casillas pressed on, "that you cooperate with us fully. No flying solo on this one. Got that?"

"Of course," I said as I took a bite of chicken.

"Are you taking this seriously?" Casillas sounded irritated.

"Absolutely, but I need to eat. I'm sure you've had the shit beaten out of you at one time or another enough to remember what it does to your body. Anyway, let's cut to the chase. Are we on?"

Sauers, the peacemaker stepped in, "We need to coordinate with the other agencies. Call me mid-morning tomorrow, and we'll take it from there."

"Mid-morning? Won't work. If the Seaview PD has a leak, we—"

"We're taking care of that," Casillas interrupted. "We—"

"Okay," I cut in. I didn't want a speech. "I'll call you, Sauers." I clicked off before Casillas could chime in.

I turned on the TV and dug into my dinner. Fell asleep halfway through.

Sauers woke me at eight in the morning. "Got bad news, bro."

"What?"

"Your sister flew the coop."

I bolted up from the bed. Every muscle screamed in pain, and the tray with my leftover dinner went flying. "What happened?" I managed to say as I gasped.

"She got hold of Demetrio's cell while he slept, called the hospital, and took off."

"But, the alarm—"

"She's a smart cookie, that sister of yours. Must've watched me deactivate it when we went in and activate it as I left. The video feed shows her entering the codes."

"Shit!"

"Demetrio took off after her and—"

"How long after?"

"The time code on the tape shows seven minutes, and—"

"How did he—"

"He turned into Godzilla. Scared the shit out of Ms. Drier."

"Did you lose her, too?"

"No. She's here."

"Sorry, Marty, that came out wrong."

"No sweat. I've sent a couple of our guys to the hospital. See if they can talk them into coming home."

"That's Carrie for you. Selfish bitch!"

"C'mon, Justin. The woman's worried about her ex. Cut her some slack."

"She's not thinking what might happen to her, or Paul, or Demetrio." I wanted to smash something to vent my anger in some physical way, but I didn't want to pay the hotel for the consequences. I took a deep breath and simmered down. "I'll swing by the hospital—"

"Are you out of your mind?"

"What—"

"You've got an intricate operation to run, and I need you firing on all cylinders. We're skirting too many laws here, and—"

"Yeah, yeah, I get it."

"Don't 'yeah' me, Pierce! Listen, calm down and don't do anything stupid. You fuck up, we're all screwed. I'll update you as soon as I can. We'll find them and bring them back, trust me. Go back to Bret's and wait for me." He hung up.

I wasn't done with him. I dialed his number, but he didn't answer. Hoping to conceal whom the call was from, I used the hotel's phone and tried him again. No answer. I slammed the receiver. At least it didn't shatter.

I dialed Demetrio's cell, but I knew Carrie wouldn't answer. She'd probably turned it off so it didn't tug at her conscience—if she had one. I left a voicemail with more expletives than I should've—I was pissed. And scared.

I checked out of the hotel and headed to the hospital. A glint of common sense seeped into my irate brain suggesting I call ahead to check on Paul and his visitors. I pulled over to one side of the road, and asked directory assistance for the hospital.

"Sorry, Mr. Pierce, but he's been moved."

"Where?"

"We don't have that information. I'm sorry."

"Damn it! Sorry, ma'am."

"That's okay, I understand."

"Did he have any visitors today?"

"I couldn't say. Sorry."

"Thank you."

Sauers' work, no doubt about it. He'd taken me out of play. I called him for the umpteenth time with the same result—nothing.

The onslaught of images coursing through my head made it impossible to weigh my future actions rationally. I had to bring my anger under control long enough to think clearly. Sauers was right. With so much at stake, any errors on my part could be fatal to us all.

Several deep breaths later, I regained control and forced my brain to focus.

Robert Dixon had won the role of the perfect conduit to entrap Braniff and Sheridan. The honor bestowed upon him came courtesy of my Jackson Pollock colorful complexion with the uneven swelling and the remaining scars over my eyebrows and mouth. I couldn't show my face anywhere. On Halloween I'd fit right in, but in the middle of June, it would scare the hell out of anybody who saw me. Makeup couldn't cover it up, so I'd come up with a plan to achieve our goal without showing my face. Next step, convincing Dixon to play his part.

After a few deep breaths, I got into character, called the college, and asked for him.

"This is Vice President Dixon," came the solicitous, effeminate voice. "What can I do for you?"

"Mr. Vice President, this is WW."

"WW?"

"Don't tell me you don't remember me? You were so helpful when—"

"Oh, God, yes…the investigator, I'm sorry." He whispered into the phone as if someone could recognize me over the line. "What can I do for you?"

"Are you alone?"

"Yeah."

"No need to whisper. Not like anyone can see me through the receiver. Right?" I laughed and snorted a couple of times to bring my image into his mind and relax him.

"Oh, yeah, right," he said nervously.

"You've been extremely helpful and will be acknowledged as such, but I need your help with something."

"Acknowledged? How? What do you mean?"

"You've been invaluable. Outstanding. When all of this is done, you'll be the hero. Believe me, a true hero." Flattery tends to bring them around.

"Oh, wow. Thanks."

"Thing is, Mr. VP, I need your help one more time. Can I count on you?"

"Sure thing. What can I do for you, WW?"

"I haven't been able to connect with Sheridan. Any chance you could help me?"

"Listen…"—he was whispering again—"the FBI—"

"Oh, yeah, my buddy Dorset told me he'd visited with the Braniff woman."

"It's been hell around here ever since then. She's gone nuts asking questions of everybody, and threatening us if we cooperate with the agents. Then, President Moore got assaulted, and now everybody's scared."

I did my best cheerleader impression. "Your evidence, buddy, that's what's done it. I hope you know that."

"My evidence? What do you mean?"

"The stuff you gave Devon."

"Do they know I'm the one who—"?

"Ah, see, that's exactly what I'm trying to find out. I need your help so I can protect you. How do I find Sheridan?"

"Oh, my God!" His voice reached a high girlish pitch. "I didn't—"

"Hey, Robert…Mr. Doctor, whoa…VP, calm down. No need to panic…at least not at this point."

"What do you mean, 'at this point'?" He'd gone from a high pitch to a whisper.

"Focus. To keep you safe, I need to find Sheridan. Can you hook me up with him?"

"Are you kidding? He hates my guts. He's Braniff's boy. They loathe me."

"That's even better. I want to get them together to show them what we've uncovered. Listen up." I pictured him shoving the receiver into his ear. "Tell them an investigator friend of Dorset, you know, Duran Dorset from the FBI…" I paused to let him gather his thoughts.

"Yeah, Dorset from the FBI. Can I tell them your name?"

"Sure, tell them I go by WW and that I called to tell you we've uncovered some evidence about both of them. Then tell them that I want to make a deal and sell the evidence to them."

"Sell? Oh, my God! How could you?"

"Robert, you offend me. You don't think I would really do that, do you?"

"Oh, no, of course not, I, well…Oh, dear God! I get it. I do get it. You're using this as a hook. Is that the word?"

I laughed, snorted, chuckled, snorted, and coughed. "You're so together, Doctor VP. That's exactly right. You're one smart cookie. Hell, you should be an agent."

"Oh, not really, but thanks." He said with pride. "I try my best. But—"

"There shouldn't be any buts here, Robert, my friend. I need you to round these two up for me. You got that?"

"What if they ask why you called me and not them? I mean, why me?"

"Good question." I sounded very impressed. "That's a question an agent would ask. So, here is the deal. Tell them I approached you first, and you've already paid me for what I have on you. You were first on account of what we have on you."

"Me? What do you have on me?"

"C'mon, Robert, play with me here. You're just trying to hook them in. Tell them I can make it all go away for the right price. Got it?"

"Oh, okay, right, this is all pretend. I get it. Yeah, I guess I could say that."

"Of course, you can. Doesn't Braniff have stuff on you? Whatever she has, I have it as well."

He gasped. "You do?"

"Robert, p-l-e-a-s-e." I added a tone of impatience.

"Yeah, of course, I get it. I keep forgetting that you don't really have it, but she'll think you do. Makes sense. She'll buy that."

"Can you do it?"

"Yeah, I think so. You don't have anything on me, right?"

"Right, buddy. You're our hero, remember? Nothing to worry about. Are you with me now?"

"Yeah."

"Good. Tell them to meet me at the Haskell warehouse this afternoon at four. Haskell, as in Al and Bill Haskell. You got that?"

"The Haskell brothers have a warehouse?"

"Yeah. Got it?"

"I do, but how will Braniff and Sheridan find the warehouse?"

"They know exactly where the warehouse is, trust me. That's part of the hook, as you cleverly said."

"What if they say no?"

"They won't refuse, I promise. But if they give you any grief, tell them I said it's about the money."

"Oh, my God! I knew there was something going on! What is it?"

"Ah, ah, ah. Can't tell you, buddy. Your life would be on the line, and we don't want that. Do we?"

"No, we don't. You know, at first, I thought that Braniff paid Sheridan to use his boat for all her hanky-panky. You know she sleeps around, don't you?"

Without waiting for my answer, he went on.

"Anyway, I kept thinking and thinking, and then I figured out she wouldn't need to pay Sheridan for that. She'd simply use it. That's the kind of woman she is. She takes and takes."

"Well, Buddy, you're absolutely right. Let's see if you've really figured it out. What do you think it is?"

"Sheridan is blackmailing her."

"Nice. About what?"

"Well, that I don't know. But I'm sure Devon figured it out."

"Is that so?"

"We were aboard Sheridan's yacht when he died, weren't we?"

"You're right on the money, but—"

"So, if—"

"Listen to me a sec, Bob. You've got to be very careful not to let on that you know so much. Too dangerous. You *must not* get involved other than to tell them what I've told you. Don't deviate."

"Yeah, yeah. I can certainly do this. Haskell warehouse, four this afternoon, to buy the evidence from WW, and it's about the money. Right?"

"Good man. I'll call in a couple of hours to check on you. I'm on the road on my way to you guys, and I don't have access to my office computer. Give me your cell number, and while you're at it, Braniff's and Sheridan's. Need their addresses and where Sheridan moors his boat. Oh, and, what's the name of his yacht again? Uh…"

"*Lady Luck*," he offered. "It's at the Seaview Marina."

"Great. Thanks. And don't worry. If anything goes wrong, I'll be there to protect you, buddy."

He gave me everything without hesitation. Weasels are all the same, regardless of age, country, or background.

Next step was to gather some over-the-counter recording equipment. I couldn't use Bret's without involving him, so I stopped at an electronics store. My shocking appearance turned out to be not only a great topic of conversation but also an asset.

I approached the geekiest looking salesman in the store, but in no time every clerk in the shop was at my beck and call. The story was that I had a company costume party playing the part of a cop who'd been beaten up by some bad guys and planned a sting operation to catch them—truth always works best. I therefore had to make it all look real because there were loads of money on the table for the best costume and act. The "amazing job" I'd done with my "makeup" hooked them in, and they got a kick out of equipping me with the best compact devices. Even gave me a discount.

I headed back to the shack to check on Bret and our captive. I tried Sauers and Carrie, but had no luck connecting with either one. Carrie and Demetrio had been missing for the better part of a day, and I had not the vaguest clue where they might be.

Unnerving.

—◆—

CHAPTER NINETEEN

As I neared the shack, I spotted Sauers and Sauers waiting for me, coffee in hand. Sitting side by side, they looked like identical twins differentiated only by age, ruggedness, and tailoring. Both were big, with dark hair and eyes, one out of *GQ* magazine, the other out of *American Cowboy*. Either could take you out with one blow if you unnerved them enough.

I didn't like the grim look on Marty's face as he saw me approach.

"You look like hell," he told me.

"You're as pretty as ever. Why haven't you answered your damn cell?"

"Turned it off. Don't want to be found."

"You could've told me."

"Hello to you, too," said Bret.

"Hey. Sorry, but this brother of yours—"

"I'm here now," Marty interrupted, "and with no news of your sister or Demetrio."

"They didn't show up at the hospital?" I asked with alarm.

"No. As soon as I discovered she'd left, I had Paul moved to a sister hospital under an alias. No change of docs that way. He's out of the coma. The swelling in his brain is still bad, but he made the transfer okay."

"Carrie didn't get to see him? Where did you put him?"

"I don't think she did. He's at Scripps Green."

"What the fuck do you mean, 'don't think so'? Did she, or didn't she?" I yelled.

Bret jumped up, uncomfortable with my tone. Marty raised his hand and Bret sat down. Moments like these I wished I had a brother and not an idiotic sister.

"Paul couldn't remember if she'd been there. Still a bit shaky in the memory department. My guys didn't see her or Demetrio. They might've missed them. I kept them there in case they show up. Sorry Pierce, I know you're worried."

I shook my head. "No, I'm the one that should be apologizing. You've done everything you could. Carrie irritates the hell out of me."

"Listen, I realize you're going to take off to look for her. But we've got Al in there snoozing, and we need to set up a sting alongside a bunch of guys with huge egos. You must focus—"

"Yeah, got it. Spoke with Murillo, the Sheridan name didn't ring a bell, but he'll look deeper and get back to us. Dixon, our errand boy, told me Sheridan's got a yacht moored at the Seaview Marina. He owns the very yacht where the college party took place and where Devon got killed. Smells to me like he's the money guy, likely ringmaster, and the connection with the cartels down south."

"Casillas thinks Haskell's involved in bringing illegals in."

"It fits. Sheridan brings them in, and the Haskells store them."

"How's this sting of yours playing out?" Bret asked.

"We'll roll little Al into the warehouse and wire him up to record the get-together with Sheridan and Braniff."

"Who are they expecting?"

"A two-bit PI by the name of WW who's selling evidence he's got on both. Dixon has arranged the meeting for four o'clock and told them that he's already paid his share to WW for what they got on him."

"I take it you're WW." Bret grinned.

"Yeah, he's one of my favorites. I only used him on Dixon, so no one else knows him."

"Since Al's never set eyes on me or WW," Marty added, "I'll play the part and handle the tête-à-tête. Al's confession and Devon's evidence gives me a full set of cards to play with. We'll put the bug on Al in case the duo decides to frisk me."

"Will he feel the wires and—"

"No. I'll set him up," Bret interrupted. "My stuff's pretty good. Plus, he's in too much pain to even guess he's wired."

I shook my head. "Sorry, Bret. Don't want you connected with this mess. I bought—"

"My gear can't be traced, Pierce. I know my business and, like it or not, I'm in it already. Hope you kept your receipt."

I smiled. Bret was every inch as valuable as his brother.

I turned to Marty. "After you take out Bret in front of Al, it won't be hard to convince him to help you seal the deal at the warehouse in exchange for his freedom and a share of your take."

"Smooth deal, bro." Brent winked at Marty. "And you'll head up the warehouse sting while the other turkeys watch and learn."

Marty smiled, then turned to me with raised eyebrows. "Where will you be?"

"I'll be far away, don't worry. My first stop is the marina."

"Whatever for?"

"Find Carrie. If your guys didn't see her at the hospital, Haskell must've snatched her. He won't go to the warehouse. I bet he's taken her to Sheridan's boat. If it all works out, I'll find a way to deliver Billy Boy to you along with some kind of hard evidence."

Marty took his cell phone out and called mine. A new phone number popped up on the digital screen.

"Answer the damn phone, Pierce."

I did. "Now what?"

"Now you have my new number." He hung up. "You and Bret, no one else. No need for names when you call. And Pierce, no solo heroics. Play it safe. We can go after Billy with Al if we have to. Grab Carrie and head home."

I nodded, stepped up to them, and shook Bret's hand with honest appreciation. "Thanks, man. Couldn't have done this without you."

"No worries. If you need me, you know where to find me."

Marty and I shook hands. "You're a life-saver."

"Remember that you owe me a tequila with *sangrita*. I mean to collect."

"You've got it." I turned to Bret. "That goes for you, too."

He winked. "Stay well."

I left the brothers to set up their act for Al and hit the road toward the ocean. By the end of the day, we'd either have an airtight case with all the crooks rounded up, or a veritable mess of bodies that none of us would recover from. I kept telling myself that we pros had the advantage. Fingers crossed.

Once on the road, I called the marina to inquire where my 'friend's' yacht, the *Lady Luck,* was moored.

As I approached the outskirts of Seaview, with an ETA of less than ten minutes to the marina, I turned on Al's cell phone. Time to get Bill on the line.

"Pierce…" His voice was eerily calm—not a good sign. "I want my brother back."

"I've missed you, Billy. What have you been up to?"

"Cut the crap."

"You've got to play nice."

"I have your meddlesome bitch sister."

I felt my blood run cold as every hair on my body stood at attention. *On this occasion, I hated being right.*

"I doubt that." I said between clenched teeth.

"Grabbed her at the hospital. Oh, by the way, don't count on those idiots Casillas had following me to come to her rescue.

Betcha they're still sitting out there wondering where the hell they lost me."

"If you let my sister go, I'll give you Al," I managed to say without conviction.

"Aw, c'mon. You can do better than that. What about the evidence you've got?"

The evidence? Is he serious? He wants the evidence and not little bro? It was worth a try. "Okay. I'll give you everything I have. Just let her go."

I could hear the rustling of clothes through the speakers. No doubt Bill was moving, but no clues as to his environment or whereabouts.

"You're a real disappointment, Pierce. I thought you took this superhero shit a lot more seriously."

"Like I said, I'm a glorified salesman."

"And you think I'm a dumb cop."

"How about it? Let her go? Where shall we meet? Just say the word."

"Hell, no. She's my insurance. You give me the discs or she takes a dive."

A dive—the ocean—Sheridan's boat. Oh, how I relish being right.

Time to stall. "Discs? What discs?" I tried to sound surprised.

"Cut the crap, Pierce! The discs little sister says she gave you."

"Oh, those discs. Thought they were music CDs. You don't really expect me to carry them with me, do you?"

"You're full of shit."

"Tell you what, I'll go get the discs and then come meet you. You give me my sister, I give you the discs."

"What about Al?"

"Hey, c'mon, even exchange. My sister for the discs. You don't mean for me to also give you Al? He's *my* insurance."

"Don't fuck with me, Pierce. It's all or nothing. What would you want with Al, anyway?"

"He's been singing for me. He's pretty good at that. Regular canary." I heard him moving again and the line crackled. "You still there, Bill?"

"Yeah, I'm here, you piece of shit! What's Al been telling you?"

He knew little bro would talk. He now wondered how much. I needed to extend our chat long enough for me to reach the marina, and this was the moment in our relationship where I needed to tape our conversation. "Listen, I'm on the road, as you can hear. I need to pull over and plug in Al's phone. The battery's almost out. I'll put you on the speakerphone so we don't lose contact."

"Fuck that, Pierce!"

I pulled over as I put him on speaker. "Hold on, man." I turned on the recorder I'd just bought. "Okay, done. It's plugged in." I revved the engine and merged back into traffic. "Bill...or should I call you Detective Haskell…can you hear the engine of your van? I'm back on the road on my way to get the discs."

"Cut the bullshit, Pierce! I want to know what Al told you."

"Hm, let me think. Oh yeah. Does a car accident on a dirt road off of I-76 ring a bell?"

"What accident?"

"The one you staged."

"I don't know anything about Paxton."

"Who? I couldn't hear you."

"Paxton, you asshole! I know nothing about him."

"Oh, but you do know who died in the accident."

"What the fuck—"

"Little brother Al says you popped him, then set up the accident to cover your ass."

"He's lying."

I'd reached the entrance to the Seaview Marina.

"He also said you killed Devon." I turned into the parking lot and headed for the moorings. "He added that you and Sheridan tossed him overboard."

Silence.

"Hello? Bill? Bill Haskell, are you there?"

"Yes, asshole, I'm here."

"You seem distracted. Hear what I said? Your brother says you killed Devon."

"Listen, Pierce—what the fuck?" The line went dead.

Something had happened. I parked the van by the dock, turned off the recorder, pocketed my phone, and raced toward the boats.

In no time, I found slip 42 where the *Lady Luck* was moored. The yacht was a quality vessel over 100 feet with a hull designed for high speed. It had a look of utter luxury with ample cargo space.

I assumed Bill to be in one of the staterooms below. After a quick assessment, I felt safe to sneak on board. I eased onto the aft deck and approached the stairs that led to the cabins below. I heard raised voices. I crouched down and sneaked a peek.

To my astonishment, Demetrio, flanked by three tough-looking Latin American men, stood before Bill Haskell in the hall between the staterooms. Haskell had been so busy dithering with me that he'd failed to look out for anyone else. Demetrio, it seemed, had recruited three *paisanos* and caught Haskell off guard.

"What's with the guns? You've got nothing on me, you—" Bill protested.

"Listen, Mr. Haskell." Demetrio spoke with authority. "We federales in Mexico do not follow the same protocols you lawmen have here in the U.S. of A. The only way you get to live is if you give us the woman now. Alive. If not, we will have no choice but to kill you. My men will not hesitate, and I will not either."

"I told you I don't have her."

Demetrio got threateningly close to Bill and said in the most menacing tone I'd ever heard from his lips, "Listen to me, *gringo pendejo*, it is easier for us to kill you right here. That way we do not have to bring you back to Mexico with us, and we don't have to answer any stupid American questions."

"But I—"

"*Compadre*," I said in a low raspy tone, *"amárrale las manos y sácalo del barco. Yo busco a la niña."*

Demetrio's companions all looked in my direction, but Demetrio remained focused on Haskell. I shifted away to avoid being seen.

"Who was that?" Bill uttered.

"Reinforcements. You think I would come with only these guys?" He turned to his friends and said, "You heard the comandante's orders, tie him up. We'll take him to a place where he cannot refuse us."

One of Demetrio's companions took off a beat-up canvas belt while the other two grabbed Bill's hands and pushed them together in front of him.

"*Amárrenlo con las manos atrás*," I growled.

"You heard the boss, tie his hands behind him," Demetrio ordered.

They turned Bill around, facing away from the stairs where I had crouched and tied his hands. I wondered where Demetrio recruited his accomplices.

"*¿Adónde lo llevamos?*" Demetrio asked me.

"Te doy las llaves de su camión. Es verde, estacionado en frente de la entrada de este muelle. Cúbranle los ojos."

His buddies chuckled at the notion of hiding their hostage inside his own van.

"What's so funny?" Bill asked.

"They are planning what we will do to convince you to talk," Demetrio answered as he eyed the knit cap of one of his assistants, nodding toward it, and silently asking permission to use it. The man handed it to Demetrio, who slipped it over Bill's head and pulled it down to cover his entire face.

"What the fuck are you doing?" Bill protested.

"Silence!" Demetrio ordered.

I scurried into one of the staterooms, grabbed a bath towel, tossed it to Demetrio, and hid away. Demetrio placed the towel over Bill's shoulders, hiding his tied hands. He shoved two fingers into Bill's lower back. "You say a word and it will be the last one you ever say."

He signaled for the guys to walk him out.

As they exited, I moved behind Demetrio. I wanted to clasp his shoulders and cheer him on, but it would have to wait. I simply patted his back and handed him the keys. *"Ten cuidado. Este cuate es fuerte y cabrón,"* I whispered.

"Te esperamos en el camión."

They escorted Bill off the boat as I made my way to the forward cabin.

I found Carrie lying on the bed in the main stateroom, feet, hands, and mouth taped, with a blindfold across her eyes. Alive, clothes intact—a good sign. A significant bruise decorated the right side of her face.

I figured I had one second to give her a piece of my mind, before she could refute anything I said. I released her feet first. "You are incredibly stupid, Carrie. You're so dammed selfish, you have no regard for others or the danger you've put us all in." I freed her hands and she immediately reached for her mouth. "Stop!" I yelled. "You'll pull your skin off. Let me do it."

I removed the blindfold. She blinked a couple of times, then her eyes opened wide and she froze as if she'd seen a ghost.

"Oh, yeah, my looks. Courtesy of Bill's little brother, Al."

She stopped struggling, her eyes fixed on my facial distortions. Tears flooded her beautiful eyes and trickled down her cheeks. And with that, my anger dissipated.

I sat on the bed next to her and gently peeled the duct tape from her mouth.

As soon as her mouth was free, she sat up and reached for my face. "Justin, my God, I'm so sorry. Did I cause this?" Afraid to hurt me, she jerked her hand back, then threw herself in my arms, sobbing.

I pulled her away. "There's no time for this now. Demetrio—"

"Oh, my God! He's terrific!" She sounded like a star-struck child overjoyed at the realization that the monsters are gone.

I snagged her purse, which had been tossed to the floor next to the bed. She took it, extricated a handkerchief, and blew her nose. She looked up at me and smiled. "I never imagined Demetrio could be so brave. Bold yes, but this act of his took tons of courage. He scared the daylights out of Haskell telling him he's a muckety muck from the Mexican Federal Police and that he'd come to fetch him."

"Bill bought that?" I asked as I got down on my knees to search for hidden compartments under the bed.

"What are you doing?"

I stood up and began a systematic search of the interior compartments of the stateroom. "So, Bill bought Demetrio's story."

"Of course, he did. He stood right here talking on the phone with you when Demetrio burst into the hall out there. All of a sudden, he rushed out, slamming the door behind him. I could hear Demetrio and those other men yelling. Haskell even stuttered, he was so frightened."

"How did Demetrio know where you were?"

"He must've followed us. Justin, I know I shouldn't have left your friend's house, but when they told me that Paul was out of his coma, I had to see him."

"And?"

"And, what? You mean—"

"I'll be damned." I'd found my gun and cell phone hidden in an overhead compartment.

"What's that?"

"The stuff the Haskell boys took from me." I shoved the gun into my belt. "Did you see him?"

"Who?"

"Paul, of course. Who else?"

"You're making me dizzy moving so fast. Plus, I can't get over how awful you look."

"Stay focused, Carrie. We have no time for—"

"Okay, okay. No, I didn't see Paul. I got out of the cab and headed to the intensive care unit of the hospital, Bill grabbed me, stuck a gun in my side, and rushed me into his car."

"Where did he park when he got here?"

"The left side parking lot—the one right off the gangway. What does it matter? What the hell are you looking for?"

"Drugs."

She froze.

I turned and smiled. "Think, Carrie, think. Who owns this boat?"

"Sheridan." She stumbled back onto a chair. "Oh, my God."

"Get up and don't touch anything." I collected the remains of Carrie's bondage, then grabbed a pillowcase to wipe down all the surfaces we'd touched.

"Fingerprints?"

I nodded. "C'mon, let's move, there's nothing here." I exited the stateroom, signaling Carrie to follow me.

I plowed into another stateroom to continue my search. She followed me as I hastily inspected the remaining cabins and compartments, salon, galley, lockers, settees, and berths. I found nothing. A vessel this size would have hundreds of hiding places. A deeper search would be required to examine every inch of the *Lady Luck.*

We went out on deck, and I checked the live-bait well, cockpit freezer, cushions, and all around the padding. Nothing.

I didn't dare spend any more time searching. Best let Marty's men conduct a more thorough search. Instead, I went about disabling the boat. I made my way to the engine room and created a hidden kill switch by disconnecting the wires and running one as a toggle. Then I removed the fuel hose from the tank and engine. I hotwired the ignition. The engine ran out of residual fuel and chugged to a stop. These were mere inconveniences, and anyone with half a brain could figure out how to fix them, but it would take time, and that was all I needed.

Carrie watched me in complete awe without interfering or getting in my way. I liked her like that, safe and quiet.

When I finished and had wiped all the surfaces clean, we made our way onto the main deck. I glanced out to the parking lot and confirmed that the van remained where I'd left it. Score another one for Demetrio. I helped Carrie off the boat. She grabbed onto the railings to steady herself. I stopped her midway down.

"Wait!"

"Oh, I'm sorry I touched—" she whispered.

"It's not that. The railing supports, they're too wide."

I hopped back onto the vessel and ran my fingers along the pipes that supported the railings in search joints. At the foredeck, I found one. I kicked it, and it sprung apart to reveal a nice cavity. I ran my fingers inside the tubing and extracted some white residue. The clear taste of cocaine rewarded my search. I cleaned all the surfaces, then yanked a section of tubing loose and took it with me.

I joined a stunned Carrie on the dock and ushered her away.

CHAPTER TWENTY

The nearly empty parking lot showed no activity. While we waited for Carrie's rideshare, I told her that Paul had been taken to another hospital for his own security. She didn't ask where. No doubt this time she'd obey. Whatever Bill had told her, accentuated by the smack to her face, plus the shock of seeing my lovely multicolored complexion, had done the trick.

The cab arrived and I sent her to the downtown Marriott to register under our mother's maiden name with strong instructions not to contact anyone. She agreed without protest. Danger now loomed too large for her to ignore.

Once she took off, I rushed to the van and eyed the parking lot to ensure there weren't any witnesses. No one around. I flung the back doors open. Bill Haskell's foot slammed into my chest, throwing me ten feet from the vehicle along with the boat's railing, which flew over my head.

The air exploded from my lungs with a loud thump. The railing crashed behind me and rolled under a car parked to the right of where I'd landed. I remained conscious enough to realize Bill's hands were still tied. As if watching a movie in slow motion, I saw him struggle to wiggle the knit cap off his head. Demetrio's limp body lay right behind him. No sign of his three companions.

I scrambled to my feet, still gasping for air in a desperate attempt to remain conscious. After a few huffs, I stabilized my breathing and looked around to see if anyone had noticed us. The lot remained deserted.

I rolled under the car and recovered the railing, lumbered back to the van, and climbed in through the passenger door, avoiding Haskell's blind thrusts into the air.

I landed the railing on his head with such force it whipped him forward and back, then side to side. I shouldn't have hit him so hard, but I couldn't help myself. With adrenaline rushing through my veins, I readied the railing for a second strike at the slightest provocation. But he lay motionless. I wondered if the blow had been hard enough to kill him or maybe turn his brain to mush.

Determining his condition would have to wait. Demetrio came first. I pulled the back doors of the van shut, put the railing next to Demetrio, and focused my attention on him. He had a steady pulse. His nose was broken and the blood from it had started to coagulate—a good sign. The swelling spread toward his eyelids, which promised to soon match my own facial decor. He remained unconscious, the perfect state to reset the bone in his nose. The sudden pain shocked him awake, and he flailed about in an attempt to beat the hell out of me.

I grabbed his arms to calm him down. *"Quieto, Demetrio, todo está bien."*

He recognized me and immediately reached for his nose. I stopped him. "It's broken, don't touch it. It'll be okay. We'll get you patched up. What happened?"

He struggled to a sitting position and glanced over at Bill's motionless body. "He hit me with his head. ¡Cabrón! Is he dead?"

I felt for a pulse as I answered. "He's alive, but I may have turned him into a vegetable."

"Good."

I shook my head. "Don't know about that. I'm off the payroll. Corrupt or not, this is a plain and simple assault on a police officer."

"Well… I will think of something. He had it coming."

I couldn't help but laugh. "I'm sure you will. Can you climb to the front seat without hurting yourself? We need to get out of here."

"I will try." He glanced around the van. "Where is Carrie?"

"On her way to the Marriott downtown. She's okay, and this time she'll behave."

He smiled and struggled onto his knees. Puffing and groaning, he crawled to the front of the van. He plopped down onto the passenger's seat with an audible sigh of relief.

"Pain is manageable?" I asked on my way to the driver's seat.

"It hurts like hell, but I will survive."

I reached for the first-aid kit Brent had given me, my stash of meds, and a bottle of water. "I'm going to tape your nose in place. It's going to hurt. Don't move." I cut a strip of surgical tape and set it tightly across his nose. Tears rolled down his eyes. "Here, take these pills. Painkillers. They'll help."

I started the van and exited the marina.

"How did you find Carrie?" I asked. "What happened to your buddies? Who were they? Where did you come up with—"?

"One at a time, *compadre*. I will tell it all to you. First, let me catch my breath."

"Okay, you do that while I chat with Sauers." I handed him the phone. "Find the last number that called me on this phone and push the call button."

Sauers answered on the first ring. I explained to him what I'd found on the boat. We agreed that a visit to Brent with my taped conversation with Bill could come in handy when it all went down and charges were filed.

I neglected to mention my cargo and how useless he might turn out to be—if he ever regained consciousness. *My bad.*

"We could leave him on the side of the road," Demetrio suggested as I ended the call.

I turned to him to acknowledge his joke, but an odd grimace welcomed my glance. He'd intended a sarcastic smile, but the swelling and bruising produced a contorted mask straight out of a horror movie. I had to pull over, he made me laugh so hard.

"What's so funny?" he asked in all seriousness, his normally nasal voice dulled by the swelling.

"You are. Your face, it's… well, let's say you shouldn't smile for a while. It—"

"Okay, I will not smile. Stop laughing at me."

I sat back and took a couple of deep breaths. "Okay, Sherlock, how do you propose we carry out the dumping of a body? And how do we make sure he's picked up by the good guys and not the bad guys, in case he's alive?"

"Well… let me think on it."

I veered back onto the road. "While you think about that, answer my questions. Where did you find those guys?"

"I got a rideshare from the Sauers house, and told José—the driver—my wife and I had just come from Mexico because her brother had been attacked and was in the hospital. When we arrived at the hospital, we saw Haskell escorting Carrie to his car with a gun at her back. I screamed 'that is my wife!' It made José angry, so I decided to ask for his help. You know how we Mexicans are—we'll go all the way when a *paisano* asks for help. So, he called Luis and Armando—his brother and uncle, and told them the story. They offered to help. José told them we were following the creep who had kidnapped my wife at gunpoint. Told them to bring their guns. Turns out they're all licensed to carry guns."

"Why?"

"They belong to some shooting club, and they carry their guns for protection. They are all rideshare drivers. Anyway, I held José's phone while we followed Haskell. The other two followed José's directions, and we came up with a plan."

"We?"

"Okay, my plan. Anyway, I came up with the idea to say we were federal agents from Mexico. They liked it."

"How do you manage that?"

"What?"

"Convincing people to do whatever you want."

"I do not do that. It simply made sense. They were all in. No questions asked. My wife kidnapped at gunpoint sealed the deal."

"So why did they leave you alone with Billy Boy?"

"Once we got him in the van, I thanked them and told them they could go, now that you, a special agent with the CIA, had arrived. I promised we would invite them for a *tardeada* at my beach house with some nice *carne asada*, my special guacamole, and of course *sangrita y tequila*. Anyway, after they left, I checked Haskell to make sure his hands were firmly tight. That's when he snapped his head back and hit me."

"*Your* beach house?"

He shrugged. "What can I say? I really got into my special agent role."

"You told them you were a special agent?"

"A little lie. Made them feel okay to help me. Plus, I liked it. No wonder you are addicted to it."

"I'm not addicted."

"Yes, you are, and now you have hooked me. I enjoyed the high of it all."

"Really? Have you looked at your face lately?"

"Not any different than yours. Anyway, our Carrie is safe, and we caught the bad guys. That is very exhilarating. The most electrifying adventure of my life."

He was so excited that he went on and on, and the more he talked, the more I realized he was right. I did get a rush saving damsels in distress, and I relished catching the bad guys. I arrived at the same conclusion—an addiction. More like a purpose, really. But the high produced by current events elicited an entirely different feeling than usual. Solving this mess had been up to me—no orders to obey, no directions to follow, no decisions by committee, no worries about the dos and don'ts of neighboring countries. This came down to my own judgment, my own choices, my own thinking, and most importantly, my call all the way. I liked it.

"How about this?" Demetrio said. "We put him in his car and—"

"His car… shit! Of course! Why didn't I think of that? Climb back there and search him for the keys." I made an abrupt U-turn and sped back toward the marina.

"How about if you stop the car? It hurts very bad when I bend down and doing it while you drive in circles makes it—"

After a loud guffaw, I pulled to the side of the road and parked the van.

"Now what is so funny?"

"You and your would-be addiction to the high stakes game. Put your head back and rest. I'll check him out."

I climbed back toward Bill's inert body. He had a pulse, but he was completely out. I felt his pockets and found the keys and… "Piece of shit. On top of everything, he's also a petty thief."

"What did you find?"

"My watch."

I climbed back to the front seat, tossed the car keys to Demetrio, and sped away.

We reached the marina in minutes and located Bill's car by simply pressing the unlock button on his key fob. Car manufacturers have made my job so much easier. The parking lot remained free of onlookers. We opened the passenger door of his car, backed the van right up to it, and eased our package onto the front seat.

While Demetrio primed him into the passenger seat, I rushed back to the boat to drop off Haskell's wallet, tie, notebook, pen, cigarettes, and lighter. I also spread around some of the personal effects we found in a small bag he carried in the trunk of his car and left the bag on top of the bed. Mr. Haskell had now set up residence aboard the *Lady Luck*.

Demetrio drove the van, I chauffeured my unconscious playmate, and in less than an hour, we delivered Haskell to a side street, one block from the Seaview PD. We transferred him to the driver's side and placed the boat's railing next to him—of course, everything wiped clean of our fingerprints. To make the scene even more believable, we added a few mementos I'd swiped from the *Lady Luck* and tossed them about.

We left Haskell behind and were on our way to Bret's place when my cell phone rang. Murillo's private number appeared on the screen. "*Hola*, Murillo. *¿Cómo estás?*"

"Justin, let's speak English. I'm in the middle of a shopping center."

"Okay by me."

"You've got a smelly package in that guy Sheridan you asked about. A Tijuana-based team here has been looking into his boat. You know it?"

"Yeah, the *Lady Luck*."

"That's the one. Drug smuggling, mostly cocaine, pot, mushrooms, and some narcotics here and there. But—and this really pisses me off—it looks like with the help of a couple of *gringo* cops, he's taken up a new venture. They're smuggling folks into the U.S. at ten thousand dollars a pop. *Pendejos*."

"Sauers figured as much. What's with you not being in the loop?"

"That's what makes my blood boil. The assholes shadowing Sheridan wanted to nail him and were waiting to ID the gringo cops. *Cabrones*, they waited and didn't tell anyone. They wanted all the glory. The info never got to me."

"Don't sweat it. We've got those dirty cops."

"No shit."

"The Haskell brothers, compliments of Casillas, Captain of the Seaview PD. Do you know him?"

"No."

"Well, he's about to pounce on them."

"How about the skipper?"

"Sauers is taking care of that as we speak. He could use whatever you've got. Casillas, too."

"No problem. I'll deliver our surveillance in person. I like to visit San Diego."

"Anyone on your side you want us to hook for you at the end of this run?" Customary quid pro quo, we eliminate some bad guys on our side, they do as well—one sting, two syndicates.

"Yeah, Ángel Rodrigo. A two-bit dealer and snitch who's double-timed us once too often. Sauers knows him."

"You got it. I'll brief him."

"*Cuídate, hermano.*"

"*Tú también. Nos vemos.*"

While Demetrio kept his head back, I called Sauers on the burner phone he'd given me. He answered on the first ring.

"We're wrapping up here." Sauers reported. "These guys may have operated under the radar for years, but they're a bunch of amateurs, and with the push of a button, they were singing and blaming each other. Quite a letdown, really."

"No need for us to swing by your brother's, I take it."

"No, we're done. Send me your recording. Usual method."

I shared the good news from Mexico.

"His intel will seal the deal for these guys." Sauers said.

"Murillo wanted Ángel Rodrigo wrapped up with this bunch. He said you know him."

"Yeah, two-timing weasel."

"I'll deliver him to Casillas for you. Text me his cell number. I'll be using this burner phone. Discard yours. I'll do the same once I'm done."

For this action, I recruited special-agent-in-the-making Demetrio Rubio Dávalos, who jumped at the opportunity. I put Demetrio on speakerphone and dialed Casillas's cell number.

"*Buenos días, hermano Casillas.*" Demetrio dropped his voice an octave and intensified his accent.

"Who is this? How do you have this number?"

"Ángel Rodrigo is my name. I call you with a favor I have done for you." Demetrio's Spanish accent had turned thicker than oil.

"What are you—"?

"Not to interrupt me, please. I have delivered to you a package named Haskell. Bill Haskell."

"What?"

"You can find him in his car one block south of your police station. He is…how do you say it?" He paused for effect and tried to wink at me, but his eyelids wouldn't cooperate. He went on, "K-noc-ked out. Maybe even a vegetable forever."

"Who are you? Why—"

"Listen. Be silent. I have no patience with you gringo cops. This Bill Haskell got what he deserved. He betrays us. No more drugs for him or his friend She-re-dan. We now look for *cabrón* She-re-dan. One day you find him dead in one of your streets or on his ship the *Lady Luck.*"

"Ship?"

"¡Cállate, *cabrón*! Casillas, you are to stay quiet until I finish. She-re-dan's big ship will not to be used to carry drugs no more.

I liked to be on it and staying at your Seaview Marina. No need for passports and no questions from *la migra*—i-mmi-gra-tion. But no more! Not welcomed in Mexico or in *mi pandilla.*"

"Pandilla?"

"My gang! He was found out by our federales and spilled the beans. So now we give you his partner Bill Haskell. He has railing of boat used to bring our drugs into your U.S. of A. Same railing we use to hit him. That is my gift to you."

"Why are you telling me this?"

"I do you favor. Now, you do me favor. I want to be on good side of Mexican federales. You tell them I gave you this shit-ass, Haskell, like proof of my good wishes. Do not forget my name, Ángel Rodrigo did this for you. Tell my federal Luis Murillo, you got that? Lu-is Mu-ri-llo, that Ángel Rodrigo gifted you with the vegetable called Bill Haskell." Demetrio turned the cell phone off, closed his eyes, and inhaled deeply.

"Are you okay?" I asked.

He opened his eyes and stared at me. "Justin, my hands are trembling, and my heart is racing. This is better than driving my motorcycle downhill at high speed. Wow! What a rush! How did I do?"

"*Perfecto.*" I gave him a high five.

CHAPTER TWENTY-ONE

Four weeks later, Demetrio remained at my side. Our wounds had healed well, and we'd allowed ourselves time to kick back, relax, and enjoy the frequent visits from Carrie and Paul. She'd asked him to move in with her so she could nurse him through his convalescence. Physically he was as strong and healthy as before the beating, but the swelling in his brain had produced some residual effects that caused him to have lapses in memory and concentration. A condition that, according to his doctors, might or might not prove permanent. Carrie resigned from the university to become Paul's full-time nurse, a role she appeared to relish and he clearly loved.

A profound change had taken place within my sister. She'd cast off the superior, standoffish attitude that I so detested and now handled herself with joy and simple self-assurance. I watched as she sat on my deck enjoying the slow sunset, relaxed, attentive to Paul's needs, and free of masks or pretenses. I wondered how, exactly, this amazing transformation had come about. Perhaps the shock of losing Paul and the realization of how much he meant to her. Maybe the fear of what could've happened to her, or possibly the dismay that both Demetrio and I would endure such violence and risk our own lives to save hers. Whatever the case, she'd finally become the woman she was meant to be. All that mattered was that every one of us, including her, felt an undeniable affection for the new Carrie.

She must have felt my stare, because she turned to me and smiled, the reddish light of sunset diffused like a halo in her hair. The kind of image that tends to burn itself into one's memory as if it were heaven-sent.

"Elizabeth Moore called me a couple of days ago, asking that I go back."

"And?"

"C'mon, Justin, you know perfectly well I said no."

"How, pray tell, would I know that?"

"I wouldn't be here if I'd said yes, would I?"

I smiled. "All's well with her at OCU?"

"Yes. She's healed quite nicely from Al's attack and is busy recruiting all-new VPs and thrilled to be rid of the likes of Braniff and company. She's hired our little jewel, Nancy, as her personal assistant. Nancy, by the way, thinks you're a superhero; she adores you. You should try to get to know her better."

A stab of pain ran me through end to end as the memory of Cecilia rushed into my mind. I must have grimaced.

"What is it, Justin?" Carrie stared at me with serious concern.

I shook my head. "Don't worry, it's nothing."

Demetrio shot me a look of disapproval that could've frozen the Bahamas. I got the message. I no longer needed to hide my feelings, or keep secrets from Carrie, especially not about Cecilia.

"Actually… that's not quite true." I sighed a couple of times to gather myself before I went on. "Fact is, I lost someone very close to me a few weeks back. It's the reason I returned to Seaview. Her name was Cecilia. I loved her… I loved her more deeply than I ever loved anyone."

Carrie rose from her deckchair and perched at the foot of mine. She reached for my hand. The type of gesture born of unconditional love, the kind we once shared a lifetime time ago when we were innocent and honest.

"I'm sorry, Justin. I didn't know. Are you okay? How did she—"

"Violently." I instinctively tried to pull my hand away, but she held on. "The hardest part is that she's dead, and I'm alive." I felt tears well in my eyes. "Am I okay?" I shook my head. "No. Not yet. I miss her terribly. As for how she died, she was killed by some very bad guys trying to save my life, during an op."

"She was doing what she needed to do," Demetrio chimed in. "You would have done the same for her."

"She was an agent, like you?" Carrie's eyes conveyed deep sorrow.

I nodded.

"She must've been very brave. I'm sorry you lost her, but I'm glad you've known love like that, Justin. Treasure it."

I smiled at her and nodded.

A few moments later, Carrie took the initiative to bring us back to the now. She stood up, kissed my cheek, and ruffled my hair, then made her way back to her deckchair. "When will the trial be? When will these creeps be put away forever?"

"They're paying for it now. They're all locked up." I smiled. "The final outcome will take time, lots of agencies, lots of lawyers, lots of crap to sift through. You mustn't worry. No one can come at you anymore. The Haskell brothers are out of commission."

"One cannot walk," Demetrio added, "and the other cannot even spell his name."

"Braniff and company," I went on, "will face criminal charges and do serious jail time. Sauers gets the credit for shutting down the drug and human trafficking ring, and—"

"Casillas," Demetrio interrupted, "will most certainly be promoted for bringing down the bad guys. Even Murillo got his man. Ángel Rodrigo was arrested for attacking an American cop."

"Who's that?" inquired Paul.

"Nobody," I said. "A two-bit Mexican dealer that rendered Bill a vegetable." A necessary white lie.

"You are not scared, are you, Carrie?" Demetrio asked.

She mulled it over for a moment. "No, not really. I'm eager to put it all behind us."

"It is, *niña*, it is already behind us in the past," Demetrio reassured her.

"Hey, Demetrio," Paul said, "I love it when you call her *niña*. I'd like to call her that myself, but she won't have it."

Carrie leaned down and kissed Paul on the lips. "That's because that word is reserved for Demetrio." She mussed his hair. "Okay, you men, I'm going in to fix us something to nibble on. Can I bring drinks for anyone?"

We placed our orders and she scampered into the kitchen.

"You two seem very close. Are you back together for good?" Demetrio asked.

Paul blushed. "We are. Better than ever. She's a new woman. We're going to go off on a cruise of the Mediterranean for our honeymoon. Oh, shit. I wasn't supposed to tell you guys just yet. She wanted to surprise you."

"We know nothing," Demetrio added quickly.

"I quit my job," Paul continued. "Carrie insisted on it, on account of my mind's not as sharp as it should be. She's decided we're going into business together. We'll be our own bosses."

"Doing what?" I asked.

"Investing our own money."

"Is that a wise thing to do, given your condition? If you can't handle investments for others, how can you—"

"Hell, Justin," Paul laughed then looked toward the house to make sure Carrie wasn't within earshot. He leaned toward us and whispered, "I'm going to milk this feeling-sorry-for-me trend she's got going for as long as I can. Truth is, I'm back on all cylinders."

"Thought so," I said with an impish smile. "Glad to hear it, Paul."

"I'm happy to keep my focus on Carrie. She's gathered a nice little sum between her inheritance, her exes, not to mention her speaking engagements. My own isn't anything to sneeze at, so I think we'll do quite well."

"Paul," Demetrio said with a look of *pay careful attention to me*, "she will need to be busy. Her mind is too sharp for you to—"

"Demetrio, I've got it covered. In a few months, once we get back from our honeymoon and settle in, I'll suggest that she head up a charity of her choosing. She's got lots of ideas on how to save the world. We'll be the primary investors at first, but she'll need to go out there, research the needs, fundraise, and do all that stuff she loves."

Demetrio and I couldn't help but smile. Paul reciprocated, and as if on cue, we all faced towards the setting sun in a satisfied silence.

Moments later, Carrie returned with drinks and some munchies. The last sliver of sun slipped into the sea as this little cadre of love, this new family, relished in the rediscovery of themselves with a simple toast.

Demetrio rose to take center stage next to Carrie. "To us, to life, to the future," he said without fanfare.

Paul and I eased out of our chairs and joined them. We touched glasses and repeated together, "To us, to life, to the future."

Dusk gave way to night and, with drinks in hand, steaks on the grill, and joy in the air, we welcomed the shining moon while we enjoyed a nice dinner and delicious wine.

We basked in the afterglow of a perfect evening. Carrie placed her hand on my arm and leaned toward me. "I'm really going to miss you when you leave, little brother."

I smiled. "I'm not going anywhere."

They all stopped doing whatever they were doing and stared at me in unison.

"Oh, come on. Don't look so surprised. You knew I was thinking of quitting. I simply made it official a couple of days ago."

"When were you going to tell us?" she demanded.

"I just did. It's no big deal, anyway."

"What are you going to do, *compadre*?" Demetrio asked, one eyebrow higher than the other.

I shrugged. "Don't know yet."

"I do," Carrie jumped in excitedly. This time the unison was directed at her. "Do exactly what you did for me and OCU."

"What? Get the shit beaten out of me? I know it *looks* like fun, but—"

"Don't play dumb, Justin. I'm serious. My God, through this whole thing, you were like…well…like a real-life superhero, like, I don't know, Batman."

"Really?" I asked incredulously. "Batman?"

"Think about it. He was a regular guy that helped those in need. Like you did. It's very quixotic."

We three men glanced at each other and mouthed, "*Quixotic?*"

Undeterred, Carrie went on. "That's it, a modern-day Batman or Robin Hood. Do what you've been trained to do and help people in need."

The idea sounded so preposterous that I had to laugh. "Sure thing, sis, thanks a lot. You can make my cape. Red's not my color, though. It clashes with my eyes."

"Batman's cape is not red," Demetrio objected. "But Carrie is right. Not a comic book hero, a real hero. A rescuer, a protector, a—"

"Okay, I get it, I get it," I said with mock exasperation. "Nice joke."

The three of them stared at me with genuine curiosity.

"Well?" Paul raised his eyebrows inquisitively. Carrie cocked her head, and Demetrio spread his arms.

"Oh, c'mon," I said at last. "Seriously?"

They all nodded.

"It is not a bad idea, *Justino*. The police could never do the things you did. They are shackled by bureaucracy and a million other controls."

"He's right," Paul chimed in. "They're both right."

Ridiculous, but they were dead serious.

"Okay," I said just to soften the stares. It didn't work. They wanted a real answer. "I'll think about it. How's that? Can we change the subject now?"

"No. I like this subject. In fact, if you are up to it," Demetrio added, "I will join you. I am hooked. Much more exciting than digging up old bones. And I bet you that Sauers would love to have you on the sidelines, and so would your Mexican buddies like Murillo. You could be very useful for them to get around all the red tapes of the agencies."

I threw my arms wide and glared at each of them in turn. "What the hell kind of conspiracy is this? Are you serious? Listen to yourselves. You've got to be kidding."

"No, *compadre*, I am not kidding. I am deadly serious. To tell the truth, I realize I have the hots for this kind of action. I have the money, and I like the idea of living the life of an adventurous beach bum. I will buy that little house down the beach from here, the overpriced one that's been for sale for a while. I am sure I can talk them into a good deal."

"But the university, your home, your—"

"I am done with teaching, and I can publish my stuff no matter where I live. I will keep my house in Mexico, and you should keep yours. With my connections, we can work in both countries. Come on, Justino, let us do this."

I sat there in awestruck silence. This turn of events took me entirely by surprise. I'd put these three people through hell, and now Demetrio wanted more. Even more amazing, so did Carrie and Paul. I gave each of them a long, hard look. One by one, they anxiously leaned toward me, as if I were about to reveal some dark, dastardly secret. "Well," I managed to say at last, "I don't know." I shook my head. "No, absolutely not…Maybe… no. I don't know…no, definitely not."

"C'mon, Justin, say yes," Carrie insisted.

All of a sudden, I realized my best friend and my sister had laid a trap, and I'd fallen right into it. I turned to Paul. "You knew about their plans?"

He nodded.

"How—?"

"*Gabacho*," Demetrio laughed, "I read your letter of resignation. So, if you are going to be a good hero type, the first step is to stop leaving important documents lying about the kitchen counter."

"A hero type…with you as my partner."

He rocked his head from side to side. "Eh, more like a… how do you say it? A kickside? No, sidekick, that's it, sidekick. You know, Batman and Robin, Sherlock Holmes and Watson… Pierce and Rubio Dávalos. Hmm…maybe just Dávalos… Pierce and Dávalos. Yes, that is much better. Anyway, you have to say yes, because I have already put an offer on the beach house, and they accepted."

As the full moon glistened off the Pacific, Carrie, Paul, and Demetrio raised their glasses.

"To Pierce and Dávalos," Demetrio said with great fanfare.

"To Pierce and Dávalos," countered the other two.

"Damn," I whispered.

That was the first night of the rest of my life.

GLOSSARY OF SPANISH TERMS IN ORDER OF APPEARANCE

SPANISH	ENGLISH
¿Qué pasa, *gabacho?*	What's up, gringo?
No, qué va	Not at all
Hasta mañana	Until tomorrow
¿Cómo estás, hijo mío?	How are you, my son?
Jodido	Fucked up
Soy todo oídos	I'm all ears
No hay pero que valga	No buts about it
Cobrón	Bastard
Carajo, sí	Fuck, yes
Escúchame	Listen to me
Cállate, pendejo	Shut up, stupid
Por Dios, hombre	For God's sake, man
Buenos días	Good morning
¿Cómo estás?	How are you?
Bien	Fine
Compadre	Buddy
Claro, compadre	Of course, buddy
Está bien	Okay
Mi niña	My child
Pobrecita	Poor little thing
No te preocupes	Don't worry

GLOSSARY OF SPANISH TERMS IN ORDER OF APPEARANCE

(continued)

SPANISH	ENGLISH
Papá, Demetrio está aquí	Daddy, Demetrio is here
Solo para ti	Just for you
Ven, cuéntame todo	Come, tell me everything
Bueno	Okay
Nos vemos	See you later
Vaya, camarada	Finally, pal
Al fin	At last
Acá	Over here
Aguardiente	Fire water alcohol
No soltó prenda	Didn't give up anything
¡Ay! ¿Por qué tan temprano?	Ouch! Why so early?
Chiquita	Darling girl – or – little girl
Por favor	Please
Ya lo sé, hombre	I know, dude
Ya era hora	It's about time
¿Dónde está mi hermana?	Where is my sister?
Tu hermanito	Your little brother
Cariño	Sweetie
Salud	Cheers

GLOSSARY OF SPANISH TERMS IN ORDER
OF APPEARANCE

(continued)

SPANISH	ENGLISH
Despierta	Wake up
Diga	Hello
No hay problema, compadre	No problem, buddy
¿Cómo está mi hermana?	How is my sister?
¿Cómo estás tú?	How are you?
Ya veremos	We'll see
Nos vemos pronto	See you soon
Suerte	Good luck
Amárrale las manos y sácalo del barco	Tie his hands and get him off the boat
Yo busco a la niña	I'll look for the girl
Amárrenlo con las manos atrás	Tie his hands behind his back
¿Adónde lo llevamos?	Where do we take him?
Te doy las llaves de su camión	I'll give you the keys to his van
Es verde, estacionado enfrente de la entrada de este muelle	It's green, parked at the entrance to this dock
Cúbranle los ojos	Blindfold him

GLOSSARY OF SPANISH TERMS IN ORDER OF APPEARANCE

(continued)

SPANISH	ENGLISH
Ten cuidado, este cuate es fuerte y cabrón	Be careful, this guy is strong and a vicious bastard
Te esperamos en el camión	We'll wait for you in the van
Quieto, Demetrio, todo está bien	Be still, Demetrio, everything is fine
Paisano	Countryman
Tardeada	Afternoon party
Cuídate, hermano	Take care, brother
Tú también	You as well
Nos vemos	See you
Pandilla	Gang

V. & D. POVALL

V. & D. Povall are a husband-and-wife team partnered in the creation of imaginative, captivating, and entertaining tales. With rich international family backgrounds, they bring to the page a wealth of experiences, different cultures and languages, interesting points of view, and a broad understanding of human nature. For more information, please visit their website at www.2authors.com.

David Povall is a producer, director, and actor who has been involved in films, television, theater, and commercials. He has written poetry, short stories, and screenplays. He has lived in Mexico, surrounded by historians, including his mother, as well as anthropologists and archeologists. He traveled to remote areas of the country and even dabbled in Nahuatl, the language spoken by the Aztecs.

Victoria Povall, born in Mexico, grew up in a family of artists and storytellers. Her father was the Director of the Classical Theater of Mexico City and Artistic Director of the Royal Theater in Spain. Her French mother was a well-known theatrical costume designer and esthéticienne. From an early age, Victoria participated in the critique process of her father's novels, screenplays, and plays, as well as her mother's designs. She wrote and staged her first play at the age of fourteen. This creative practice propelled her lifelong passion for teaching—or as Victoria calls it, storytelling. Her doctoral dissertation focused on transformation, stimulating one's audience to imagine the future.